ECHOES
DARK GODDESS BOOK 1

NIKKI BROADWELL

ECHOES

Dark Goddess
Book 1

Airmid Publishing

ISBN: 978-1-7326173-7-7

❀ Created with Vellum

EPIGRAPH

"There is a crack in everything. That's how the light gets in."

~Leonard Cohen~

PROLOGUE

A splash of water, ever widening circles as leaves stirred in the gentle breeze to land delicately, bright spots of color on an otherwise dark expanse. I bent to cup water into my hands, splashing my face before moving deeper until I could no longer touch the bottom. And there I floated, eyes closed, suspended as though held by invisible hands. I wanted to stay, the task I'd been assigned grating as I tried to calm my fast- beating heart.

The woodland behind the pond was singing with summer sounds—the chatter of birds, the chirp of frogs and crickets, the snuffle of skunks and other small creatures rooting on the forest floor. Turquoise dragonflies flitted across still water, iridescent wings catching the light. Symbolizing change, self-realization and the deeper meaning of life, the whir of their wings was another source of solace, my eyes opening for a moment to watch them. This was my home. The place where I felt safe and protected. But looming up in my mind was the quickly approaching future that I had no say in.

The day lengthened and stretched, the sun hovering in a

cerulean sky. No clouds marred the slow trajectory, shadows growing longer as the life-giving orb moved slowly toward the west. I roused, wondering how long I'd been here. The water rippled as I shifted. The forest felt my sigh, the animals perking up to listen. I saw them hovering, waiting for me to pick up the mantle of my future, the shadows of my family. It was time to go. I rose from the water and looked around at my home. The house that lay just beyond the trees was a dimly lit shape in the gathering dusk. I'd said my goodbyes, clinging to those I loved. There was no more to say or do. I squeezed water from the tunic, smoothing out the wrinkles. The light fabric would be dry by the time I reached my destination.

Dark eyes found me where I paused, the weight of the future landing heavily upon my shoulders.

"Take care my daughter. Do not fall prey to what lurks in the shadows."

My mother's words echoed as I stepped into the unknown.

I

Patterns of darkness moved across my vision, taking the pale crescent moon, the calming pool and the feeling of comfort along with it. I gasped and opened my eyes. Two walls so tall I couldn't see the top. Dirt under me, rats scurrying, beady eyes meeting mine. When I rose to my knees the beautiful visions ticked away, one by one, replaced with the miasma of rot, garbage and unwashed bodies.

"Hey! You okay?"

I looked up to see a man hovering over me, mahogany skin gleaming. Soft brown eyes surrounded with crazy dark hair held back with a bandana met mine. "Um...I don't know," I answered, taking the hand he held out.

He grinned, revealing straight teeth that gleamed white as he pulled me up. "What's your name?"

I stared at him, trying to recall my name or anything else about me. "I...um...Feirin, that's it!" I said as though remembering a question on a test. "It's Gaelic."

"Gaelic? That's not a language I've ever heard. Where you from?"

I shrugged, looking around as we emerged from the alley. Fires lit up the dark street, hunched people sitting around them. In the background were hulking buildings that reminded me of malevolent creatures poised to pounce. I could feel them leaning in to see who this newcomer might be. "Where am I?"

"Have you heard of Hell? This is basically it. I'm Jeremy, by the way. Welcome to my world, Feirin."

"Fee," I muttered, meeting the gazes of the others as they took in my appearance. "I go by Fee."

Jeremy laughed. "Either a fairy or a debt to be paid. Which is it?"

"I don't know," I said seriously, glancing down at the rough tunic I wore, my bare feet covered in dirt.

"I'd say fairy, since you have an otherworldly aspect, especially with that crescent moon tattoo on your forehead. Come meet Isabelle, my sister."

"What tattoo?" I asked, my fingers going to my forehead.

Jeremy turned. "The one right there," he answered, placing a finger on a spot near my hairline.

When he turned again, I followed him toward a thin dark-skinned girl with big eyes who sat next to one of the fires. She had metal hoops in her ears, and a wide band of striped material around her head to hold her braids back—not one but many. I heard the words, *who is she* and felt fear coming from the young woman. But Jeremy was already next to her whispering in her ear, "nothing to be afraid of, little sister."

THE DARK-SKINNED PEOPLE took me in, sharing their food and blankets and their wisdom. I was with them for six months before I moved on. They were exotic and beautiful, with earrings made out of twisted scrap metal, piercings in their noses and lips, and wide woven metal bands around their upper arms and wrists. Strips of bright material had been woven into their dark hair, that was either braided or held back with wide bandeaus. Their clothing consisted of pieces they'd sewn together into strange asymmetrical skirts that hung on their hips, belly's exposed and piercings in their navels. The men wore loose-fitting pants in the same materials. Some upper bodies were bare and others covered in light-weight tunics. At least during the hotter months. When it grew cold, they added capes and shawls made from blankets. They used found items from the dumpsters, turning them into things of beauty as well as tools. But to them *I* was exotic, the indigo moon tattoo, along with my sudden arrival and lack of memories confirming it.

When I asked, Isabelle told me about the old beliefs, the spiritual ways they'd held onto as a group. They used dance as a way to connect with something greater, and they laughed a lot. Many played instruments they'd put together with wood and strings made from wires. "We look to each other and the wise ones for our strength," she confided.

"Wise ones?"

"The ones who can see. The drumming puts them in trance and they get visions."

I learned a lot from them as well as the other ethnic groups who came and went. They were all slightly different in appearance and customs, but they managed to get along. Maybe it was the struggle to survive that simplified their lives. And because I knew nothing about them, or myself, I soaked in everything they had to say. But eventually I had to move on, if only to discover my own identity.

Gift...gift...gift...Feirin means *gift in Gaelic.* I roused from a reverie, and as always, annoyance of not being able to remember rose to the surface of my mind. I'd been living in this world for a few years now and I still could not recall where I'd come from or how I got here. My memories, if that's what they were, were always like this—hazy, ethereal and enigmatic, merely echoes. But lately I'd come up against a brick wall behind which a little voice whispered, *you have a purpose here.*

I let out a sigh and stared up and down the street. It was night and I could already hear the raucous music coming from the bar on the corner, as well as the screaming argument in the alley between where I was standing and the neon lights announcing <u>Peyton's Place</u>. Apparently, this name was a play on the owner's name and some show that had been on a watched screen called television back in the twentieth century. When I asked Peyton about it, he just shrugged. "An old dude suggested it. He's a history buff. Way before my time."

Peyton and I had been meeting off and on in his small apartment above the bar to do the beast with two backs. He was a good lay and I guess I was too, considering the roaring expletives that poured forth from his mouth nearly every time we arrived at the finish line. It filled the time between work and sleep, I supposed. Better than the constant barrage of propaganda that played on the screens in our heads provided by IRIS, the Immediate Retinal Imaging System we all carried with us. Thank everything holy it could be switched off.

I was outside waiting for Peyton to close up when I heard the shouting turn into gunshots and then saw a gun-wielding man exit the dark alley at a run. I ran too, straight for the bar. I felt the fear wafting from him, the anger under the surface. He was poised to shoot anything that moved.

Strong hands grabbed my shoulders. "What the hell, Fee?"

"Murder," I hissed, pointing. "That guy's crazy."

6

Peyton laughed. "Yeah? Pretty much a daily occurrence. You want to investigate?"

When I shook my head, it loosened my pinned up dyed blonde hair, tangled curls falling around my shoulders. Peyton's fingers were immediately combing through it, his throaty whisper in my ear. "You know what this does to me, woman."

I pulled away and pinned it up again, fastening it with a clip.

"When are you going to let this shit grow out?" he asked, his fingers tracing along the dark roots.

I frowned. There was something about the natural dark color that disturbed me. "Never," I whispered, taking his hand as I glanced around the empty room.

He took the hint, locking the door before dragging me toward the stairwell behind the bar.

It was morning before I knew it, my muscles aching from the extremely athletic night we'd had.

"You stayed," he whispered, waking to gaze at me sleepily.

"I was too exhausted to leave." I heard the words in his mind, *you are beautiful*, as he rose from the rumpled bed.

"Coffee?"

"Yes, and make it strong." I watched his narrow-hipped backside amble toward the pullman kitchen. I rose and was partially dressed when he returned with two steaming mugs. But what I noticed would delay my departure if I didn't get hold of myself. "No, Peyton."

He grinned. "Just a goodbye kiss, that's all." *Want to ravish you, lady.*

I glanced at him. "That looks like more than a goodbye kiss to me. You didn't get enough last night?"

He chuckled. "What can I say? You worked your magic and the spell remains."

"There's no such thing as magic," I grumped, sitting on the bed to take a sip from the mug. "And I have to get to work." Since the bar didn't open until four, Peyton had all day to laze around. But my job was in construction—a day job.

"Tonight then," he said, waggling his eyebrows. "You're a witch, Fee—there's no doubt about it."

"I am not!" I yelled, nearly dropping the mug.

He laughed. "Dropped out of nowhere with no memories? That tattoo on your forehead? What else could you be? And your eyes—I swear I can see other worlds in them. Look at yourself in the mirror."

"What do you mean?" I asked, rising to take a look in the mirror in the bathroom. My angular face was flushed, my normally violet blue eyes turned blue-green because of the green sweater I was wearing. I was still trying to figure out what he was talking about when he came up behind me and put his arms around my waist, his head on my shoulder. Our two faces stared back at me. His was square-jawed with a two-day growth, gray eyes and shoulder-length brown hair mussed and falling across his forehead. The crescent moon on my fore-head picked up the light, shining bright indigo as though it had been recently applied.

I pulled away and hurried into the other room and grabbed my bag and the keys to my bike. "See you later, crazy man."

I was out the door and pounding down the stairs before he could reply.

I was on my Harley and speeding down the road full of traffic when the vision came. I nearly ran off the road as the startling images flew by, one after the other. Fields filled with wildflow-ers, whimsical huts made out of tree limbs, hand-made chairs that looked like they came from a children's book, a woman with dark brown hair and eyes shaped like mine standing with a tattooed man with hair so black it reflected light. I let out a sob and careened across two lanes of traffic, coming to a screeching stop on the edge of the sidewalk. "Who are you?" I shouted, startling several pedestrians who skirted quickly around my bike. I heard their thoughts as they hurried by: *she's crazy-- why don't they lock these people up?*

I sat there for several minutes before I was able to put the bike in gear and continue on my way. I was going to be late for work. I tried to calm my fast-beating heart, worried that some other vision would come, but as I drove on all I was aware of was the layer of smog, the smell of rot and trash and the crowds of people wandering homeless up and down the alleys, their possessions slung in bags across their backs. I could feel the desolation and fear wafting off them.

Bright neon lights caught my eye, blazing in ever-repeating lines of text along the buildings as I drove past. Ads for all the wonderful things being done for us. But behind them I could feel the people who designed them, the ones who were getting rich. Their sneering faces moved in and out of my mind, their thoughts drifting in the air: *Going to make a bundle on that one. What a bunch of morons. Who buys this shit?* Laughter that made the hair on my arms stand up. The city was a living thing, the mirrored eyes of closed windows reflecting a foreboding dark-ness. I'd never been in those buildings, nor had anyone I knew.

"WHERE IN HELL HAVE YOU BEEN?" Bill shouted when I drove up and cut the engine. "We have a big job to do today!" *I'm going to lose everything if I don't get this building done on time.*

I felt bad as I climbed off the bike, hurrying toward the truck packed with pallets of building supplies. I'd never been out of the city so I had no idea where this stuff came from, obviously manufactured elsewhere. Bill and the rest of us were erecting a twenty-story apartment building and we were barely finished with framing the first five floors. The deadline was in four months. It was heavy work and I'd grown stronger because of it.

"You better get your act together," Bill hissed, watching me grab the hard hat. "If this happens again, you're fired." *I don't want to fire her, she's my best worker. And that body. Love watching her up there hanging on a cable.*

I let out a sigh and pushed the hard hat down over my tangled hair. Not enough sleep, a terrifying vision, not to mention whatever Peyton saw in my eyes. And I hoped to hell Bill didn't come onto me. He was way too old and not my type.

It was dark by the time I left work. Fall was upon us, the days creeping into night

way too soon. But who could really tell with the towering buildings and the smog that filled in any areas where light might penetrate? The sky was a smudge of polluted darkness, my acute sense of smell picking up the rot of garbage left too long and the darker odors that lurked around the fringes. The street people were already drunk or drugged, staggering down the sidewalks. Their thoughts were blurred from too much drink but occasionally I picked up a word here and there. *Feel sick. Why did I spend that fucking last credit? Where will I sleep?*

The streets were awash with the homeless and the half-humans who'd been created to do the dangerous work in the underground sewers and the computer systems no one knew how to deal with. Education had gone by the wayside in the rush to keep the rich happy.

The mechanical humans walked stiffly their eyes flat. Their thoughts and feelings were muted, barely discernable. I felt sorry for them, knowing that inside they still retained a fragment of humanity, their brains connected to wires and metal limbs. And yet they were treated like automatons, living their lives in service to the city, their deaths only coming when they broke apart or suffered some catastrophic accident. I'd seen one of them hit by a car, heard the muffled cries of pain. But when the authorities arrived and looked them over, they were taken apart and thrown into trucks like so much refuse.

There were a few of these in Bill's crew, their ability to straddle inch-wide struts and use tools at the same time, putting the rest of us to shame. When I'd tried to speak to one, I'd seen something in the eyes buried beneath the computerized systems. It disturbed me so much I'd steered clear from then on. Who would do this to a human being? But I knew the answer to that—a person who had no regard for human life. These workers had been put together for one thing and one thing only and fashioned from the broken, the sick or the poor who couldn't speak up. I'd worked hard all day, but the tiredness in my muscles did not extend to my mind, which whirled, questioning what I'd seen in my vision and angry about the injustice of this world brought about by the ones who ran things here.

My bike roared to life. There was something satisfying about this black beast I rode, the raw power and the purring engine soothing some deep place inside. An image of an enormous dragon came to mind and disappeared just as quickly. I knew that dragon. *Must be a story I read as a kid*, I thought, easing away from the curb and entering the line of traffic, trying not to breathe in the fumes.

Instead of going to the bar as I usually did, I headed home. I rented a tiny

apartment along an alleyway several blocks from Peyton. It was barely big enough to accommodate me and the black cat I'd found starving on my stoop when I first moved in. Apparently cats this color were considered bad luck. I climbed the four flights of stairs and slipped the key in the lock, not surprised to hear the meow. He streaked by me, getting inside first and headed straight to his empty food dish. "What, no rats today?" I asked. He didn't answer, waiting until I poured soup into his dish. It was as hearty as I could manage, with a few pieces of chicken, or what passed for chicken these days. I shuddered thinking about it. While he was eating, I poured a glass of wine from the bottle I'd bummed from Peyton and collapsed on the threadbare couch. My mind spun with the day's activities, but beneath it something lurked. And I did not want to look at this lurking thing. Luckily a ding in my head saved me. *Peyton calling*, a voice announced. I touched my arm, activating a tiny screen that showed his face.

"Are you coming over?"

"Maybe, maybe not. The cat needed me."

"Have you named it yet?"

"Cat's fine. He comes when I call."

"I need you too," he said in a husky tone.

"We're getting too hot and heavy."

"You're scared you're a witch."

"Don't be stupid." I took a hefty swig and coughed.

"I've had a lot of women, and you...well, let's just say I've never

experienced sex like what we have," he continued.

I scoffed. "Sex is sex, Peyton. We have good chemistry, but so do a lot of people."

He let out a sigh. "Get your ass over here, all right? I *need* you badly."

"I'll think about it," I muttered, ending the call with a wave of my finger. I

glanced at the cat who stared back at me out of all-knowing green eyes before settling down to clean himself. Sex softened the clamoring in my head, I thought as I grabbed clean underwear and a pair of jeans, stuffing them into my backpack. "You're on your own tonight," I told the cat before swigging down the rest of my wine. I placed the glass in the sink, turned off the lights and opened the door.

"JESUS," Peyton moaned, pulling me on top of him. He was inside me before I could decide if I liked this position. But a second later I didn't care what position I was in. By the time we were finished I was sweating, my nerve endings all on fire. But as I eased off him, I was suddenly thrown into a twilight world. And someone was there with me. I let out a shout and fell off the bed as a face loomed into view. A second later it was gone.

"What was that?" Peyton asked.

"I don't know. It felt like someone pushed me."

"Someone? In the room?" He glanced around the darkened bedroom, scanning across the candle flickering on his dresser, his gaze arriving on me still sitting on the floor. He tugged me to my feet. "What did it feel like?"

I frowned at his overly interested expression, and the gray eyes widening in delight. "You love this, don't you? The idea that I'm being stalked by some alien entity."

His eyebrows rose innocently. "Did I say that?"

"No, but I..."

"Perhaps it was my prowess in bed that threw you to the

floor." He grinned, watching me. *Man, it feels good inside you, lady.*

The candle flame caught my attention, flickering in a non-existent breeze. "I was here and then I was somewhere else," I muttered. "And then I felt hands on me and next thing I was on the floor."

"And this somewhere else—what was it like?"

"It was dark and scary. I felt helpless."

"Maybe you were a baby."

"I need wine," I muttered, heading for the kitchen. I found the red we'd opened the night before and took a swig straight from the bottle.

"Hey, are you planning to share?"

I walked back to where he was propped on his elbows watching me. His thoughts wafted around me, a miasma of want, almost overpowering. "Don't even think about it," I hissed, handing the bottle over. "I need to..." A second later I was no longer in the room. But this time it was light outside and I was toddling down a hill toward a meadow of flowers. I was here and not here, my baby thoughts taking over the me that existed in this place. Shimmering colors hung in the air, like magical entities. A sky so blue it hurt to look at it.

"Feirin, where are you?"

The voice penetrated into my baby brain. It was my mama, the person I loved most in the world. But when I turned to answer, I was flung into the present. I lay on the floor panting, Peyton bending over me. "What happened?"

I pushed myself to sitting and stared up at him. "I was...a baby, and I was..." I burst into tears.

Peyton lowered to the floor next to me. "You never cry."

"I know!" I sobbed, leaning against him.

2

I sat on the bed next to Peyton, telling him everything I remembered from my childhood, which was pretty much zilch. The sounds of traffic, sirens and screaming slowly faded away as deep night blanketed the city.

"So, you don't remember anything?" he asked, astounded.

"My last memory is basically someone yelling about sending me away. I swear I went from around three years old to fifteen in a split second."

Peyton scoffed. "Someone took your memories."

I frowned, wiping at my swollen eyes. "Took my memories? How does that happen?"

Peyton smiled. "You don't believe in anything you can't see, hear, touch or smell, do you?"

I thought about that for a second. "I guess not, if you're talking about magic or witchcraft. I wish it wasn't possible to hear thoughts, though."

"What? What thoughts?"

"Thoughts—you know. People's thoughts."

Peyton frowned. "I can't hear thoughts."

"Oh, common on, Peyton. Yes, you can. Everyone can."

He shook his head. "No, Fee. No one can do that."

"But..."

"I've had some strange experiences in my life that I can't explain, but hearing thoughts isn't one of them. Tell me what I'm thinking right now." *I love you, you crazy bitch.*

"You just called me a crazy bitch."

He stared at me. "What the hell? How long have you been able to do this?"

"Since forever? I thought everyone could. It's why I blank my thoughts when I'm around anyone. I always wondered why people weren't more careful."

"So, when someone's lying you know it?"

"Everyone lies, Peyton."

"They do?"

"Yes. What they think and what they say is almost always in opposition."

Peyton chuckled. "Something else about you that proves what I was saying. You're...different. What do you think spiritually...do you believe in something greater?"

"Greater? You mean like the God people talk about?"

"Not God, per se. But something more, something you know deep down. Like what happened tonight. How do you explain that?"

"It's my lost memories."

"Maybe you should go to a hypnotist."

I shook my head. "What if it's something weird? I'm having a hard enough time getting used to the idea that no one else can hear thoughts."

"Maybe you're from another planet."

"Very funny."

Peyton stared at me. *God, I want you right now.*

I was suddenly very aware of his heat, the visions he had of the two of us locked together. I didn't want him. I was more worried than turned on. "I heard what you thought and I saw what you planned to do to me."

He grinned. "You do know that men think about sex at least nineteen times a day?"

I WAS DOZING LATER when his fingers began to explore. My body responded and a second later he pulled me into position. His thoughts were muddled now, the physical taking over. I couldn't stop him—it felt too good.

I SPENT THE NIGHT, waking to soft light sifting in through the dirty window. I felt satiated, aching in all the right places.

When I disentangled myself, he opened his eyes, gazing at me sleepily. "Where are you going?"

"Shower and work. Boss man told me I'm fired if I'm late again."

Peyton stretched, his arms over his head as he let out a soft groan. "You did me in last night, lady."

I ignored him as I picked up my strewn clothes and the pack with my clean underwear. I headed to the shower. With water sluicing down my back I revisited the realization that I was unique. Sex was a distraction. I didn't want Peyton to fall in love with me.

I was drying off when Peyton came in carrying a mug of coffee. "Don't know how you have the stamina to go to work after what we did last night."

"I'm superwoman," I murmured.

I pulled on underwear and wiped the fog off the mirror, staring at my face. My cheeks were red and chapped from his two--day growth, my lips swollen from kissing. I had love bites on my neck. I had to wear a scarf today or I'd hear if from Bill and the rest of the crew.

I was on my way out the door when I heard him. *I'm falling in love. That woman could fuck me over good.*

"Do not fall in love with me, Peyton!" I called. I heard an expletive and the sound of the bathroom door slamming.

I PRIDE myself on my strength. I'm tall for a woman, with wide shoulders. My body is well-proportioned and muscular because of my construction work and also because I work out at the gym; sometimes I even wrap my hands and spar with the men. Kickboxing. And I usually win. I have a Celtic knot tattoo on one arm, a raven on the other. I'd had them done recently. Both had come to me in a vision, as though they needed to be there to remind me of something.

I liked my life. I was a free agent, had a job, a place to live and a man to fuck. It was perfect.

That's why I was so disturbed about the recent visions and the ability to read thoughts. And not only that, Peyton was falling in love me. I was suddenly vulnerable to something I didn't understand. Control. I was losing control over my life. I could feel it brewing behind my eyes, the need to kick or hit something.

When I arrived at the construction site Bill was already there, but a quick look at my watch told me I was not late.

He grinned when I walked toward him. "Guess you took my threat to heart. But Jesus, Fee, you look like something the cat dragged in. Another late night?" *What the hell happened to her? She must have been up all night screwing—wish it was me fucking her.*

"Get your mind out of the gutter, Bill. What I do with my

time is none of your business." I grabbed the hard hat off the back of the truck and climbed the scaffolding, hoping the hard work would ease the knot in my stomach.

It was noon by the time I stopped for a break. Sweat poured down my face, my hands swollen from wielding the hammer. I shaded my eyes to look up, catching sight of two androids balancing on a beam at the top. It was hot today, a cloud of yellowish pollution hanging in the still air. Dizziness made me sway, my surroundings disappearing as a field of flowers appeared. This time I was older—me and not me at the same time. A dark-haired woman with intense eyes was telling me something about my fate or destiny. I strained to hear what she was saying.

"Fee!" Bill's voice broke through my reverie. "Are you free over the weekend? We need to get this project completed before the backers cut off our funds." He opened his hand, producing a screen, his finger moving the images. "This is what has to be here in thirty days. Capiche?"

I glanced at the screen, the mock-up of the finished building in all its glory, my mind still back in the sunlit open field. "Um...yes, I guess so. Nothing better to do."

He closed his hand, the screen disappearing. "Great. You're one of my best workers when you arrive on time."

I nodded, contemplating this latest assault on my consciousness. *Fate? Destiny?* Those words were not in my vocabulary.

The rest of the day went by in a brown haze as the pollution seemed to ripple over everything. I was coughing up stuff as the day progressed, finally covering my mouth and nose with a bandana. By the time I quit I was so tired I could barely walk. My lungs hurt, as well as every muscle in my body.

"For god's sake, get some rest!" was Bill's parting shot as I climbed on my bike. I closed my mind to any thoughts that might have come after, putting it in gear and roaring out of there. I was stuck in traffic when the thoughts of others began to swirl through my brain, making me want to scream. *Why can't I get ahead? That bastard is screwing me. I'm so fucking tired I can't move. Where is she? She said she'd be here. God, I hate my fucking life.*

The thoughts spun until I closed my mind to them, putting my attention on the far distance and ignoring the misery of the people in cars and on the sidewalks. When I reached my apartment, I parked in the alleyway and locked up the bike.

"Hey, Fee!" a male voice called out.

I turned to see my friend Jeremy. I slipped him money when I had it, and bought groceries for him and his sister occasionally, depending on my income that week. His dreads were nearly to his waist now, his ebony skin contrasting with his very green eyes. "Hi," I answered back, stopping my hasty retreat toward my apartment. "What's up?"

He frowned and shook his head. "We're being rousted. Don't know where in hell we'll go. I can't find a job to save my soul. It's as though robots all marched in and took over." He laughed humorlessly. "Did you ever ask your boss about me?"

"I did, Jeremy. He has a full crew and he said he can barely manage to pay us. I guess the guy who's bankrolling the project is a cheap bastard. Have you searched the net?"

Jeremy's face fell. "None of us have access any more. No money for it. I have a feeling we may be deported. The bastards that control everything are on the rampage."

"Can you hide?"

He glanced up and down the street. "Where?"

I shrugged. "I don't know. Maybe out of the city?"

"Have you been there? It's all farms and barns. I guess I

could wrestle down a pig, but even if I managed to kill it, I'd be caught when I tried to roast it, and that's after skinning it, cleaning the carcass and cutting it up."

I laughed at the image. "Doesn't sound good."

"At least here we can raid the dumpsters." He grinned, his eyes meeting mine. "And we have you."

I smiled. "Wish I could help more." I touched his shoulder before heading toward my apartment. My exhaustion came back as I climbed the stairs. I had to get a good night's sleep or I'd be useless. Once inside I locked and bolted the door, not because of Jeremy and the other homeless, but because of the weirdos who ran around waving guns and shouting about Jesus Christ and some dude they called the All Mighty. I imagined him dressed in chain mail and carrying a sword, the image strangely familiar. I fed Cat and then threw myself face down on the couch. A second later I was fast asleep.

'You are the dark goddess, sweet girl. Embrace your future.' She leaned in to give me a kiss, and behind her I saw the raven-haired man with the tattoos. He was my father.

I WOKE BLEARILY, my mouth as dry as a desert. Someone was banging on my door. *What time is it?* I asked IRIS. *It is 2:06 a.m.*, the voice in my head replied. I pushed off the couch and went to the door, hearing Peyton yelling my name.

I unlocked it and stared at the red-faced man standing there. He burst past me, a worried expression in his gray eyes. "Where have you been? I called you at least a dozen times. Is your chip broken?"

"I don't think so. I just asked what time it was and she told me."

Peyton shook his head, frustrated. "When you didn't come over tonight, I started worrying. Especially after the shit that went down yesterday. I was afraid you had an accident." He waved his hand and a large screen appeared on my wall. "Look at what's going on out there. I've never seen it this bad," he muttered, pointing.

On the screen I saw an angry mob shouting and holding signs that said: **Stop hiring Robots! Hire real People! Let us work again!**

"I just talked to Jeremy about it. They're desperate."

"But if they keep this shit up, they'll be deported. It's happened before."

"Jeremy mentioned that too. But what's the reason?"

Peyton stared at me in surprise. "For rioting. Robots cost less and don't need food and they don't complain. The homeless population grows with every day—they make up over half the population down here. And they're not white, Fee."

"It's not their fault that robots and androids are taking all the jobs."

He sighed and closed his hand to shut the screen down. "I can barely stand this crap, but there's nowhere to go. I've seen the world outside the city."

"I've wondered. There's that wall out there. Does it surround the entire city?"

"Haven't you been to the wall?"

I shook my head. "One time I took a drive on my bike but once I got out of the city limits, I got weird vibes and turned around."

"Once you get away from the city proper the network stops working. I've heard there's some underground military installation out there beyond the factory farms. And who knows what they're up to—maybe you picked up some electromagnetic weirdness."

I let out a sigh and glanced out the window at the neon ads blinking on and off. IRIS was emblazoned in enormous letters, and on another building it was Apple, and Google on another. According to Bill, news had been whittled down to propaganda and ads. Less conspicuous ads for smaller companies blinked in magenta and purple. The people I knew were only able to afford the barest level of IRIS, and now Jeremy said they couldn't get any access. With my payment plan all I had was the ability to call people, and to ask the web questions. Even Peyton being able to bring up screens was way above my pay grade. I didn't want to think about any of it.

"Hey," Peyton said, noticing my expression. "Are you all right?"

"I'm fine, just tired." I tried to smile, but the wisps of the dream were still with me, even though I couldn't weave them together. "I...I had a dream, but I can't remember it now."

"You need to find out why this is happening, especially with this thought power you have."

"Maybe I don't want to know," I muttered, heading back to the couch.

Peyton sat next to me. "We've known each other for what, four years, five years now? And I hardly know anything about you. What was your childhood like? Where did you grow up? I know you said you couldn't remember, but Jesus...you have to remember *something*. I still think your memories were taken. But one thing I know for sure--you dropped into my life and I haven't been the same since."

I glanced at him.

"You can tell me anything, Fee. You must know that by now."

"I told you I don't remember my childhood. I don't even know for sure how old I am. The authorities seemed to think I was around fifteen when I was picked up for loitering and spent a couple of nights in jail. That was after I lived on the streets with Jeremy's people. I'd been planning to look for work but who wants to hire a girl who barely knows her own name? When they released me, they suggested I seek help, since, apparently, I had a bad case of amnesia. The jails are full of girls like me—runaways, drug addicts, unmarried mothers. You name it." I rose and went to the table where I'd stashed the necklace I'd been wearing when I arrived. "This was the only thing of value I had." I held out the black faceted stone.

"It looks like obsidian, a volcanic glass. It's a protective stone--keeps the wearer safe." He glanced at me. "Whoever gave this to you wanted to keep you from harm."

"But who? Where did I come from? These visions, or whatever they are, are beginning to bug me. I was doing okay and now I'm freaking out."

Peyton let out a sigh. "If it were me, I'd want to get to the bottom of it."

"I want control over my life," I muttered, taking the stone from him and pulling the strip of leather over my head. When the narrow stone settled into the hollow below my breast bone it seemed to take away some of my anxiety. "Lately I've had the feeling that some terrible dark energy is coming to get me."

"There's terrible energy right out there," he said, gesturing with a nod of his head to indicate the street below.

"I know, but this feels more personal."

Peyton watched me for a moment before he leaned closer, his lips moving along my neck and up to my ear. "The stone will keep you safe," he whispered.

I tried not to respond. I was exhausted and in a weird mood, not ready to be physical. But a few seconds later he'd removed my shirt and we were stretched out together on the couch. His fingers roamed and mine did too, removing clothing that remained. My couch thumped against the wall as we did the deed, barely coming up for breath until we'd reached the point of no return.

I pleaded with Peyton to go home but he insisted on spending the night. When I opened my eyes in the morning and rolled off the couch, I was thoroughly disgusted with myself. Since when did I need a man's arms around me the entire fucking night? I hurried to shower and dress, worried about the job and being tardy.

When I came into the living room twenty minutes later Peyton was gone, fresh coffee waiting on the counter. He'd left a note: *See you tonight?* Hanging in the air were his other thoughts. *You have to get a grip, girl. You can read minds and now I'm scared to be around you. But your body—Jesus. I can't do without it.*

No, I thought, shaking my head as I lifted the mug to my lips.

3

The weather was out of control, cold storms rushing through, followed by blistering heat. I'd read in a web article that the ozone layer was gone, the sun's rays, when it ever showed itself, sending seriously damaging radiation down. People were sick and dying from pollution, cancers caused by radiation, and many other things, including starvation and the crap they put in the food. The ones who ran things turned a blind eye to everything that didn't benefit them financially.

The street in front of my apartment was empty now, trash blowing wildly as the wind came up. Jeremy and his sister and the others had all disappeared, their absence worrying. I was walking to the grocery store when I came upon a food line that stretched at least a mile down the sidewalk. Some kind soul was handing out free soup and bread. I stopped to give a woman with a child in her arms a few credits, feeling guilty that I had a job. She thanked me and put her hands together in the sacred position, her eyes welling. Despair entered my heart, winding around it like a thorny vine.

It had been three days since I'd seen Peyton, his missed calls using up my bandwidth. I didn't have the heart to delete them. I felt like a drunk trying to stop boozing, my sex addiction burning inside me as the sleepless hours rolled slowly by. I hadn't had any more visions, but I was now considering consulting the police to find out what I could. Surely, they had records.

I'd been given the day off, my boss actually worried about how shitty I looked. "Rest up, Fee," he'd told me. "I need your strength."

I laughed, thinking about how he assumed one day off would bring me

back to the woman I'd been before the visions began. I was no longer that person; something was breaking apart.

The store shelves had been emptied out by the time I reached the little

market on the corner. The clerk told me there was some virus going around and everyone was panicking, grabbing everything they could. I grabbed cans of cooked beans, freeze dried bread, and a vegetable I couldn't identify, transferring the credits from my phone to pay. At least I still had coffee, because that item was nowhere to be found.

On the way home a guy tried to steal my backpack, but when I swung in a circle and kicked him, he took off. The witnesses gave me a wide berth, staring with wide eyes as I walked by. *Scary woman. Look at her crazy eyes.* I smiled. At least I could defend myself. When I reached the corner, I turned left instead of right. The police station was only a block away.

"YOU WERE HERE five and a half years ago for two nights, you say? What is it

you'd like to know?"

I put my pack on the floor next to my feet. "Is there more information about

where I came from? I had amnesia. I was here for six months before I got picked up."

The dark-skinned woman grimaced, swinging her head in disbelief. I watched

her braids, listening to the tinkling of the beads clicking against each other. "Yes, we have it in the system but it won't be easy to find. What's your name?"

"Fee. Feirin."

She struck the computer keys, glancing up again. "Last name?"

"I don't have one."

She pulled her hands off the keys. "Do you have a driver's license?"

I sucked in breath. "Uh, no." I'd been driving for three years without one and

hadn't yet been caught. "But Feirin is an unusual name, isn't it? It means *gift*." Like she cared.

The policewoman laughed. "How have you managed without a last name? You can't work without one; you need a number."

"Can you just look up *Feirin*? F-E-I-R-I-N. It was around this time of year, I think. 2319?"

She pursed her lips and began to type as she watched the screen. "Okay...I do see a homeless girl of that name. She was picked up on the street and brought in. Spent two nights with us. She seemed disoriented and not all there." She looked up.

"Anything else?"

"They released her because there was no charge they could hold her on, and they couldn't locate a parent or another relative. There are a lot of homeless kids out there. If we kept all of them, we'd be overflowing."

"I understand. I didn't expect to be taken care of indefinitely. I only wondered if there was something more—maybe a bag I was carrying or even something I might have said?"

"This Feirin told the officer that she couldn't remember anything about her past. She said she'd been living in a homeless camp with someone named Jeremy and his people. And from the notes written here, she seemed out of it, as though she might be slightly retarded. As far as a bag, let's see. Ah, yes. She was carrying a pack and she had a black crystal," she looked up, "Like the one you're wearing." She glanced back at the computer screen. "And some herbs, it says here. They didn't identify what they were."

"Herbs," I muttered. "Oh yeah. Jeremy gave them to me."

"Apparently not weed, though. As a minor that would have brought a lot of trouble."

"Is that it?"

"I'm afraid so. If I were you, I'd find a way to get an identification card. You can't be wandering around the streets with only one name. If you get picked up you could be held on charges related to illegal immigration. You could be deported."

"Immigration? But..."

"If they think you don't belong here, they'll send you back. No one is allowed to cross our borders without I.D."

"Where would they send me? I don't know where I came from."

She glanced around the empty room. "They'll either hold you in a detention center, or you'll be taken beyond the wall," she whispered. "I'm surprised you've managed to keep off their radar for this long. Take care now," she said, handing me the printed-out copy of my intake papers.

I stuffed the papers into my pack before turning toward the door. As I exited, a cop was man-handling a young handcuffed woman up the steps. She glanced at me as they went by, her eyes pleading. I kept going.

As I walked back to my apartment I passed by mothers with small children, hollow-eyed men, and old folks who seemed half crazy. They huddled in doorways, had set up camps in the alleys where rats scurried by, sharing the thrown-out food. They were more downtrodden than Jeremy's group. I heard their muddled thoughts as though they were my own. *Please someone help me. I'm starving. I can't be bringing up no child without work or money or a place to live. Where do I sleep tonight? It's cold and I don't have a blanket.* I gave a woman a few credits, transferring them to her I.D. number. "Bless you," she murmured.

Along the streets I noticed the beautifully crafted street-lamps that stood like holdouts of some magnificent time in the past. But shining glass and seamless metal buildings were in sharp contrast, as though those living on the streets were nothing compared to the ones who worked and lived up there.

Most shops were boarded-up, trash plastered against their walls. But the skyscrapers boasted their high-end stores in neon. Self-driving cars sped by with well-dressed people inside smiling and talking. Judging by those elegant lamps and some smaller brick buildings still standing, the streets had once been a good place to live. I suddenly felt sick, gagging with the reality of what I was seeing. If there was a hell, this was it.

I hurried the rest of the way, rushing up the stairwell and into my apartment, panting with the effort. Inside I ran for the half empty bottle of wine and poured a glass before flopping onto the couch. I tried to get the whispering and the images of the ragged people marching across my vision out of my head. I felt responsible but I didn't know what to do. Maybe there was a reason I could read thoughts...but if so, what was it?

I was at work early the next morning after another nearly sleepless night. I put on make-up to cover the dark circles under my eyes, hoping Bill wouldn't make a comment. The streets were empty when I left, the bike roaring to life as I set off without breakfast. This machine used a pricey liquid to keep it going, a cost that I was losing the ability to afford. When I reached the site, Bill was there, his gaze worried as I hurried toward him.

"You need to fill out papers today," Bill told me. "There's been another crack down on illegal immigration. Everyone needs to prove they belong or they get deported."

I stared at him. "But..."

"I didn't ask any questions when you arrived at the office like a starving cat a few years back, but now you need to be legal. Not a big deal, Fee. You have a bike, you must have a license, which means you belong here. Just fill it out." He handed me some papers which I took in shaking fingers.

I stared at the blank spaces where I was supposed to insert first and last name and identification number. When I looked up again, he was watching me with a frown. "What?" he asked.

"I...don't have a number and I don't have a driver's license. As far as I know I don't even have a last name."

His brows rose. "You can't be serious. How did you get that bike?"

"I bought it from a guy."

"And it's not registered?"

I shrugged.

"Fucking hell, Fee! I'm going to have to let you go."

"But...can't you let me work under the table?"

"That's what I've been doing. These guys are serious now. I could lose my license. I'm really sorry."

We stared at each other until my eyes began to well. I turned away and walked back to where I'd parked my bike. "I'm sorry!" he yelled just before I turned the key. I waved as the bike rumbled to life, passing the other workers on my way out of the yard. They all stared at me wide-eyed as I roared past. Being alone right now was an impossibility. I headed to Peyton's Place.

"Say that again?" Peyton asked. "You went to the police station and...now you're fired?"

I gazed around the half-full bar, trying not to attract more attention than I already had. "Can I have a drink?"

"Sure. What do you want?"

"Something strong."

"Long island ice tea it is." He turned away to collect a glass as I stared at the scratched surface of the bar, turning to look at the tattered sconces on the walls covering over lights that no longer worked. This had once been an upscale bar in a neighborhood that catered to working people. I was on the verge of tears and furious because of it.

"Hey, little lady. Can I buy you a drink?"

I turned to the older man who was easing onto the bar stool next to me. "She *has* a drink," Peyton said, handing me a glass. "And I'd be careful about calling her little lady. She's not little and she ain't no lady."

I laughed, grabbing up the glass to take a swig. I almost choked on the strong concoction. Meanwhile the guy next to me was watching us with a perplexed expression. "You two together?"

"No," I said at the same time Peyton said, 'yes'."

The guy turned to me. *I would love to get in her pants.* "Which is it?"

I glanced at Peyton who frowned. "We like to fuck each other," I answered.

The guy nearly choked on his beer. "Okay...I'm backing off," he muttered, picking up his glass and heading to a table.

Peyton shook his head and grinned. "You love to shock people, don't you?"

I shrugged. "Whatever works."

"Drink that and then tell me again what happened today," he said before heading down the bar to a waiting customer.

The tea was delicious and the buzz it was giving me was extremely pleasant. I no longer cared about much of anything. "What in hell is in this?" I asked when he came back.

He chuckled. "Gin, vodka, rum, tequila and triple sec. You like it?"

"I'm drunk, if that's what you're asking."

"Good. You need to be drunk right now. I'm about to leave Tim in charge and take you upstairs."

Being *taken* upstairs sounded heavenly I thought as I eased off the stool. I waited while Peyton talked to Tim, glad when he took my arm and led me past the bar and up the back stairs to his apartment.

Our clothes were off a minute after the door closed behind us. I was as ravenous as he was after three days of abstinence. He threw me down and pinned me to the bed, kissing me before pressing inside. I was more than ready and putty in his hands, his lips grazing mine before moving to my neck.

When he pulled me on top, my stone swung between us, a mystical light shining from it. Peyton's face changed, all high cheekbones and angles, his normally light eyes as dark as the stone. The hands that held me were pale, the fingers long and tapered. I let out a shriek and pulled away.

. . .

"You say I turned into someone else? Is it someone you know?"

I shook my head. "He...he's kind of ethereal with really dark eyes."

Peyton stared at me. *Should I be jealous?* "Sounds kind of creepy if you ask me."

"He isn't...wasn't creepy...it was just weird." And then I told him everything,

from my arrival at the police station and what I learned, to being fired for not having a proper number. I was still drunk and overwhelmed by the strange vision.

"You're telling me you've been driving around on a giant hog without a license? Three years, Fee? Three fucking years and you haven't been stopped for speeding or parking in the wrong place? What about fuel? You need special credits for the stuff that bike needs."

I shrugged. "The bike plate is the one it had when I bought the thing. Maybe it's because of this," I said, holding up my necklace. "Didn't you say it's a protective stone?"

"So now you believe in magic?"

"Something was going on when we were screwing. Did you notice?"

"You mean the light blazing out of it? How could I miss that?"

"And it didn't bother you?"

"Bother me how? I was focused on you."

I pulled away and sat up. "This city is a cesspool. But it used to be beautiful. What happened?"

Peyton's gaze drifted away. "From what I've heard, the old city was great. But that was way before my time. When the highrises went up that was basically it. Businesses on street level went belly up and anyone who could afford it moved to Uptown."

"It's horrible—there are a million homeless." I shivered. "And those high-rises are ugly--soulless."

"Yup. I know all about it. My parents live in one."

"Your parents...you've never mentioned them."

His eyes turned opaque. "They aren't worth mentioning."

"I told you my sad story, it's your turn now."

Peyton rose to get the wine bottle, coming back with two glasses. "I can't have more alcohol," I protested.

"Just sip it, Fee. What I have to tell you requires it." *God, I wish I didn't have to revisit this—but I owe it to her to come clean.*

4

I gazed out Peyton's dingy window at the buildings rising up into the sky. Light blazed out of every window, contrasting with the darkness below. Bridges lit with strings of sparkling lights united one to the other, making sure that all residents never had to take a step into the squalor below. More than a million residents could live up there. *Elysian City*. Paradise. What a joke.

When I turned back, Peyton was staring at his hands, his expression brooding. He felt my gaze, his troubled eyes meeting mine. "Beautiful isn't it? The lights, the bridges. That's where I grew up. My parents have tried several times to convince me to move home. Did you know that the residents have everything they need? And I mean everything. I hated it there, couldn't wait to get down to the street, even if it meant low pay, illness and seeing the suffering, even being one of those who suffered. Living in a perfect world is false and dishonest."

When I reached for his hand he pulled it back, continuing. "The world up there is fed by the bots who have taken over nearly all the jobs. The wealthy live in air-conditioned splendor, using all the energy to run their systems. Every need is taken care of. A few businesses on ground level still survive, but not many. A couple of markets, bars, cleaners. You must have noticed the lack of food. It all goes up there," he said, pointing. *Those bastards couldn't give a shit about anything but themselves.*

"Peyton, I don't want to hear this if it's too painful."

He glanced at me, his eyes bleak. "It's time you knew who I really am. I grew up wealthy and I never thought about anyone but myself. My parents and everyone we associated with were either sociopaths or narcissists. I went to school with them. It's like these psycho conditions come through in the water up there. I thank everything holy that one day I just decided to walk out. Not sure what prompted me to do it—I just took the elevator down and left. But it was their dirty money that allowed me to buy the bar."

I took another sip of wine and watched him lean over to retrieve his wallet. He pulled out a card and handed it to me. "This is my key to that world."

I stared at the picture of a much younger Peyton with his I.D. number listed under it. Under it were a bunch of numbers and letters that made no sense. "What are these?" I asked, pointing.

"That's IRIS and the rest are associated with my parentage. I can go there anytime I want."

"And I can't?"

He shook his head and scoffed. "You wouldn't get past the first door."

"What if I was with you?"

He shrugged. "I would have to get a special temporary card made for you. It would only last a few hours."

"I have IRIS but I don't have I.D.," I muttered.

He nodded. "They must have chipped you in jail. Do you remember?"

"Yup. It hurt like hell. They told me it was in case someone who knew me came looking for me."

"And they never suggested you register?"

I shook my head. "Do they watch us through the chips?"

"Of course. It's their main function. Being able to call by voice, and ask any question day or night is secondary to keeping track of where everyone is and what they're doing at any given moment."

I glanced at him. "I don't get why I haven't been picked up. I don't have any of the necessary papers to live here legally."

"I know. It's odd. I wonder if there isn't more that the police didn't tell you."

"Or it's because of this," I said, taking hold of my stone.

He smiled sadly. "I do believe in the mystical, but I sincerely doubt that stone is protecting you from being deported."

"Deported. Should I be scared?"

Peyton sighed and looked down. "I don't know, Fee. It's been hard enough for me to stay here without my parents sending the authorities to round me up."

"They would make you live up there against your will?"

"I know too much," he muttered.

"About what?"

His eyes met mine. "About everything—all their illegal activities, the way the

system works and how they've turned the city into a hell for those who live outside the high-rises--not that knowing gives me any power to change things. I guess they worry that one day we may all get together and rise up against them."

"Doubt you have much clout from what I've seen of your bar and the life you lead."

"There are still avenues that could lead to their downfall. It would take a tremendous summoning of energy, but it could be done."

"Summoning—are you talking magical?"

"No. I'm talking will of the people."

I waited but he didn't say anything else, his unfocused gaze going to the window and the lights blinking in the distance.

When I rose to leave, he grabbed my arm. "Stay here tonight."

"I can't. I need my own space. We have a good thing going, but I don't want to get in any deeper."

"And what do you plan to do when you get evicted?"

"I haven't thought that far in the future. I just paid rent, so I have a month, maybe two with the deposit."

He shook his head. "I just opened up to you. I thought that might count for something."

I reached for his hand. "It does. But I...I don't know what to say."

"You don't love me."

"Love? We've never even said that word to each other. Let's not get ahead of ourselves."

"What did you *think* would happen?"

I pulled out of his grip and grabbed my pack. He didn't try to stop me as I headed for the door and opened it. A second later I was clattering down the stairs, something heavy sitting on my shoulders.

THE STREETS around the bar seemed oddly alive with the homeless squatting by fires and drinking from bottles. Peyton sometimes handed out booze. Not the best idea, but on a cold night like this, I suppose it helped. Laughter and shouting in equal measure accompanied me down the sidewalk in the dark. I heard sirens in the distance and for the first time the shrill noise made me nervous. I was an illegal and if they found me, I would be deported. I hurried toward where I'd parked my bike, but before I reached it, some guy wearing a bandana over his mouth and nose appeared out of the shadows. He pointed a gun at me. "Backpack."

I carefully removed it from my shoulder, watching him the entire time. He was nervous, his eyes flicking about. And when his attention was off me for a second, I kicked out, catching him in the knee. He buckled, the gun sliding away. A moment later I was on my bike, the roar of it seeming louder than usual as I spit gravel and took off.

By the time I reached my apartment I was thoroughly freaked out, wishing I'd stayed with Peyton. I could feel an energy that I hadn't felt before, dark and malevolent. Something nasty was at work here.

I thought about my early days and the education I got once I met up with Bill and his crew. It was through him that I learned how the city worked and how to navigate the streets and life in general. He'd explained the mainstream culture, the slang, and the religious fervor of many of the residents, pointing out the dingy places of worship and the crosses I wouldn't otherwise have noticed. When he asked about my religious preferences, I had nothing to say, only telling him that I had no memory of my previous life. He was like a father or a big brother to me, giving me a job and calling in a favor to help me rent an apartment. He'd even given me an advance on my first paycheck. But when he and his crew tried to take me to church, I balked, despite their talk of original sin and what would happen if I didn't believe in the god that they claimed sat up above the clouds watching everything.

Like a stray baby bird, he'd taken me under his wing and taught me everything he knew. It was because of Bill that I'd turned from an amnesiac waif who didn't understand anything into who I was now. But when I told him about Jeremy and my time with his people, Bill's expression soured. "Don't get mixed up in that. Those blacks are drug addicts. They steal and they lie. They're on the take."

I argued, but there was no changing his mind.

I'd worked for Bill for two years before I met Peyton, coming upon his bar by accident one day when I was heading home from the market. There was an immediate attraction between us, a chemistry mostly missing from the many one night stands I'd had since I arrived. We fell into bed together that first night and I hadn't strayed since. But the word love scared me. The idea that I was tied to him and he to me, made my stomach hurt.

I hurried up the stairs and let myself into the apartment, sighing with relief. This was my fortress, my place of safety where I could think without interruption. I fed Cat and sat on the couch, going over what Peyton had told me and trying to see my future. I took hold of the stone--I either had a guardian angel or the best luck in the world. And what about reading people's minds? How did that fit in?

Good luck or not, I had a sinking sensation that it was all about to change. A second after this thought went through my mind, Cat jumped up on the couch next to me.

"Cat? Did you say something?" But when I leaned down, he jumped off the couch and stalked away.

5

When I expected change, I didn't think it would arrive so quickly. But being awakened at six and dragged out of my apartment was evidence of just what I'd feared the night before. When I asked what it was about, I was met with stony stares, my captors wearing mirrored sunglasses and frowns as they led me to the waiting squad car.

Once inside the brick building, I was told to empty my pockets and produce my I.D. When I told them I had none, I was taken into a room with a table and two chairs and left there. It was a long while of fidgeting before the door opened and an officious looking man arrived to sit across from me. "I've been told that you have no identification number," he said.

"No, I don't. I had amnesia when I arrived and I still can't remember where I came from."

"And yet you've been working and living and driving a very expensive motorcycle. Where did you get that?"

"I bought it from a man. It wasn't that expensive."

"And no license on that either. We checked and the plates expired three years ago."

"I...I didn't know I had to get new ones."

"You are either an idiot or you're lying through your teeth." His eyes went to the stone hanging around my neck. "Where'd you get that?"

"I had it on when I arrived. I didn't steal it if that's what you're implying."

He eyed it before his gaze rose to mine. "That's gold filigree wire wrapped around that stone—impossible to get these days unless you live in Uptown."

I didn't say anything.

He looked me over disdainfully, continuing. "So, where did you come by something like that? You are obviously not a resident of the Uptown apartments, nor are you rich enough to afford a necklace like that."

"I already told you I had it on when I got here. Haven't you looked at my records?"

"I've read all about you, Feirin with no last name. I doubt your story. And the man who's been paying you under the table? He's being charged with aiding and abetting an illegal."

I felt a pang under my ribcage. "Bill let me go when he discovered I had no papers."

"After working there for years? Highly doubtful that he only just discovered your status." He glanced at the file folder in front of him. "And this man you see, this Peyton Rankin, what's his role?"

Rankin. I'd never known Peyton's last name. "His role? We sleep together occasionally, that's all."

"He seems to care for you. He told us that he'd vouch for you, even offered to provide for you. But sadly, that isn't how the system works, despite his affiliation with Uptown. I doubt he can pull enough strings to get *you* released, Feirin with no last name. You will be kept in jail until we look further into your background, and then you will be taken across the border and left there. Do you understand?"

I nodded, fear tangling my tongue.

"Good." He rose from his chair. "The system does not look kindly on those who try to cheat it." He smirked. "Enjoy your time behind bars. It will not be pleasant for you."

He gave me one last hard stare before he headed for the door, opening it and closing it carefully behind him. I suppressed the scream that rose into my throat, my fingers clasped tightly together to stop them from shaking.

A uniformed female officer took me down to the cells in the bowels of the building, leaving me with two other women who huddled into the corner. The entire place smelled of feces and urine. When I noticed the bucket, I knew why. I sat on the bench on the other side of the cell and stared into space, my mind whirling.

"What did you do?" one of the women asked. She was dark skinned and very thin with almond-shaped haunted eyes.

"I had amnesia—I still do. I don't have any papers."

"Likely story," the other woman muttered. "Amnesia is a great excuse, though. Good luck with it."

"It seems they don't believe me," I muttered.

"Without papers you're out," the first woman said. "And the other side is worse than here. I came from there a year ago and now I'm going back."

"What's it like?"

She shook her head as though it was too awful to describe. "You'll see soon enough."

I shivered and pulled my arms around my middle, trying to fend off the deep chill. I thought of Peyton, wondering what he was thinking right about now. They'd questioned him at some point—maybe last night after I left his apartment? Maybe that was the reason for the sirens I heard. He'd basically said he loved me. And he'd offered to take me in. It wouldn't have helped even if I'd agreed to stay with him. I still had no papers.

It was sometime in the afternoon that I was taken from the cell, handcuffed and transported by van to another prison. The cell where they left me was filled with hardened women who looked ready to kill. And I was the prey. When they attacked, I fought back, my skills with kick-boxing coming in handy. But six against one was too much for me. Only one young woman did not participate, her dark eyes distressed as she watched from the shadows. My screams brought a guard who watched impassively as they beat me to a pulp.

I was lying on the floor barely able to move when the guard came in. I expected him to help, but instead he fastened handcuffs around my wrists. When he looked down at me and unzipped his pants, I began to fight, grabbing him with my legs and twisting until he lost his balance and fell. But before I could kick him again, he'd grabbed my ankles, his look hard as he stared at me. "Help me, Patsy," he hissed. One of the women came forward to hold my legs as he pulled down my jeans and moved on top of me.

I heard an anguished cry from the woman in the back, but after that the pain took over, his grunts and fetid breath making me want to puke. If he hadn't put the cuffs on, I would have scratched his eyes out, but with my hands restrained and Patsy holding my legs all I could do was lie there like a dead fish.

Blessedly, it didn't take long, his last grunt of release loud in my ears just before he rose to zip up. Patsy waited for his nod before she let go of my legs and headed back to sit with the others. "That's only the first of many," he stated, reaching for my stone and ripping it from my neck. He bent down to undo the cuffs. "If you're lucky you'll be one of our breeders." *And I'll be the one fucking her.*

After he left, I lay huddled into a corner, too numb to cry. I was out of the city

proper now, far from anything familiar. And my protection stone was now in the hands of the guard. When the dark-eyed woman came close I drew away from her, but her murmured, I'm sorry, made me stop. She was young, just a teenager. Her name was Mirabelle and she'd been picked up in one of the homeless camps. I noticed the swell of her belly. "You're pregnant."

She nodded. "They raped me too. I'm a victim just as you are."

Victim was not a word I associated with myself, but in these circumstances it rang true. "What will happen?" I asked, glancing at the bulge that pressed against the orange suit.

"They will take the baby and sell it to one of the rich people in Uptown. After that I will be deported."

I stared in shock, not sure what to say.

"In here there is no power, nothing but waiting until they decide your fate. I hope he didn't make you pregnant."

I shook my head, hoping the device I'd had inserted into my womb was still working properly. I curled up and closed my eyes, wanting to shut out this place and the pain that radiated from what he'd done to me. I was dizzy, my head throbbed, my sense of self diminished to a drained and frail shadow.

. . .

I THOUGHT I was asleep when I opened my eyes to Peyton's bedroom. He was in bed, a scowl on his face as he stared out the window. He felt me and turned, his eyes widening. "Fee?" He was off the bed and rushing toward me a second later, but when he reached for me, his hands went right through. "What the fuck?"

When I tried to speak it came out garbled as though I was underwater, but I did manage to convey where I was and what had happened.

His expression went from surprise to fury in an instant. "I'm coming for you," he muttered.

Sometime later I woke to shouting, the women in my cell banging on the bars as smoke filled the hallway. I pushed to standing, trying to see what was going on, but the women were blocking the view. I had no desire to tangle with them again. When a guard appeared and unlocked the cell, they all rushed out. I trailed behind them, holding my side where I figured my rib was broken.

"You come with me," the guard muttered, grabbing my arm. He smiled, showing rotten teeth, his breath like a sewer.

The other women were being herded down the hall, but he took me in another direction, opening a door into a stairwell that led up. We climbed two flights before he opened a door into another hallway and dragged me toward a door that stood open. "Here she is," he said, pushing me through.

When I saw Peyton standing there I nearly fainted with relief, but the look on his face was not encouraging. When I tried to go to him, I was restrained by a matron, who held me back with a vice-like grip. "No, you don't, missy," she hissed.

Peyton frowned, his worried gaze going over the cuts and bruises on my face and arms. "What have you done to her?"

"The ladies down there had a go, that's all," the matron said. "It happens to all the new ones."

"And the guard had a go, too," I muttered, looking down.

Peyton stared at me. "Did he rape you?"

I nodded, my arms going tight around my middle as I looked at the ground.

"This is outrageous," he said, turning to the matron and the officer. "Whoever did this will answer to my father."

The officer's eyes narrowed. "No one who works in this prison would abuse one of the inmates."

"Fee? Were you raped?"

"Yes," I whispered, not trusting my voice. "And he took my stone."

Peyton turned toward the officer in charge. "You will return her stone and fire the guard who did this to her. If you do not, all hell will rain down on all of you. I want her released into my custody."

"Are you willing to pay the bail, Mr. Rankin?"

He glanced at me. "I am."

"She will need to be back here in three days to stand trial."

"Fine. And I would like her stone returned."

"We will have to examine her before we let her go," the matron said. "Don't want her to get out of here because of a false rape claim."

Peyton glanced at me, waiting for my small nod of assent before agreeing. "Find the man who did this and get the stone."

"His name is Carl," I said, remembering the tag on his shirt from when he was on top of me. When I met Peyton's gaze, his eyes had filled with tears.

It was another hour before I was released into Peyton's custody, his threat seeming to take root throughout the department. The exam was quick and easy, the matron's frown telling me all I needed to know as she attempted to clean me up. Peyton signed a paper promising the bail, and when we walked out, he had my stone in his pocket. He didn't own a car but he'd managed to find the keys to my Harley. "Do you want to drive or should I?" he asked.

"I think you should. I'm not feeling up to it right now."

"Jesus, Fee. I've been going crazy trying to find you. You weren't at the local station and they refused to give me any information. I would never have known where to look if it hadn't been for that trick you pulled last night. You teleported. How in hell did you do it?"

"I thought it was a dream. Can you take me home? I need to clean that man's filth off my body and feed Cat."

Peyton grimaced before nodding.

At home I scrubbed every inch of my body and squeezed vinegar water into my vagina until I felt satisfied that Carl's sperm was gone. I felt the tears against my eyes but held them back, a part of me closing off. I dressed in clean jeans and a sweater and pulled my hair back, securing it with a band before meeting Peyton in the living room. The cat was on his lap when he looked up to see me standing there. "You look better."

I shrugged.

"My place now?"

"I guess. Can I bring Cat?"

"On the motorcycle?"

"He's been on it before."

His eyebrows rose. "Yeah, it's fine with me. But when there's customers he has to stay upstairs."

Cat rode under my jacket, snuggled against me as I clung to Peyton. He parked in front of the bar and helped me off. I extricated the cat and lifted him close to croon to him. My legs were like rubber, my back and ribs aching from being slammed against the cement floor of the cell.

When Peyton tried to put his arm around me, I backed away, not able to handle the physical connection. He sighed and went ahead to unlock the door, standing aside to let me in before locking it again. "I'd say a drink is in order."

I put the cat down on the wooden floor and perched on a stool as he poured wine into a glass and handed me a bowl of peanuts. "Did they feed you at all?"

I scoffed and shook my head, reaching for the bowl.

"Those bastards will pay for this," he muttered. "Are you really okay?"

"I don't break easily, Peyton. I've been beaten up before."

"What about the other thing?"

I stared at my glass. "It was over quickly."

"I'd like to kill him for what he did."

"I know, but it's done and we're here now. Did you really talk to your father or were you bluffing?"

His gaze lifted. "I don't have that many credits on hand."

I snorted and took a drink of wine, relaxing for the first time. "How long do you have to get it?"

"I told the guy at the desk that I could get the credits from my father."

I stiffened. "Are you saying what I think you're saying?"

He stared at his half-full glass of whiskey. "My father will never agree to it."

My nerves returned, my empty stomach rebelling from the wine. For a moment I thought I might be sick. "What are we going to do?"

He reached into his pocket and pulled out my pendant. "You need to wear this."

I slipped the leather loop over my head, but I didn't feel

any safer. If he didn't pay, they would come for me. And after what happened at the station, there would be revenge.

"If you can do again what you did last night maybe there's a way to trick them."

I shook my head. "I was asleep when that happened. I didn't control it."

Peyton picked up his glass and downed the rest, his eyes as dark as my thoughts.

It was an hour or so later that he brought up the idea of heading over to his parents' place. "Maybe if they meet you, I can convince them to help. If I don't do something you'll get deported." His pale gray eyes welled as he stared at me.

"You're still drunk."

"Maybe so, but I have to try. Are you game?"

"I guess, but I'm not looking forward to it."

He nodded. "Do something with your hair and put on some lipstick."

"Are you serious? I don't wear lipstick." I pulled the band off my wrist and wrapped it around my hair to make a makeshift bun. "Should I go out and buy a ball gown?"

"Very funny. I have a shirt you can wear. It's linen."

I put up with Peyton's nervous fussing, slipping his shirt on and tucking it into my jeans. I gazed at him. "Better?"

He nodded, his eyes narrowing. "A skirt would be better, but..."

"I don't own one."

We took the Harley, him driving. I was still feeling weak and ill, and with all the alcohol I'd consumed it was even worse. When we reached the apartment building, he handed the keys over to a guard and produced his I.D. The cold-eyed uniformed man nodded and gestured to the wide glass doors. Another guard looked us over as he examined Peyton's I.D., finally making a temporary card for me. "One hour," he said, his eyes meeting mine. *Can't believe I have to let this skank in.*

"One hour?" I hissed as we walked through the marble entryway toward the elevators. When the elevator arrived, we stepped in, the mirrors surrounding us showing my disheveled appearance and the bruises and cuts on my face. "I look like crap."

He pulled me to him and kissed the top of my head. "You're beautiful."

I grimaced and pulled away. "None of that mushy stuff, okay? I won't be able to keep up the pretense if you do that in front of your parents."

"Pretense of what?"

"Of being a respectable citizen."

He laughed and a second later the doors slid open. He led me down a white marble hallway carpeted in deep maroon. Every ten feet or so a lacquered table holding an intricate flower arrangement was set against the wall, gold framed mirrors above them. Sconces with pale linen shades and soft lighting were set here and there, everything perfect and pristine. There wasn't a sound. When we arrived at the number 26, he stopped and took in a deep breath. "Here we go," he said, running his hand over a plate set into the wall.

When the door opened an older dark-skinned uniformed maid was standing there, brown eyes staring at us in surprise. A second later she broke into a smile. "Mr. Peyton," she gushed. "Come in."

Peyton took her hand between both of his. "Good to see you, Martina. Are they here?"

She nodded. "Wait here a moment."

While she was gone, I scanned across the dark oil paintings to the marble and bronze sculpture on tables and the thick Persian rugs that lined the marble floors. I'd never seen anything like this. The opulence reminded me of books Bill had lent me about bygone eras.

When Martina arrived, she had an unreadable expression on her lined face. "You may follow me," she said.

"Are they annoyed?" Peyton whispered.

She turned to look at him, her expression giving him his answer before leading us into an enormous high-ceilinged room. Windows looked out on the darkened sky, a lighted bridge in the distance. A wide screen on the wall flashed pictures of waterfalls and forests. Two white couches faced each other, a woman with a drink in her hand sitting hunched into the corner of one of them. A man on the other couch stood when we arrived, his frowning eyes on Peyton before resting lightly on me. "I assume this is the woman the authorities called me about earlier today?"

Peyton blanched. "I told them I would talk to you. They had no right to..."

"To tell me that my son lied to save some indigent woman? They had every right, Peyton. She has no papers, no means of identification. What were you thinking?"

"Fee has amnesia, Father. She has no memory of her past. She needs our help."

At that moment the woman stood and walked unsteadily toward her son. Peyton took after her with his gray eyes and dark hair, but the expression on her face was not one I'd ever seen on his. She wore a gray silk dress with a high collar, her dark hair piled into intricate knots and curls.

"How dare you, Peyton," she said shrilly. "We've given you every opportunity and you've refused us, and now you decide to rescue a stray cat?" She looked me over, narrowed eyes assessing. "This one is obviously not worth the bother. I thought you had better taste." Her hand went to touch her perfect hair before she turned to glare at him.

"I suggest you take stock of your life before it's too late," his father chimed in. "Big changes are coming and those who aren't prepared will be churned up in its aftermath."

"What are you saying?"

"I'm saying that if you don't join us you will be swallowed. And this one is already slated for a future she will not enjoy," he added, gesturing with his thumb.

"Her name is Feirin, Father. I'd forgotten how intolerant you are. What about all the people who live down there?"

His father gave me a cold glance before his gaze went to Peyton. "The high court has decided to remove them from the city. You do know there is disease down there. We cannot risk the spread of such a virus."

"How will you get your precious deliveries?"

"We've shifted to full robotics."

"Robots can't bring the food in, Dad. The deliveries come from other places, across the sea by real life human beings. And from what I've heard, this city has been cut off due to greed and improper management. The rest of the world has lost confidence in our ability to pay our bills."

His mother frowned, ignoring what he'd said. "You are a fool if you don't abandon that silly bar. Soon there will be no one down there to buy from you. You could get sick. Is that what you want?"

Peyton's face went red with fury, his lips white from pressing them together. "I should have known how you'd be. It's why I left in the first place."

"And yet your brother lives here and is as happy as he could possibly be," his mother said.

"Never had much in common with Blair." He grabbed my

hand, tugging me backward. I glanced over my shoulder after I heard Peyton's father say, "Bar— martini dry with olive." He was standing in front of what looked like a real bar, glasses of every sort hanging from a rack and several bottles of different liquors displayed. There was a whir and a martini glass appeared in the opening at the bottom. It filled with clear liquid, an olive falling into the glass. Peyton's father took it and drank it down, ordering another a second later. I saw him turn back to his wife, her cold eyes meeting mine briefly before she covered the distance to the door and slammed it in our faces.

Martina glanced at us wide-eyed before she opened the door to let us out. She looked behind her and then hugged Peyton, her eyes welling. Once the door closed behind us Peyton's hands fisted. He swept his arm across one of the flower arrangements, sending it crashing to the floor, glass and water streaming across the carpet. "Those bastards!" he shouted.

I glanced down the long hallway, noticing several doors opening. "Come on," I muttered, pulling him toward the elevators.

ON THE GROUND floor we walked in silence to the front doors, Peyton's face set in a stony frown. Once we reached my bike, he broke down. "We should never have come," he mumbled, wiping at his welling eyes. "I'd forgotten what assholes they are. I'm sorry, Fee."

"Meeting them makes me admire you even more. If they were like that when you were a kid, I can't imagine your childhood."

"They were. My brother was their golden boy and still is. What I consider important is as far from their values as the stars in the sky. I can barely stand knowing I'm related to them."

When he got on the bike, I clambered on behind him, my arms going around his waist. I felt his juddering sigh before he turned the key, the bike roaring to life. He peeled away, ignoring the shouts from the guards monitoring noise levels around the high rises, and shot into the late-night traffic.

6

Peyton didn't try and touch me that night, his forbearance allowing me to relax. He was still reeling from his encounter with his parents, his jaw rigid as he pulled off his shirt. The bed was narrow and with two of us in it, it was narrower still. But our bodies were not touching when I finally fell into an unsettled sleep. When I woke in the night, he was curled around me from behind, his arm slung across my middle.

It was morning when I woke again, the spot next to me empty. I looked up to see a naked Peyton spooning something into a dish for Cat. I smiled when I heard him whispering sweet nothings to my cat. He turned, feeling my gaze, his gray eyes soft in the early morning light. "He was hungry."

I pushed up to sitting, watching him move around the kitchen as he heated water for the French press and retrieved the can of coffee. His body still drew me like a moth to a flame, but I was sore and also felt some emotional crap that I didn't want to think about. I noticed that Peyton had set up a cardboard box as a litter and filled it with uncooked rice. "Cat appreciates your efforts," I said.

He glanced at me. "I didn't want him peeing all over my apartment. And besides, you may be moving in here for a while; he needs to get used to it."

"Not if your parents have anything to say about it." I pushed back the covers and headed toward the tiny bathroom.

Before I left the bathroom, I reached for his robe, tying it tight around my waist. Parading around naked would give him the wrong idea, especially because he was in need of comfort. And right now, I was incapable of giving it.

He was standing by the bed when I came back and handed me a mug of steaming aromatic brew. I let out a sigh of pleasure as I took a sip. *The little things*, I thought to myself. *Concentrate on the little things.*

"Are you okay?" he asked, climbing back into the narrow bed.

I shook my head. "I feel like something sacred has been stolen from me."

He nodded, lifting the covers so that I could sit with my back to the wall next to him. I moved carefully into place, trying not to spill coffee all over his sheets.

"Rape isn't an easy thing to get over. It's a violation, a desecration. Not to mention the physical damage he did. Do you need to see a doctor?"

"No. I'm okay. I'll heal."

"That part will, but what about your psyche?"

I shrugged and stared out the window at the bird that had landed on his sill. It was bobbing its head, watching me. My mind quieted as I gazed at the iridescent feathers. Pigeons were common, but in this landscape of little to no wildlife, they had taken on a more important role. "I should be asking you the same question. What happened last night must have hurt."

"It did, but it was foolish of me to expect anything. I was living in a dreamworld when I thought my father might help."

"I didn't like them, but Martina was nice."

He nodded, his brows knitted together in thought. "Known her a long time. She basically raised me. Listen, Fee, I know a guy who can get you an I.D. He works underground."

"Like the ones who manufacture those drugs everyone takes?"

He shrugged. "Like anyone who strives to make a living in this god-forsaken shithole."

"I'm willing if you think it will keep me out of jail."

Peyton opened his hand to produce a screen. He turned his back, walking distractedly around the kitchen, his mumbling voice too low for me to make out the words. A minute or two later he was back by the bed. "Randy said come by this afternoon around three. Is that good for you?"

"I don't have anything going on, so yes."

Peyton sighed, his sad gaze meeting mine. "I want to make love in the worst way, but I know it's too soon."

I tried to smile but I wasn't in a smiling mood. I was upset in so many different ways and it bothered me when he referred to what we did as 'making love'. I'd never thought of it like that. To me it was sex or banging, humping, getting it on, or fucking. I cared about him for sure, but love? That was an alien concept.

WE WERE PREPARING to leave for Randy's when the knock came, turning into banging when neither of us answered. "Mr. Rankin?"

Peyton glanced at me, gesturing toward the bathroom

before he headed to the door. He looked over his shoulder before he opened it, making sure I was safely out of sight.

"What is it?" I heard him ask, followed by the sound of boots.

"Where is the girl?"

"If you are referring to Feirin, she isn't here."

"In that case you won't mind if we take a look around."

"I do mind. Do you have a warrant?"

"Actually yes, we do," the officious male voice answered.

"Why do you want her? She's not due in court for two days."

There was a moment of silence before the same voice said, "Because you did not return with the bail money, and when we contacted your father, he knew nothing about it. It was his suggestion that we pick up the girl. He told us she's illegal and should be deported with the rest of the scum."

"I'll have the credits by tomorrow."

"All lies, Mr. Rankin. Your father confirmed that you barely have a pot to piss in. You're lucky we don't arrest you for lying to the police. Now, where is she?"

I stepped back when the bathroom door opened abruptly, revealing a burly man with a nasty expression. "Got her," he announced, grabbing me by the arm.

Peyton watched them haul me out the door, his expression bleak. "Be assured that I *will* call my father. You will not get away with this."

The two cops laughed as they put the cuffs around my wrists and pushed me ahead of them down the stairs.

"Take care of Cat!" I yelled. At the bottom of the stairs they steered me away from the bar to the door that led outside. And when we reached the squad car my heart dropped. Behind the wheel, smiling a sickening smile, was my rapist.

Lucifer felt it. A change in the ether, the inner sense of something coming. "Prince of darkness, my ass," he muttered, turning into a beacon. Dazzling white light spun out into the night, lighting up the people huddling around fires, the barren landscape of dirt and rock. Radiance penetrated into the shadows, illuminating gaunt faces and weathered hands held to hearts. A cry went up, a shout of astonishment as the people stared at the hill in the distance where he stood. "It's an angel!" they roared.

"I am no angel." The whisper rode on the wind, winding down the hill and spinning through the crowd who still stared upward.

A voice went up and then another. "If he's not an angel, what is he?"

Lucifer smiled, his inner focus on the girl he knew was coming.

7

I spent the night in a tiny jail cell by myself. It was cold, drafty and smelled just
as bad as the others I'd been in. At least there weren't other angry women to contend with and the bucket was empty. I was sure Carl would come by, but he didn't. Perhaps Peyton's threat had stuck. Something nagged at me, as though I was supposed to remember something that hid along the edges of my mind. But I could not bring it into focus. The whispers of fear and panic wafted all around, energies from former occupants that hadn't been cleared out, and thoughts from other prisoners that I didn't want to hear. My necklace buzzed with energy, as though something had lit it up, but it didn't reveal its secrets. And when I glanced into the grimy mirror the crescent moon on my forehead glowed with an inner light.

I was awake all night, so when morning finally came my head lolled and I finally lay down and fell into a light doze. I was still on the floor with my jacket under my cheek when the metal door rattled. I looked up to see the matron.

"Time to go," she muttered, swinging it open.

I pushed myself up and grabbed my jacket. "Where are we going?"

"First to the judge so he can make it legal, and then you'll be transported to the

border. From there, who knows? It depends on what you have to trade."

Her gaze scanned across my body. I got the drift. She put the cuffs on my wrists

before we entered the stairwell, pushing me ahead of her as we climbed.

THE JUDGE WAS a stony-faced heavyweight man in his fifties, his narrow-eyed

gaze less than friendly as he pronounced my fate. When I protested, he

interrupted.

"You have no last name, no papers, no I.D. of any kind. How you've managed to keep off our radar for the past six years is astounding. People like you are the ones who make the system bad for the rest. Breaking the law is no small thing, young lady. Where you're going there are no laws, and you will find out very soon exactly what that means. I wish you luck." *You'll get exactly what you deserve.*

The way judge looked at me was like a man watching a bug die under the heel of

his shoe. "But I have no memory of how I got here or where I came from."

"I can't help that. I guess they took pity on you the first time. But

no one has claimed you and you've been living off the system ever since. There should have been a follow-up regarding your case years ago."

"But I had a job. I never lived off the system...."

He waved his hand. "Get her out of here," he growled, glancing at the matron. *Little bitch deserves a beating. Too bad Carl's off today.*

"This isn't fair," I muttered as she herded me down the hall. "I didn't have any

representation."

The matron made a sound in the back of her throat. "Fair? You have to be

kidding. We do what we have to with indigents such as yourself. The ones who pay get off; the judge has kids in college. If you'd asked nicely, perhaps he would have taken another sort of payment."

I gagged at the thought of it, swallowing down the bile that rose into my throat.

"But instead you were rude and talked back. You'll get yours soon enough."

"Get my what?"

She gave me a nasty smile. "What you deserve for cheating the system, missy."

"Call Peyton," I muttered. A second later there was a loud buzzing in my ears.

The matron laughed when she saw the look on my face. "You've been cut from

the net. There will be no more web use, calls or information available. You will be in a lawless land with nothing but the clothes on your back."

THE VAN TRIP through town was chilling. The homeless camps were gone, bits of cardboard, newspapers, clothing and trash all that was left. Loudspeakers blared from the tops of trucks that rumbled by, warning anyone who was living off the system to either self-deport or report to the nearest police station. "No more welfare!" the voice shouted. Skinny dogs ran by, their furtive glances going from one side to the other as they kept to the edges of the buildings. I might never see Peyton or my cat again.

The van carried at least twenty other men and women who had been beaten

down by life. Their eyes were downcast, their expressions grim as we left the city and bumped along the unpaved roads that covered the miles between the city proper and the border. Factory farms providing food for the city dotted the landscape, mechanized machinery moving up and down the rows of vegetables. Beyond them were enormous barns housing milk cows, and fields of cattle, pigs and other creatures being fattened up for market. I saw only one worker wearing high black rubber boots. Maybe he was there to oversee the mechatronics and robotics. Other than that, it seemed to be pretty much automatic everything.

Beyond the acres of green and the many barns, there were mountains of trash, machinery parts and abandoned vehicles of every kind, dust rising into the air as the wind came up.

I WAS half asleep when I felt the van slow, my eyes opening on an ominous black wall rising twelve feet into the air. I shivered, glancing at the terrified faces of those around me. We piled out and were herded toward a gate guarded by four uniformed men. I scanned in both directions seeing no end to the wall. If it surrounded the entire city it had to be hundreds of miles long. "How many gates does this thing have?" I muttered.

"This is the south gate," one of the men beside me answered. "It's the worst place to be left."

"What are the other ones like?"

He huffed. "All bad, but at least there are trees to shelter under and a few small

settlements if you travel far enough. The sun here can kill you. There are no deliveries through this gate since the area out there is a vast wilderness. Trucks come through the north gate and sometimes the east gate but not through this one. The ocean's too far away."

We arrived to the smirking grins of those who guarded the wall, the

chuckles making my skin crawl. Two of them undid the heavy chains and slid the gate open, ushering us through. There was no window where we could show papers, no machine where we could enter I.D. numbers, nothing but the grim expressions of the guards and the knowledge that we were heading into a very uncertain future.

"There's disease in there," I heard one of the guards say, flipping his thumb toward the emptiness.

"We've seen the virus here too," the van driver replied, producing a cigarette. He

lit it with a lighter and leaned against the wall, pulling smoke into his lungs.

"Vaccine?"

"Nope, but they're working on it. A big reason we were ordered to get the

homeless out of the city is because the higher-ups are worried that the sickness will spread and infect those at the top. From what I've seen most of the ground dwellers would have died anyway. Thousands have already been incinerated. Those of us in law enforcement are taking old prescriptions for a flu from a couple of years back. It may or may not work, but at least it's something."

The gate guard nodded, his gaze going to me as I walked by. He raised his

eyebrows, eyeing me up and down. "Now that one I might have to detain a bit longer," he murmured. *Like to get my cock in that.*

The smoker shook his head. "She's a fighter--nearly broke Carl's balls when he

had it off with her."

The guard laughed. "I enjoy the feisty ones."

When he sauntered toward me, I turned on him, my hands in fists. "If you touch

me, you'll regret it," I hissed, poised to kick.

He stared at me for a moment before splaying his hands in mock surrender. I felt

him watching me as I hurried to catch up with the rest of the group.

"Move away from the wall!" another guard yelled. "Anyone loitering will be

shot on sight--we don't want to see your sorry asses ever again!"

I ignored the laughter behind us as I weaved through the group. "Have any of

you been here before?" I asked.

"Oh yeah," a grizzled man with a thick beard answered.

"And?"

His rheumy eyes met mine. "You ever read about hell? This place is worse."

We began to walk with no discernable goal in mind. I scanned across the desert

of red sand and rock that led toward low hills in the hazy distance. There were no roads or signs of habitation anywhere. A thick miasma of brown hung over all of it and there wasn't a blade of grass, the chirp of a bird or even signs of a lizard. And when I looked around at my companions, I realized that at least half of them were sick.

There was nothing much to head for, no mirages or line of spindly trees. "Since you've been here, which direction should we go?" I asked the man with the rheumy eyes.

He pointed vaguely. "There's a hill out there that isn't visible yet. It has a few caves. You'd be surprised by the look of this place how the ground goes up and down. It isn't as flat as you'd think."

We'd been walking for nearly three hours when I felt a gust of wind, looking up to see a billowing cloud of brown heading toward us. "What is that?" Before I got an answer, the sand hit us. I screamed a warning before crouching to cover my face, but it didn't stop the gritty substance from getting into my eyes, mouth and nose.

How we made it through that first night I do not know. We formed a tent with

our bodies, huddling together with our heads down as the wind howled and screeched. In the morning we were covered in grit, our faces reddish brown, and our clothes shredded and covered in dirt.

"Haboob," someone muttered.

"What does that mean?"

The man sought me out, his face pale under the reddish sand that covered him. "A haboob is a desert sand storm. They happen all the time. There was once a river out here. There were animals and plants. But when the city diverted it for their farms it created a dustbowl."

"Water," a woman moaned.

And that's when the truth of our situation really hit me.

Along with the crazy weather, we had no water, no food, nothing to keep us alive. "*You've* been here and lived through it," I said, seeking out the man I'd talked to the day before. "There has to be a water source somewhere."

He glanced at me, continuing to shake the sand off his shirt. "There is, but it's a day's trip from here." He looked around, lowering his voice. "Not sure if some of these folks can make it that far."

"If we had something to carry it in, we could leave them here and bring it back."

"It's possible you might find a plastic jug along the way, but not guaranteed."

I glanced around at our group of twenty or so. A few from the bus had struck off alone, their silhouettes hazy in the far distance. "How about I recruit a few volunteers and head out?"

He shrugged. "Suit yourself."

"Can you point me in the right direction?"

He raised an arthritic finger. "It's over that hill there. Probably a good six miles, maybe more."

"What's your name?"

"Sam," he muttered, now working to free the sand on his face and in his beard.

I moved away and clapped my hands. "I need some volunteers to accompany me to the water source. Anyone game?"

Two men moved toward me, as well as a woman who looked to be in her early forties. "Good. Let's go before the sun gets too hot. Sam here says it's about six miles away."

"But what about us?" a pasty-faced older woman asked, coughing as soon as the words were out of her mouth. She was definitely sick.

"We'll try and bring water back, but that depends on finding a receptacle to carry it in."

"I've got one," another man with salt and pepper hair said,

reaching into the pack on his back. He pulled out a collapsible camping jug. "I'm Joseph, Joe. I'll come with you."

"Anyone else have a jug or a jar?"

No one did. A single gallon jug would not suffice. "I hope we find some discarded containers along the way," I muttered, nodding to the people who'd agreed to come along.

THE SUN BEAT DOWN, unrelenting. I tied my jacket around my waist and ripped a strip of fabric off the tail of my oversized cotton shirt, wrapping it around my head and over my face. I'd learned most of my companions' names as we walked and asked if any of them knew my friend, Jeremy. One of them did. "He was rounded up the week before us. His sister too," Ted told me.

"So, they're out here somewhere?"

"Possibly, although he could have been taken to another gate. It's hard to say."

"Are there towns? Everything seems so bare."

"There are towns, if you want to call them that," Adam with the shaved head answered. "But you need a weapon if you plan to go there." He reached under his shirt and pulled out his Glock 18, eying me. "I was prepared for this, and if you're smart, you'll let me lead. This gun may be an antique but it's deadly. I've been in the military and I know how this shit goes."

I only knew about this gun because of Bill who had one and always raved about how with an extension it could shoot 1200 rounds a minute. "It shoots real bullets, not like the zapping ones that turn people to ash," he'd told me. The one Adam held looked like the same model but with a 33-round clip. The man was covered in tattoos of skulls and weapons, his arms bulked out from lifting weights.

His eyes narrowed as he realized that I wasn't intimidated. "Girls do not take lead in a lawless place like this."

"This one does. Shall we fight for the privilege?"

"You should watch out for Adam," Ted warned. "He fights dirty."

I shrugged, waiting for Adam to make up his mind.

"You're a fucking idiot, lady," he muttered, removing his sleeveless vest. His muscles rippled across his bare chest, glistening with sweat.

I was pulling the makeshift scarf from my head when he came at me so fast that I barely had time to react. He'd surprised me, but his bulk kept him from being quick on his feet. I sidestepped away. When I saw him make a move I turned and kicked out, catching him in the upper thigh. It didn't seem to faze him as he rushed toward me and twisted me to face away, his arm around my neck. I was choking when I managed to wriggle free, but before I could turn to face him, he did a one-two punch into my back that would probably have killed me if it had landed on my kidneys.

I was on my knees gasping when he grabbed me by my hair, hauling me to my feet. "Let's see what you got, girlie," he hissed into my ear, bending me backwards as his fingers dug into my neck. I gagged as he pressed into my trachea, his other arm around my chest in a vice grip. I was unable to breathe, seeing black spots when I flung myself against him, loosening his hold and moving away to face him.

I pushed the hair off my face, bent my knees and wiped the sweat out of my eyes, watching him to see what his next move might be. When he rushed me, fists raised, I quickly backed away, setting myself up to kick him again. And this time I aimed for his crotch. I felt my boot make contact in the soft vulnerable part of him, his moan of pain the most gratifying thing I'd ever heard. He doubled over and was on the ground before I could kick him again.

"Shit!" he screamed, his expression contorting. "You fucking bitch!"

Ted took hold of my arm and pulled me away. "Adam's a bully and he doesn't like to lose."

"I don't give a crap. If he wants to fight again, then so be it." I left Adam lying in the dirt, pulled the cloth around my head and face and headed toward the hills in the distance.

"You're a good fighter." The woman held out her hand. "I'm Elena." She was Hispanic with deep-set brown eyes and a kind expression.

"Fee. As far as fighting, I've had to be."

"Well, I pick you for my leader. That guy can go to hell as far as I'm concerned," she said. "Big bully goes down hard."

I scoffed. "Hard? He may not be hard for a long while."

When Elena let out a roar of laughter I grinned, glancing over my shoulder to see Ted and Joe about twenty paces behind us. "They're leaving him back there," I said, surprised.

"Couldn't happen to a nicer guy." Her gaze met mine. "But I'd be careful if I were you."

"I always am."

WE HAD REACHED the base of the distant hill when I held up my hand and signaled a stop. The sun was directly overhead, burning whatever skin was exposed. I was covered in sweat, panting and so thirsty I couldn't think of anything but my dry mouth and throat. I could barely swallow. The hill we faced was a lot bigger than I'd thought, the idea of climbing its steep and rocky sides impossible to contemplate. Jagged rock and slippery gravel reached upward into a sky white with heat. In the distance I spotted Adam trudging toward us, his dark form hazy and shimmering in the heat mirage.

"It's a miracle!" Elena cried out.

I turned back to see her lifting a gallon plastic jug to her lips. "No!" I screamed, running toward her. I ripped it out of her hand, sloshing cool water over my wrist. "It could be contaminated."

"And how do you plan to figure that out?" Ted asked, grabbing it out of my hands and tipping water into his mouth.

I sniffed the second jug and placed a drop on my tongue. "If it's poisoned it's tasteless," I muttered, handing it to Elena. She drank for a long time before she handed it back. I drank and drank, only stopping when my stomach reacted to all the liquid.

"Nothing could be worse than the thirst I felt," Ted muttered. "I was ready to die for that water."

I tried to smile, but my face was so parched that my lips refused to lift. "Those poor people we left behind. I can't imagine how they feel right about now." I glanced at the two nearly empty jugs. "But where did these come from?"

We all looked at each.

"I know," Adam said, arriving suddenly.

I jumped when I saw him. He looked terrible, his face bright red, his lips blistered and bleeding. He was hunched over, his arms around his lower belly, as though what I'd done to him was still painful. When I saw the goggles he was wearing, I wished I had a pair for myself; my eyeballs ached from the brightness and from squinting. When he held out his hand, I grabbed a jug and handed it over.

When he was finished drinking, he wiped a gritty hand across his face. "There's a myth in these parts about an entity that does favors. They call him Lucifer."

Elena's eyes widened. "Lucifer the fallen angel?"

Adam shrugged. "I don't know fallen angels from devils. All I know is what I've heard from others who've encountered whatever this thing is."

I glanced around at the sand and rock, the places where there might have been some sign of another person, wondering if what he said was true. The water had been cool when we arrived. If it had been here for more than ten minutes it would have been hotter than Hades. "No sign of anyone, not even a hint of footprints."

Adam reached into his pack, producing four more pairs of sand goggles. "Found these on my way here. Military grade."

"They just happened to be left on the route you took?"

He shrugged. "That's what I'm sayin'. With the dust storms out here, we'll need 'em."

I thought about the people we left behind. Would this good Samaritan leave more for them? And where in hell do you come up with military grade sand goggles in the middle of fucking nowhere?

"I know what you're thinking," Adam said, watching me. "But I'm telling you, this is what happens out here. And if this entity, or whatever the fuck he is, doesn't like you, watch out."

"What happens?"

"I've heard gruesome stories."

I grabbed his arm and pulled him away from the others. "I can handle it."

He shook his head and looked down. "Let's just say that by the time he got finished with them, they were happy to die."

I felt a chill despite the blistering sun and the sweat trickling down my neck. "Has anyone seen this...whatever it is?"

"Not any that I know of." He turned away and headed toward Ted and Sam, leaving me to my terrible fantasies.

We were half way up the hill and I was gazing toward a few trees on the far side when Ted came up behind me. "Don't be surprised if it takes longer to get there than you think. Distances are deceptive out here."

"How far do you think it is?"

"Could be another two miles."

I let out a sigh and adjusted my makeshift scarf. "Two more miles...and then we have to walk all the way back."

Ted didn't reply, only squinting into the distance.

"There's a settlement out there," I said, pointing to the left where a cloud of dust had risen. It was at least ten miles away, maybe further.

"I would steer clear of that place," Joe said, catching up. "I've heard stories."

"I have too," Adam agreed. "They're well-armed and hate newcomers."

"What *is* this place? Are we in another country?"

"Borders mean nothing out here," Ted answered. "It's just one crazy free-for-all. You ever see the movie called Mad Max? You can search it on IRIS. Made a couple hundred years ago, but pretty accurate."

I hadn't heard of it, nor had I watched anything entertaining on IRIS. That level was way above my paygrade. "But how big is it? Has anyone explored those mountains?" I pointed toward a haze of blue probably two-hundred miles away.

"Not any of us, but I'm sure someone has. People have been living out here since way before the city was built."

"Who are they?"

"Desert nomads? I haven't met any of them so I can't say. Getting across that desert would take some serious know-how, like the Australian Aborigines."

"I...I haven't heard of them." I was beginning to feel really ignorant.

"They were wiped out a long time ago, their culture

subsumed and their people scattered," Joe mumbled. "Just like the Indigenous peoples I descended from."

I glanced at him, noticing his mahogany skin and dark eyes for the first time. He looked exotic with his high cheekbones and dark straight hair.

"You and your indigenous crap," Adam muttered. "This place is a shithole filled with assholes who would stab you or shoot you before you could say a word. It's time to face facts."

"Where's Elena?" I asked, looking around. When no one answered, I turned, scanning for her. She was still on the upward climb, and from what I could see she was struggling. I hurried toward her. "What's wrong?"

She looked up. "I hurt my ankle. It slowed me down."

"Is it okay now?"

"Not really, but I can manage."

I put an arm around her waist, helping her forward. "If it's bad I'm sure one of these burly guys can carry you."

"But not Adam, please."

I scoffed. "Adam has an injury of his own," I whispered, making her chuckle.

WE RESTED FOR A WHILE, letting the water saturate our cells before heading upward. Another two miles didn't sound nearly as bad now. And as we climbed, I thought about our environment and how harsh it was—a place where life balanced on a knife edge. For some reason the idea of that motivated me. When my necklace buzzed and grew hot, I removed it from around my neck and stuck it in my pocket. The stone was absorbing the heat. Or at least that's what I figured was happening.

8

Peyton was growing more and more agitated. It had been weeks since Fee was taken, his one trip to the police station giving him next to no information. He stared out the window at the empty trash-filled street, the gray sky, the sense that life as he'd known it was crashing down. A call to his parents only left him feeling more upset, his father's clipped tone and snide remarks regarding Fee giving him the strong sense that he had orchestrated whatever had happened to her. She was either in jail and had been taken to the prison outside the city, or she'd been deported. Judging from what he noticed on the streets, the latter was most likely the correct scenario. The homeless were gone, their makeshift houses turned into compost and burned in the incinerators under the city.

Something had changed in the past weeks, as though a new order had begun. Every day he saw uniformed men on the streets carrying heavy weapons, their faces covered in gas masks. He'd begun to suspect some kind of toxin had escaped, his strange cough persisting and his lungs burning whenever he left the bar for supplies. The other thing he'd noticed was a distinct lack of necessities, including the basics for the bathroom, plus the fake stuff that replaced meat, cheese and soy. When he asked about the shortages he was met with blank stares and sideways glances, as though the store clerks had been sworn to secrecy. The people in the stores he'd known before, the ones who would give him credit, were all gone now, replaced with robots and hybrids.

Amidst all this his bar was doing a rousing business, but the clientele had changed, men in business suits and other more white-collar workers coming in for drinks or a beer before heading toward the high rises for the night. Gone was the easy comradery from before. He merely mixed drinks and collected the money, trying to ignore the conversations that centered around life in Uptown. But he couldn't ignore overhearing that leaders had been replaced, and that Uptown was planning a complete take-over, including redoing this street on which he lived. Robot workers would pull these buildings down and new high-rises would go up in their place. No one would be allowed to live on the streets.

Peyton was depressed. The world had altered. His girl was gone and with her absence his heart had closed down. He hadn't realized how much he counted on her and craved her body to soothe his dark moods.

IT WAS EARLY one morning about three weeks into the new reality when he decided to head out to see Bill, Fee's former employer. Fee's bike was where she'd left it and the key was still on the table from the morning the police had come for her.

The project on the far side of town was nearly completed,

Bill barking orders to the hard-hatted men and androids scaling the scaffolding along the front of the building.

"Bill? I'm Peyton, Fee's boyfriend. Remember me?"

Bill turned, his eyes narrowing. "Your gal left me in the lurch. She was the best human worker I've ever had."

"Fee's disappeared. The police took her away three weeks ago and I haven't seen her since." He glanced around at the empty streets. "What the hell is going on? The homeless are gone and my bar regulars have all but disappeared."

Bill looked wary, scanning behind him. "Why are you asking me?"

"According to Fee you have your finger on the pulse of things. I need to find her."

Bill scowled. "I saw the busses loaded up weeks ago. They rousted everyone who wasn't essential. You do know about the virus, right? From what I gleaned, that was the reason for the deportations. Fee was probably among them. Either that or she's in federal lockup. I wouldn't wish that on a dog."

Peyton ran a hand over his three-day growth. "My father is high up in the council, but he wouldn't give me any information."

"The virus is all you need to know. If you don't have it already you will soon. We all will. There's no cure. My human crew has dwindled from twenty down to seven."

Peyton stared at the older man. "They died? And yet here you are working. That makes no fucking sense."

"If we don't work, we get deported. It's as simple as that." He swiveled to yell at one of the men and then turned back to Peyton. "If you want to find her go up to the federal prison. If she isn't there, there's only the desert. Good luck." With that he turned and hurried toward the scaffolding, yelling as he went.

Peyton stood there for a while before he mounted the bike and took off to the north. Toward the federal prison.

"No one by that name is incarcerated here," the heavy-weight matron told him two hours later. He'd only managed to get answers because of his family name.

Peyton left the squat cement building surrounded with razor-wire feeling even more down. The drive back along the deserted strip of road where trash clung to chain link fences and long dead animals festered, did not improve his mood. He knew now that whatever was going on was because of the council and his father. They were hunkering down, getting rid of the trash, so to speak, and keeping themselves safe until they could find a cure for the strange virus that had appeared two months before. The only bright spot was the hope that Fee was in the desert and hadn't come down with it. As far as he knew she'd never been sick.

9

"We need to find water and get back!" I shouted, scrambling up the hill. "Think about what we just experienced and double it for our friends back there."

Elena struggled upward to climb beside me, the oversized goggles hiding half her face. "If we wait until it cools off it'll be better."

I glanced at her. "You mean wait to head back?"

She nodded. "The afternoon heat is worse than this."

I let out a sigh, glancing at the nearly empty water jug in my hand. "And we need more jugs," I muttered.

I heard Adam, Joe and Ted muttering behind me, unable to catch their words. But I knew this reprieve from Adam would not last. I was poised, alert to any move on his part as I struggled for footholds on the slippery rock formations. He'd answered my questions willingly enough, but I felt his animosity like waves of energy rolling over me.

I passed several caves, longing for the shade and coolness

they would afford, but I kept going, hoping Sam was right about an oasis on the other side.

BY THE TIME we reached the top I was thirsty again, trying hard not to drink the few ounces left. With my goggles on I could see the base of the mountain where a few straggly trees and some willows surrounded what looked like a spring. My energy returned as I realized how close we were. I started down.

We were closing in on the small copse of trees when a sudden commotion took our attention. Several men ran toward us with black scarves tied around their faces, their eyes the only part of them we could see. They had guns.

I stopped in my tracks, signaling to the others with my raised hand. The gun wielding group stopped too, watching us. "We need water!" I yelled.

"So does everyone else," the apparent leader called back. "Find another source. This one's ours."

"We have things to trade," I called back, hoping that was true.

"What do you have?" he asked.

I pulled the stone from my pocket and held it up, glancing at the others behind me. "Find something," I hissed.

Elena pulled off a gold ring and Ted produced a telescope and a collapsible camping cup. Joe pulled a hunk of cheese out of his backpack that he'd neglected to share, as well as a pair of scissors and a small towel. Adam did nothing. "Adam—what about your gun?"

"Are you fucking kidding me? I'm not giving that up. It's all that stands between me and these mofo's."

He did have a point. I shook my head when Joe offered the cheese and the scissors, knowing that they would both come in handy at some future time. But I took the ring and the telescope and held them out, along with my pendent, and walked slowly forward.

"Watch out," I heard Ted whisper. "These people are savages."

The leader walked forward to meet me, his brows knitted together in a frown. He was thin to the point of emaciation, but he looked wiry and I could tell he was strong. His clothes were tattered strips of cloth revealing tattoos and dust covered skin, and he had a belt of bullets around his waist and a knife on his hip. Out here weapons were primitive. Anything high-tech needed energy to run, resources that did not exist outside the city.

He took the items I held out and looked them over. "The only thing of value is this," he said, holding up the telescope. "Your jewelry is worthless out here."

"But how do we barter for things? I saw a settlement out there," I said, pointing vaguely. "Cars."

"Some have motored vehicles but I wouldn't call them cars. They've been pieced together from found parts. This is a dumping ground for obsolete military equipment. You do now about the underground military installation. The smart ones have taken advantage of that."

"Like you and the water here."

"That's right. Water is a precious commodity. I will give you two jugs of water in trade."

"I need two more jugs and a camp jug filled as well," I said, holding mine out. "There are twenty people in our group."

He was suddenly wary, his gaze scanning. "Where are the rest of 'em?"

"We left them miles back. Most are sick and weak."

"If you're smart, you'll cull 'em now. All they'll do is slow you down and get you killed."

"Thanks for the advice. Now how about the water?" I signaled to Ted to bring Joe's and the second jug we'd found.

The rest of the ten men watched us out of narrowed eyes, guns pointed, as the leader took the jugs. "Don't do anything stupid," he muttered, disappearing.

I tried to see where they lived but there was nothing there but trees and some low growing desert bushes.

When the leader returned, he was carrying four full jugs of water. "I'm keeping the other one," he said, handing them over as he eyed me and glanced at Elena. "And FYI there's more to trade than shit like that collapsible cup and the telescope," he muttered.

"Thanks for the tip." I wondered when it would come to that. This was a dangerous place with scant resources.

WE CLIMBED BACK up the mountain and rested in a shallow cave, discussing our uncertain future. Ted and Adam seemed intent on outdoing each other with tales of bizarre happenings. Strange lights, unexplained deaths, water and food left without explanation, people disappearing never to be seen or heard of again.

"We need more weapons," Adam announced after Ted relayed another gruesome death he'd heard about.

"If you haven't experienced this shit first hand I suggest you shut the hell up," I hissed, watching Elena's face pale. "We don't need to freak out until we have to."

"We still need weapons," Adam muttered under his breath.

He was right, but I wasn't about to put him in charge of finding them. He was a hothead who didn't have the sense to think before acting.

I leaned against the wall and dozed as the sun sank lower and lower, my consciousness sinking with it. I was so tired.

She's made her mind up, Bran. I can't dissuade her. And we ought to trust her intuition. After all, she is the dark goddess.

My eyes flew open, the words 'dark goddess' stirring some buried memory. But as soon as I was fully awake the wispy threads unraveled and were gone. My companions shifted around me, ready to be on their way. The sun was finally gone, leaving an orange glow in the west. Black hills rose up in the distance, the stillness of the moment feeding some need I hadn't known I had. For that few seconds I forgot where I was, staring at the horizon and taken by the ethereal beauty of the sunset.

"Get a fucking move on," Adam hissed, jostling me as he moved by. "The desert gets cold at night, girlie. And none of us are dressed for it."

I followed him out, checking on Elena. "How's your ankle?"

"It's better. Resting helped."

"Good." I smiled at her and strode quickly by Adam to take the lead. I heard his muttered oath as I moved past, ignoring him as I scanned into the deepening dark. When I glanced at the sky a million stars twinkled back, the sight so startling that I had to stop for a second, causing Adam to run into me. "What the fuck, lady? You leading or what?"

I pointed upward. "That's incredible," I whispered.

"You've never seen stars before?"

"Not like this." But I *had* seen them like this; I just couldn't remember where or when.

He scoffed. "Just another reminder of where we are. Nowhere. We're tiny ants who will die if we don't get our shit together."

By now the others had caught up. "What's happening?" Ted asked.

"This idiot bitch is staring at the stars," Adam scoffed, taking that moment to stride ahead.

I let him lead, content to ask questions of those who would answer honestly and not spout negativity. I was negative enough without listening to an overgrown man-child fill my ear with garbage. "How big is this place?" I began. "Is there an ocean or something over those far mountains? What about another city or at least a few towns?"

Ted was next to me and answered first. "Being on foot is kind of limiting, but it's not like the world ends here. There are many towns and cities somewhere out there in the vastness of the planet. As far as the mountains go, I've never made it that far, but Sam has. This is his third stint here and he knows a lot."

"Guess I'll question him when we get back."

"If he's still alive," Adam said, dropping back. "That dude has cancer and he may have the virus as well. Not long for this world."

I glared at him. "Why don't you keep your nasty thoughts to yourself? It's bad enough without listening to your unhelpful crap."

"Someone has to tell it like it is, girlie."

"My name is Fee, not girlie."

When he sniggered and strode ahead into the darkness, I knew he was baiting me. The more I reacted the worse it would get. We were headed for another fight.

THE SKY WAS LIGHTENING by the time we reached the spot where we'd left the others. Most were asleep, heads resting on arms or jackets. But when they heard us there was a collective shout, hands reaching for the jugs. They drank and passed the jugs around, finishing every drop. When they handed them back, I wondered what we would do now. Water was gone, there was no food unless someone else had a hunk of cheese, and there were the sick to take care of. Adam must have realized my mood because he was suddenly whispering in my ear. "What now, *leader*?"

"Fuck off," I muttered, shoving him away.

He sneered at me and went to talk to Joe while I sought out Sam who was in the midst of talking with Ted. "Ted here was telling me what happened out there," he said, glancing at Adam in the distance. "He says you know your way around thugs."

I laughed. "Well, yeah. I'm a woman and I lived in the city. I heard you've been out here a few times. Any ideas for what to do? There's no shelter close by and the mountains are too far for most of these people."

His eyes darkened as he ran a hand through his graying hair. He pointed in another direction that seemed to lead into flat desert, no mountains or trees to be seen. "The last time I was here I found a series of caves out there. There's wildlife too —scant, but it exists. The problem is water."

"If there are animals there has to be water."

"That's what I thought too, but I never managed to find a reliable source."

I gazed into the early morning haze. "How did you end up getting out of this place and being sent back? Ted said you've been here three times."

He let out a humorless laugh. "I needed a doctor's attention, and since I had things to trade, they took me out to see one. That was trip number two. This trip will be my last."

He was saying he would die here. "If you're sick..."

He shook his head. "Nothing to trade this time, and besides there's nothing more they can do for me."

I glanced at the ground, trying not to become emotional. Must be lack of sleep and exhaustion that was causing my eyes to well. I didn't even know this guy. "How long to get to the caves?"

"With this group? A full day and night, maybe more. And since I haven't been there in a while, I can't guarantee they're still available. The natives lay claim to whatever they come upon."

They've been living here forever, right? If we could make friends with them..."

He shook his head. "They are fiercely independent, not to mention ferocious. You do not want to mess with them."

"But how do they live?"

Ted moved close to join in the conversation. "They know this desert and where to find water and food. It's kind of mystical how they manage."

Sam nodded his agreement. "This is their home, but you'll never see them."

"Like the one who left the water for us at the base of the mountain?"

"The nomads do not share. If water was left for you it was not their doing."

We left less than an hour later, making our way slowly in the direction Sam had pointed out. I heard coughing, sneezing and sniffling, worried about the rest of the group catching whatever this was. "Do you think they have the virus?" I asked Sam who struggled beside me.

"No way to know for sure until the rest of us come down with it. It's a virulent son-of-a-bitch."

"Well, that's encouraging. We need to do something, don't we?"

"Wear your scarf and tell everyone else to do the same."

I did as he suggested, stopping to make sure that everyone had some article of clothing they could pull over their nose and mouth. "If you have a fever let me know!" I shouted before heading off again, leading into the no man's land spread out in front of us.

It was late when we stopped. Dehydration had taken over, the sick slowing us down so much there was no point to it. There was not a tree or a bush or a weed in sight as we settled in. I watched the ones who knew each other huddle together, trying to keep warm, the others lying down around them. I took myself well away from the group, hoping to have a moment's peace before the whole thing started up again in the morning. If we didn't find water tomorrow, we were doomed.

10

I woke to a penis in my face, my arms pinned. "Say ahh, bitch," Adam hissed, his eyes glittering with malice. He was naked, straddling me with his knees on my arms. His fingers pried my mouth open as he shoved his hips forward.

I gagged and turned my head away, using all my strength to arch my back and bring my legs up to wrap my feet and ankles around his neck. I didn't manage what I intended, but it dislodged his hold long enough to wriggle out from under his heavy bulk. I thought of yelling for help but decided against it. This thing between us had to be settled or it would go on forever. I jumped up to face him.

His naked body glowed blue in the sliver of moon hanging low in the sky. He faced me with knees bent, poised to fight. And when I moved, he lunged, grabbing me around the neck. "Should have done what I asked, girlie," he hissed. "A lot less painful than what I plan to do to you now." He grabbed my hair and jerked, twisting me into position on my knees, his fingers working on my jeans.

I kicked and fought hard, but he held me around the waist in a vice grip. He had my jeans down and was nearly there when Ted appeared, wrenching him off me with a roar. I rolled away and pulled up my jeans, my head spinning with what he'd almost managed to do.

"You fucker!" Adam yelled, pulling out his gun. A second later a report pierced the silence and Ted dropped. Sam was now awake as well as several others, all rising to their feet. Adam was like a crazed lunatic, the whites of his eyes showing as he waved the weapon around. "Stay back!" he screamed.

I watched him scan, waiting for just the right moment to rush him. And then I charged like a bull, head butting him and knocking him to the ground. When the gun dropped and skittered away, Sam picked it up and pointed it at Adam. "You're out of here," he stated flatly. When Adam didn't move, he shot into the air. "Now!"

Adam watched him with narrowed eyes. "You won't shoot me," he muttered.

"You want to test me?"

By this time, I was next to Ted, feeling for a pulse. He was still alive, but a red stain had spread across his shirt. The bullet had gone in just below his ribs on the left side.

Out of the corner of my eye I saw Adam moving backward to where he'd dropped his clothes. "You'll regret this," he muttered, pulling on his fatigues.

"Get the hell out of here and don't come back," Sam hissed.

There was a moment of tension before I saw Adam's shoulders drop. He turned and walked into the darkness and a few minutes later he'd disappeared into the shadows.

Sam hurried to where I knelt next to Ted. "Is he alive?"

"Barely. We need to get the bullet out."

He bent to take a look, gently moving Ted to examine his

back. "It went straight through." He glanced at me. "That's lucky."

"But what did it hurt on its way?"

"Anyone here a nurse or a doc?" he called out.

Elena walked toward us. "I've dealt with bullet wounds." She kneeled and examined Ted, probing carefully with her fingers. "I can't say for sure, but it seems it may have missed everything important. I'll need herbs to treat the wound. It could get infected."

"Anyone here have herbs of any kind?" I called out.

When no one answered, I let out a sigh. "Maybe they grow around the mountains. The natives must know."

"The natives won't help," Sam said. "But if they grow here at all, that's where they'll be."

Something skittered by in the dark. "What was that?"

"An animal of some kind, maybe a coyote," Sam answered.

Joe nodded. "Smelled blood."

"We need to flush out the wound," Elena said. "Which means using up the tiny bit of water we have left."

I stared into the dark night. The mountain was still very far away. We'd walked for two full days with nothing to eat but a few nuts and some cheese. Sam's estimate of a day had stretched into at least three. The water was nearly gone, despite having found another jug of it the day before. If only whoever was leaving water would leave food too.

My gaze went to the sky, something about that vastness of stars calming my juddering nerves.

"Fee?"

I brought my attention to Elena.

"Ted's awake."

By the time I reached him Ted was attempting to sit up. I pushed him gently back. "You need to rest."

"That bastard shot me."

I nodded. "He's gone now, hopefully for good."

"Don't count on it. Did he hurt you?"

"Nope."

Ted smiled and then winced. "Glad to hear it. I had no idea what he was capable of."

I scoffed. "I wouldn't have chosen my sleeping spot so far from the group if I'd had any inkling."

"Safety in numbers, Fee. We need to stick close together."

I thought about that. Many were sick, which meant that the rest of us could catch it. Since I was leading, I had to make sure I stayed healthy. "The sick ones are getting worse," I whispered, listening to the hacking coughs around us.

Ted nodded. "A few will die. They know it and we know it."

I glanced into the dark, scanning for Sam. "You and Sam saved me, Ted. What can we do for him?"

He shook his head. "Nothing but a miracle will save that old bastard."

We rested until just before dawn and then headed off again, Ted supported between Sam and another man called Daryl. The sun rose blessedly late because of the mountain range to the east, but that meant that the heat was worse once it appeared.

Elena moved to walk beside me, her expression grave. "I need herbs to pack the wound before it festers." She glanced at Ted whose head was lolling as he stumbled between the two men. "He's losing blood. He could die."

I nodded, gazing at the still distant mountains. "It will take me several hours, Elena. And what if I don't find what you need?"

"Yarrow is a many blossomed white flower that grows on a long stalk with feathery leaves. It has a spicy smell when you crush it. If you can't find it look for aloe. It's thick like a cactus, with green stalks filled with liquid."

I let out a sigh. "I'll do my best." I left her and headed toward Sam. "Can I borrow the gun? I'm on my way to the mountain to look for herbs, but maybe I can shoot a rabbit or something on the way."

He handed it over but his expression was skeptical. "The time to find animals is just before dawn or dusk. They've gone to ground by now."

"Snakes?"

"Possibly. Be careful out there."

My fingers went to the stone around my neck. If it was protective, I needed it now more than ever. I tied my shirt around my head, winding it over my mouth and nose, donned the goggles and jogged away, my breathing rhythmic and slow. There was something otherworldly about the red sand stretching away, the boulders dotting the landscape like ancient extinct animals, and the feeling that we'd never come to the end. The space was vast, enormous, empty, so unlike the confinement of the city. I felt it inside me, the sensation of mystery, something unknowable. It was in my stomach, tight, like something coiled and waiting.

WHEN I SAW THE MAN, I was sure he was a mirage. He wasn't wearing goggles nor was he dressed for the weather. He was barefoot wearing a long black coat and jeans, his dark hair pulled back and tied at the nape of his neck. His face was striking and full of planes and angles. Androgynous. He stopped when he saw me, waiting as I approached. Instead of fear I felt curious about who he was.

When I was six feet away, he put up a hand as though in

welcome. I stared into eyes the color of onyx. I couldn't seem to speak.

A slight smile lifted his lips. "I've been waiting for you."

Those words made no sense. I opened my mouth but nothing came out.

"I've been leaving breadcrumbs."

"Breadcrumbs."

"Clues to follow." He shifted his stance, settling onto one slim hip as he gazed at me.

"You're the one who left the water jugs."

He nodded. "Take off your scarf and goggles so I may look upon you."

"It's too bright," I argued, glancing briefly at the sun, but my fingers were already busy unwinding the material. I slipped the googles up onto my head and turned to face him.

He moved closer, his long fingers lifting the tangled hair off my shoulders to examine my necklace and the crescent on my forehead, before his eyes sought mine.

Did he like what he saw? Did I care?

"Do you know who you are?"

What a weird question. "My name is Feirin, but I go by Fee."

He shook his head. "A name is not who you are."

I was mesmerized by his eyes, unable to look away. "I...I lost my memories—amnesia they called it."

"That's what I was afraid of. You come from the past, Feirin, to do a job, but you have forgotten your mission."

Was this a dream? "A job? I guess I'm doing one now."

"Yes, you are a leader, but not in the way you think. You are the dark goddess."

The words *dark goddess* drifted through my brain. "I dreamed about this," I whispered, my mind loosening as a sensation of floating took over.

"You are trying to remember."

The dreamy feeling disappeared as I focused on him. "How do you know all this?"

He smiled, transforming his serious expression. "I am Lucifer, timeless and here for one purpose."

My gaze traveled his face, his dark coat, the ethereal beauty of him. There was not a drop of sweat on his face. "What purpose?"

"I think you already know."

The answer was there before I could think. "For me."

"Correct. I have come to help you do what you came to do."

He was the one Ted and the others were talking about, the one responsible for death. "They call you a devil, a fallen angel. You kill people."

He looked surprised for a moment. "I have not killed anyone. As far as being a devil, or 'the prince of darkness', the other name used to refer to me, religion took what I am and perverted it to suit themselves. Lucifer literally means 'light-bringer'. I am the original bringer of light, an avatar who exists between worlds."

I frowned, trying to wrap my mind around his words. "What's an avatar?"

"It's an ancient word that means descent, as in a deity who comes to the Earth."

"So, you *are* a god, or at least an angel."

"Not in the strictest sense, but I am an entity who, as I said, exists between worlds. Sometime I will elaborate on this but for now it must suffice. You traveled three hundred years to this future time and it is imperative that you remember."

My hands prickled with foreknowledge, something in me lighting up. I nodded slowly as the dreams I'd had made themselves known. When my eyes met his, I saw that his swirled with light. "Your eyes..." I began, leaning closer. I remembered falling to the floor, Peyton's face changing, seeing the dark eyes I now gazed into. "You were there...in the city when..."

He nodded as though he could read my mind. But when I tried to read his, I heard nothing. "What about this?" I asked, pointing to the tattoo on my forehead. What does it mean?"

"It is the symbol of who you are, Feirin."

I was suddenly aware of how much time had gone by and my urgent need to find medicine for Ted. I looked around frantically, noticing how high the sun had risen and the distance to the mountain. "I..."

He placed his hand on my arm. A second later we were standing at the base of the mountain. I gasped in surprise, my body trembling. I took in a deep breath.

He pointed toward a steep path leading up the mountain in zigzag lines. "This is where the plants you need grow. Do you know what to look for?"

I tried to answer but my voice came out in a squeak before I stopped to clear my throat, beginning again. "Elena described a flowering plant called yarrow. But I know nothing about herbs."

"Are you sure?"

I saw the plant in my mind, just as she'd described it. I glanced at him with what must have been a surprised look.

"You learned it as a child," he explained. "Yarrow grows in a shady spot just where the path twists to the right."

I wrapped my face, pulled down my goggles and headed up the mountain trail, leaving Lucifer standing at the bottom. As I climbed, my thoughts tangled, turning into a snarled ball of confusion. Should I believe this guy? What if this was just some made up story to lure me into a trap? This day had begun with a near rape, it could happen again if I wasn't careful. I patted the back of my jeans where I'd stashed the gun in my belt.

I took in a deep breath and turned my attention to the job at hand. Although seemingly bare from a distance, the mountain was covered in plants. They grew in cracks and crevices, flowers poking out to receive the sunlight. There were animal tracks along the path, big cats, coyotes, smaller creatures. Water pooled in places, tiny springs bubbling. This is where we need to be, I thought to myself. And that's when I heard flute music. I was suddenly alert, my gaze going upward. I saw nothing to indicate human habitation. A moment later I spied the yarrow. I picked several, tying it all up in my shirt before I turned and headed down.

"You found it."

I jumped and glanced behind me where Lucifer hovered. "I did. And I also heard flute music. Who lives up here?"

"The natives come and go."

I glanced at the rocky terrain, the spots of green, the trickling water, the earthy miasma reaching my senses. "This is the perfect spot for my group. Will the natives mind?"

Lucifer shrugged, a motion that seemed incongruous with the long black coat and his unsmiling expression. "That I cannot say. But I would be mindful of their position here."

"Are they dangerous?"

"Dangerous in attacking for no reason? No. But they've been here a long time."

"These are the nomads I've been hearing about."

Lucifer nodded. "They are hunter gatherers, and they know where to find what they need."

I continued down the hill, being careful not to trip on the rocks. I felt better now, not so nervous about Lucifer, glad that I'd found the yarrow. "Are there towns out there somewhere?"

"Your kind have built up settlements, yes. And further on there are cities similar to the one you came from."

I thought about that for a minute. "How far?"

"Over a month's travel on foot, possibly more."

I stumbled, and when he grabbed my arm to steady me, I felt a tingling sensation on the spot where his fingers made contact.

"Shall I take us back quickly?" he asked once we reached the desert floor.

"Can you heal?"

He stared at me for a moment or two. "If you are asking me to heal your shooting victim, I cannot. I am only authorized to reveal myself to you."

He knew about Ted? I turned from the fuzzy green plant I was examining. "Authorized by who?"

Instead of answering he placed his hand on my arm and a second later we were back where we'd started. "I will leave you here. In the next few days you will have many questions. When you are ready for answers I will come."

He disappeared so fast I wasn't sure if he'd ever been there. I hurried off with my herbs. I felt Lucifer as I ran, as though he was watching me.

II

I lay on my back staring up at the stars, my head on my jacket. Some were blue, some white, some a gold white, and others reddish. The big dipper, little dipper, Orion the hunter, Taurus the bull. I could pick them out now, tracing their shapes with my eyes and thinking about what it must have been like for the first humans. *They thought of them as Goddesses*, a voice whispered. *And gods.* There were so many of them, a haze of billions of stars that made up the milky way-- other galaxies with other planets and other beings who lived there.

I heard the others talking around the fire, their voices muffled. It had been a week since my return from the mountain. Ted was better now, although still very weak. On my way back that day I'd managed to kill a snake. My eyes teared up at the memory. Despite being tough with humans I did not like killing animals. But it had provided a meal for which everyone was grateful.

After losing two to the virus we were down to eighteen. Sam had insisted that we strip them and leave them for the crows and ravens and the other desert animals. There wasn't much choice since we had no digging tools and the ground was rock hard. Their clothes provided rags and shirts for the others who were sick; fevers made them shiver on the warmest of days. Five more were on death's door, their hacking coughs keeping me up at night.

We were heading toward the mountains, hoping we'd reach them before our last supply of water ran out. Lucifer had left more, his continuing help keeping us from dying of thirst. Sam had promised to do the next animal killing, assuring me that he could find a wild boar lurking around the base of the mountain. Now all we had to do was reach it before we starved.

My musings about Lucifer had gone from non-belief to tepid belief, to certainty. My time with him seemed steeped in a mystic light. I had many questions, but they were still forming; I wasn't ready to see him again. When I thought of him it was as though he was encased in light. Had he been? I had no idea anymore, as though my normal way of thinking had been stripped away, leaving me with mysteries impossible to solve.

My eyes closed, a momentary sense of peace washing over me. Adam was gone, we were close to reaching the mountains. Mostly, we were surviving.

I WOKE TO SCREAMING. It was dark as pitch, the only light coming for the stars. The moon had set. *Elena*, Elena was shrieking. I jumped up and ran to where the sound was coming from, shocked to see Adam with his hand around her throat, a gun to her ribs. Sam and Joe, and the other men in our group watched, unable to do anything. "Let her go," Sam growled.

"Make me, old man," Adam responded. He began moving

NIKKI BROADWELL

backward, Elena stumbling as he dragged her with him. "If you come after me, she'll die," he warned. Adam held her tight and backed away until they disappeared into the night. I heard another terrified shriek and then utter silence.

I stared at Sam. "I need to go after them."

"You still have the Glock and the extra clip?"

I nodded.

"I'll go with you."

"No, Sam. This feels personal. Where'd he get that weapon?"

He shook his head. "Probably murdered some poor sap and stole it. Kill the son-of-a-bitch."

"Oh, believe me, I will."

Sam and another sandy-haired kid named Brad, as well as Maisie, a thirty-something woman, offered to come along, but I said no. I needed to do this by myself.

It was dark when I left, so the only way to track was by the scent of Elena's perfume. For some reason the Hispanic woman dabbed cologne behind her ears every morning. An earthy floral. I chuckled, thinking that my perfume was Eau de Sweat. And by now it was nearly too overpowering to keep track of hers.

By the time the sky lightened I'd lost the scent. But now I could look for tracks. I was tired, my thoughts tangling around Adam's motivation. But then I got it. Elena could be used to barter for things. A whore on a leash. I felt sick picturing it. I hoped I reached them before he had a chance to put her to use. Adam was only one of many hardened men who would do anything to keep their power in this lawless place. If it required using another human being to get what they wanted, then so be it. Anything was disposable.

It took me an hour to find the tracks again, Elena's reluctant sliding steps obvious in the marks left in the pebbles and dirt. They were headed toward a rocky hill in the distance that rose up from the desert floor like a temple of some kind. Adam seemed to know his way around the place and also how to take advantage of what was at hand. He wasn't as dumb as I had first thought. He had to be a mile ahead, maybe more because of the extra hour it took me to find the trail again. I set off after them.

THE SUN WAS DIRECTLY above when I spied them in the distance close to the hill. Adam was talking to another man and gesturing. A moment or two went by and then Elena was handed off and the man headed away, dragging her behind him. Her hands were tied and the rope acted like a dog leash. Adam sat down in the shade cast by the wall of rock. I figured he was waiting for the man to take his fill and bring back the reward of gun, knife or whatever he'd bargained for. I ran in a crouch, trying to stay out of his line of sight. Sweat ran down my body. I had no fucking water along. What an idiot.

I was within forty feet when the man appeared carrying something heavy. He handed it over, their voices carrying on the dust-filled wind. "She's staying with me," he said. "I can use her."

"She belongs to me," I heard Adam growl. "We made a bargain."

"And I gave you your fucking gun."

"I didn't say you could have her."

They stared at each other until I shouted and headed toward them. Neither one had a gun in his hand, but I had the Glock, and it was pointed straight at them. They turned at the same time, the other guy pulling a gun from his back pocket as

Adam unwrapped the high-tech weapon the guy had just given him. Before either could do anything, I fired, winging the new guy in the arm. He dropped the gun and gave a shout. And that's when I noticed Elena creeping around the side of the red rock, hands tied in front of her.

Adam's weapon needed to be primed before he could fire and he was still fiddling with it when I reached him. "Don't bother," I said, kicking it out of his hands and pressing the Glock into the back of his neck. I "Just give me Elena and we'll call it a day."

The guy I'd winged was reaching for his gun when Elena ran up behind him and grabbed it.

"Get out of here and we'll let you live," I told the guy on the ground, motioning for Elena.

He was burly like Adam, not used to being bested by a girl. His face was bright red, his eyes narrowed in rage. "I'll find you and kill you," he muttered.

"Not if I do it first," I answered. "Hand me that gun," I said, turning to Adam.

"Fuck you."

"Would you rather die? Because I can make that happen."

Adam glared, furious, his gaze darting from me to the guy on the ground back to Elena. "How do you expect me to survive without a weapon?"

"How is that my problem? You nearly raped me, and what you planned for Elena is beyond heinous. I should shoot you just for that."

"You deserve to die for what you did to me," Elena hissed.

"What did I do, bitch?"

"Kidnapping and whoring me out?"

He scoffed, rubbing a hand across his filthy face. "I could have done worse," he muttered.

I was white-hot with rage. "Do you want to live, Adam? Because Sam told me to kill you and I promised I would."

He stared at me. "Take the fucking thing. I'll find another one." He threw it at me where it landed in the dirt.

"Go, and take that slime-ball with you," I said, bending to pick up the heavy weapon.

Adam gave me a scathing look and walked away in the other direction. I let him go. "Okay, you. Undo her hands," I ordered.

"I'm shot."

"Too fucking bad, asshole."

Elena pulled a knife out of his belt while he glowered at her. She carried it back to me. "You can do the honors."

I sawed through the rope and tucked the pieces into my belt loop before I took off my shirt and wrapped up the knife. I stashed it in the pocket of the jacket around my waist. "Yarrow's good for wounds," I called over my shoulder. "Did he hurt you?" I asked, afraid of the answer.

She let out a bark of laughter. "Adam didn't have time—too focused on the weapons he would get in trade."

"And the other guy?"

"Let's just say that if you hadn't reached us when you did, I would have been passed around until I was used up. Adam was planning to leave me there until they all had a turn. There were five more and they were all mean. My body isn't that strong."

I glanced back, glad when I didn't see a bunch of angry men running after us. I put my arm around her hunched shoulders. "I'm sorry, Elena."

She smiled. "No need to be sorry. It didn't happen."

I didn't say anything but I knew those men would be gunning for us soon.

12

Anorther month flew by. The only way I kept track was from the phases of the moon which also heralded my menses. It happened like clockwork on the full moon despite what was going on. It was always an annoyance with no modern ways to deal with it, but Elena had found a source of moss on the mountain, and we both used it, handing it out to the other women in our group. And because of certain biological oddities we all began to menstruate at the same time.

Elena's early life had been one of poverty, working in the fields outside the city—that is, before the workers were replaced with robotics. Her family had taught her about herbs, mosses, natural toothpaste made from peppermint and salt, things to use instead of the store-bought items she couldn't afford. Talking to her seemed to stir some knowledge I'd hidden from myself, the herbs she mentioned as familiar as my own hand.

There was something primitive and satisfying about how we managed. Nothing unnatural, nothing to throw away. And in other things that came up I was almost glad that IRIS was not available. It gave us a reason to puzzle things out for ourselves, not that we were always able to do so, but at least there was a community effort involved in solving problems.

Maisie hung around us, starry-eyed, taking in what each of us had to offer and adding small bits of her own experiences. She'd grown up on the streets, a thief who was able to pick-pocket before she was ten years old. "No need for that out here," she told us, making a little moue of disappointment. I liked the scrappy girl with the wide eyes who took everything in and stored it for future use.

WE WERE NOW CAMPED out at the base of another temple hill similar to the one where I'd last seen Adam. There was a barely running spring and we'd caught a few small lizards and roasted them over a fire, but everyone was hungry and the thirst never ended. Our two new guns had come in handy several times to keep looters at bay. Sadly, two more of our group had died from the virus and been left behind for the crows and ravens.

Before the sun got hot I left camp to climb to the top of our temple mountain, hoping to find a few more herbs and possibly a rodent or two. The rocks were sheer with barely any footholds, the pebbles loose, but I pushed on. I was bent over gathering wild thyme when I felt a presence, glancing back to see Lucifer standing behind me.

"Thought you would have contacted me by now," he said, unsmiling.

I straightened. "I had to let it all sink in first. I do have questions."

He waited while I arranged the herbs inside my torn shirt. "But right now, I'm too absorbed in what I'm doing. We've had several run-ins with raiders as well as the constant food problem. We're starving, Lucifer. And it's been weeks since you left water."

"Are you expecting me to act like your guardian angel?"

I frowned. "No, but you said you were here to look out for me."

"To *guide* you, Feirin. To help you discover who you are. Not to bring food and water for twelve people."

I stared at him, annoyed by his impassive expression. "I'm a woman in a desert wilderness faced with keeping a group of human beings alive. Remembering some past life isn't going to help with that."

"No, but it will help you understand why you're here."

"Do you know? Because if you do, I suggest you tell me. I'm leading these poor people in circles trying to stay alive and every day makes it clearer how precarious our situation is. If we don't die of hunger or sickness, a gang will murder us all in our sleep."

Dark brows pulled together over his brooding eyes. "I cannot answer a question you haven't asked."

Heat rose into my face. "I just asked if you know why I'm here."

"I know where you come from and who you are. Shall I tell you or would you rather not know?"

"You told me already—I'm from three-hundred years in the past and I'm the dark goddess."

"And those words have no meaning to you."

"Why should they?" When I looked up again, he was gone. I left the herbs and climbed to the very top of the rocky hill, anger still simmering. I was sick of his enigmatic answers. Why didn't he just say whatever was on his mind? I found a boulder and clambered up to stare across the desert. The flat expanse stretched into the distance—seemingly without end.

Small upright mountains similar to this one dotted the landscape like temples to the sky. I felt tiny, unsubstantial, just as I did when I gazed up at the stars. The view was breathtaking. My nerves calmed and settled as I let the silence and the vast emptiness wash over me.

"Fee?"

I started and turned to see Ted huffing up the hill toward me. "You're well enough to climb?"

He grinned, wiping the sweat from his face with his shirt. "I made it, didn't I? I came to tell you there's a dust storm on the way and I saw some vehicles out about twenty miles or so."

I turned to look where he pointed. A dark yellowish cloud billowed in the distance obscuring the view. The distant whine of engines could be heard over the wind that had just come up. I moved past him to climb down to the flat shelf where I'd left my shirt. He came behind me, his sandals scraping along the stone as he slid. "Did you notice the cave on your way up?" I asked, keeping an eye on the fast-moving storm. "It could be large enough for all of us."

"I didn't see it, but I trust you. Shall I head down and tell them?"

I glanced at his sweaty face. "Why don't you check the cave out while I alert the others?"

Ted nodded, letting me take the lead before following carefully behind me.

WE WERE ALL SAFELY STUFFED into the cave when the haboob hit, the wind like the howl of wolves as the dust and dirt surged over. We had moved as far back as we could get, but it didn't stop the sand from finding us, the grit getting into our eyes, our mouths, our noses and ears and under our clothes. By now most our clothing was rotted from sunlight and ragged from wind, our shirts in tatters, and our jeans full of holes. Anything we'd taken from the dead was used for bedding or to keep warm at night. I regretted using what was left of my shirt for the herbs as I lifted my ragged camisole and attempted to remove the sand from my sweaty skin.

It was hours before we emerged from our partial safety, surprised to see two water jugs sitting outside without a grain of sand on them. No one questioned where'd they come from, just grateful to drink. I thought of my earlier conversation with Lucifer, his denial of being our guardian angel. I also remembered the way I'd spoken to him. "Thank you," I whispered. I heard engines a moment later, gazing down to see several strange looking vehicles circling our hill. They were somewhere between motorcycles and dune buggies, their riders heavily armed and wearing goggles. "Back to the cave!" I shouted.

I went to stand watch, viewing the idiots zigzagging around our island of safety on their contraptions, laughing and shouting. They seemed drunk. But when a gunshot rang out, I thought again. I hurried back inside. "We need the guns!" I called out. "Ted? Do you have the other pistol? And where is the other weapon? It needs to be loaded."

When Ted stood, his face was sweaty and very pale. His exertion had taken a toll. "I have the other pistol. You have the Glock. I think Sam was carrying the other one."

I hurried into the back in the direction of coughing. When I reached him, Sam was bathed in sweat, his eyes rheumy and dark with pain. "I need the weapon," I whispered.

He shook his head which set off another bout of coughing. "I'll deal with it, Fee. You've never handled one."

"Sam, you're in no condition to..."

He pushed himself up. "Don't tell me what condition I'm

in. I know better than anyone. But I'm still capable of defending these people." He pulled the weapon out from under him. "It's already charged," he said, noticing my questioning expression.

I sighed, watching him rise unsteadily to his feet. He threw off my held-out hand and headed unsteadily toward the front.

THERE WERE SIX OF THEM. They'd stopped playing around and had begun to climb. Sam, Ted and I watched from behind a boulder, weapons in hand.

"I'll scatter them once they get within a hundred feet. If any get closer than that use the Glock and the pistol," Sam muttered.

I glanced at his rigid jaw and the pain etched into his eyes. Ted wasn't much better with his ashen face covered in a sheen of sweat. I took off the safety and waited, trying to keep breathing. Joe lurked in the cave entrance, waiting for me to give the word, but he had no weapon, no way to defend himself against armed men. I waved him back.

When a head popped into sight Sam fired, the odd zinging sounds ricocheting in the silence. There was a shout and a scream and then nothing. We were still looking in the same direction when I heard a noise behind us. When I turned, two men were standing there with guns pointed. Before I could get a shot off Sam fired the thing again. They dropped instantly, turning to ash a moment later.

"If my calculations are correct, that's four of six," Sam said, breathing hard.

"Sam..."

"Shut-up Fee and pay attention."

By now it was getting dark and we were losing visibility. "Stay here," I hissed, moving quietly to where the two men had snuck up on us. I went into a crouch as I followed the path they'd taken, alert for the others in their group. I was near the outside cave wall when I was thrown backward by the butt of a rifle, sprawling in the dirt to see a man standing over me. He cocked and pointed, but just before he fired, a blinding light split the shadows, his rifle going off while it was careening through the air. It landed with a crash and skittered away down the hill.

Ted came running, Sam limping behind him. The man lay dead on the ground, but I hadn't fired a shot.

"One more to go," Sam said, nodding to me as if it was my doing.

"I have a feeling he took off," I whispered.

"What the hell was that light?" Ted asked.

"Lightning," I answered, meeting his gaze. "Heat lightning."

Inside I watched Sam head slowly into the back and collapse onto his blanket.

"He's not long for this world," Ted whispered.

I glared at him. "You won't be either if you keep pulling stupid stunts like you did today."

His eyebrows lifted. "What's with you?"

"Nothing," I hissed, pulling my arms around my trembling body. Lucifer had just saved my life.

THE CAVE WAS cool and dark, the interior of tamped earth redolent with the pungent odor of animal dung. I heard Sam coughing and handed the thyme over to Elena. "Can you make a poultice using some of the water? Sam's bad today."

Elena nodded. "Others are sick as well."

"Sam doesn't have the virus, he..."

Her brown eyes met mine. "I know what he has, Fee. I'll do what I can. But don't get your hopes up."

When she said those words, I realized how fond I'd become of Sam. He was my mentor, the one I talked to when I reached the end of my tether. He knew things the others didn't. It was Sam's advice that had led me here to begin with, the promise of caves and small rodents and lizards driving me on. If he died... but I knew there was no *if* about it. He would die and probably within the month unless a miracle happened. And as far as I could tell there were no miracles here aside from Lucifer's comings and goings. But then I remembered Lucifer admitting to being able to heal. Could I convince him to do it? I let out a heavy sigh, my mind on our last conversation. He was pissed at me.

Two days later I was crawling along the ground at the base of our temple mountain, hunting for lizards, when I heard a muted voice mutter, "Don't ever do that again."

I spun around with the knife pointed and ready to throw, surprised to see Lucifer behind me, his eyes swirling with rage. "Do what?"

"Nearly get yourself killed."

"I wasn't planning on it, Lucifer. The guy snuck up on me and he had a rifle."

"You should know better, Feirin. You were born to this."

I stared at him. "Born to live in an uninhabitable wilderness and fend off attacks?"

He frowned. "Do you have any idea who the dark goddess is?"

I smirked. "Me?"

His eyes narrowed in annoyance. "The dark goddess is the

destroyer of evil. She demands equality in all systems and things. Her message is clarity and she will not back down when she's confronted with those who want to make her subservient. The dark goddess brings the world into form and embraces all parts of it and herself. She embodies clear vision, exults in her own sexuality and her power. She is powerful, Feirin, and is not taken in by deception."

I watched him gesture, his hands expressive as he wove the words into something more. I saw myself fighting in worlds where I'd never been. I heard shouts and children crying as I fended off angry mobs.

"The darkness is rich with possibilities. It is where the answers lie. You must embrace it and bring who you really are into existence."

I was overcome for a moment as an image of the meadow appeared. I'd envisioned it many times, but this time it was vividly clear, my family standing amongst the flowers and smiling at me with love in their eyes. "My home," I murmured.

"Yes, your home, your family. You left them to do this. It was your choice."

"This? Not the city, but this?"

His swirling eyes bored into mine. "All of it."

Before I could ask another question, Lucifer was gone. I stood there like a zombie for several minutes, unable to process his words. And then it all came, the dreams, the power I'd been given through my heritage. I felt dizzy, and lowered to the ground to sit cross-legged and let the truth roll over me, an enormous tidal wave I couldn't stop.

WHEN I GOT BACK to where I'd left my group, I felt different, changed in a way I couldn't explain even to myself. A door had opened, showing me a world that was hard to comprehend.

My father and my grandfather were both gods. My mother was a demi-goddess. I had an uncle who was shockingly powerful and I also had a Fae half-brother. I'd been powerful since my first baby steps, able to move things with my mind, to see things that others could not see, and to destroy. Reading minds was just a small part of who I was. My memories were stripped when I walked through the portal into the future, repressing my gifts. But why was I here now?

I had several large lizards to cook for dinner, my talents for hunting coming alive after my talk with Lucifer. I thanked them for giving up their lives to feed us, sending a prayer out into the universe as I gathered them up and tied them into my shirt.

"Lizards!" Ted exclaimed when I appeared, his eyes widening. "Didn't know there were any that big."

I shrugged and set about making a fire, still in a state of shock about my nascent talents.

That night there was a festive feeling among us, the cooked lizards bringing hope where there'd only been exhaustion and starvation. Even Sam looked better after the meal, his wan cheeks turning rosy in the firelight.

13

Peyton woke to the smell of burning. When he sat up, he realized his entire room was filled with smoke. It burned his nose and eyes and made him cough. Grabbing a bandana from the side table he tied it around his mouth and nose, rushed to the door and flung it open, only to be engulfed with flames and more billowing smoke. He shouted but there was no answer. He ran back and flung open the window, grabbed the cat and climbed out, trying to gauge how far to the ground below. The street was deserted, the crack of the bar's timbers crumbling loud in his ears. He jumped and rolled, something he'd learned to do when he was a teenager. The cat flew out of his arms as Peyton rose to his feet. "Cat," he whispered. "It's ok." But the black cat was gone.

Peyton called the fire department and waited, watching his livelihood burn away. The bottles of alcohol were like small bombs, bursting as they overheated. The fire department never came. Peyton was still there when the flames finally burned out, leaving only smoldering bits of toxic smoke. He stared at his bar and the only home that was truly his, and cried. Someone had set the fire.

WHEN PEYTON CALLED HIS FATHER, he got the answering machine. He left a message letting his parents know that he was now homeless and penniless. After that he brought up the screen where his security footage had been saved. He saw the hooded figure who lit the fire. Despite his face being turned away from the camera, he recognized the way the man moved. It was the guard from his parents' apartment complex. His father was behind this—he'd hired the guard to set the fire, but it was his idea. His own father had just ruined his life.

He wandered the streets for a long time trying to decide on a course of action. When night came, he huddled in a doorway shivering. By morning he'd made up his mind. It was time to find Fee.

14

I practiced in private, moving small stones with my mind and sending rocks crashing with my raised hand to split apart against the solid boulders that lifted from the desert floor. I scared myself, my mind balking at the sheer power I wielded; I much preferred my kicks and my choke holds to the supernatural

Our group had dwindled to ten and Sam was growing weaker by the day. In the wake of my strange new mood, I had decided to find others who were struggling against the tyranny of those who wielded weapons. Today I had traveled far afield, seen hazy groups in the distance, but so far no one had threatened. I discovered and climbed another mountain temple, this one full of small caves and springs with a profusion of mosses and tiny flowers and herbs growing in niches. I climbed to the top, deciding that this was to be our new home. Unless, of course, I came upon natives or others who had already claimed it. So far it was silent as a tomb.

When I came upon the pool nestled within a circle of boulders, I let out a whoop. It had to be spring fed. Anything else would have dried up by now since there hadn't been a drop of rain in months. My body was caked in sweat and dust which had turned to mud, my hair a mass of dread locks that I'd given up trying to untangle. Every single person in our group would give up a tooth to have this within reach. Now if I could find a cave, we'd be set.

But before I went searching, I absolutely had to get into that water. It shimmered in the dappled sunlight reflecting off the rocks and the spindly bushes around it, calling to me in dulcet tones.

I quickly stripped off my filthy clothes and bent to rinse them, rubbing the fading and thinning fabric together to release the dirt and sweat. My clothes were now pared down to a skimpy camisole top, a leather jacket I'd found along the way, jeans with holes and heavy boots that chafed my sockless feet.

When the garments were as clean as I could get them, I laid them out on the rocks and stepped into the water, feeling carefully for the bottom. I had never in my life felt such exquisite pleasure as the water closed over, enveloping me in coolness. I hadn't had a bath in months, my skin like leather as I rinsed and rinsed in the soft cool spring water. No soap, but I didn't care, just the water was enough to take off the main grime and loosen the dirt from my dreads that began to untangle as I worked my fingers through them. I pulled the ends around to examine them, realizing that the blonde was gone. I'd been slicing the ends off every few months when it got too long, and now my dark hair had grown out.

It was a while before I stirred myself to rise from the pool, aware that my group was probably wondering where I'd gone. But they had guns and strong men to wield them; I wasn't worried. Bright droplets, like tiny kaleidoscopes, slid down my belly and legs as I stepped out. I squeezed the water out of my hair and ran my fingers through it, shivering as the sun reached me, my skin pulling tight as it dried. I closed my eyes, allowing myself this moment in the filtered sunlight, standing with my face raised and my arms at my sides, safe in the knowledge that I was alone.

And that's when the atmosphere shifted. When I opened my eyes, Lucifer was standing right in front of me. His long coat was unbuttoned, revealing his lean chest, and his flat belly above the waistband of his jeans. He stared at me and I stared back, uncomfortably aware that I was stark naked.

"Do you want me?" he finally asked.

What a strange question. But when our eyes met again, I realized what he meant. Yes, I did want him. Badly. My entire body had begun to tremble in anticipation. "Yes," I answered.

He moved a step closer and lifted my pendant. When he touched it, bright shards of light skittered outward in all directions. It hummed and sang, as though his touch had awakened it. He let it drop and touched my cheek, pushing the strands of wet hair back before his fingers trailed downward across my jaw, my neck, pausing at the pulse in my throat as he met my eyes again. "And this?"

The trembling intensified. "Yes."

One step closer. "And this?" he asked, his fingers moving lightly across my breasts.

"Yes," I whispered, closing my eyes.

"And this," he murmured, his fingers like feathers across my belly and headed lower.

"Oh gods," I moaned. "Yes."

"And this?"

His fingers felt like pinpricks of light as they traced downward to where my

thighs had parted. "Yes," I somehow managed to whisper.

"And this."

His thumb moved gently against the part of my body that was beyond a verbal response. My eyes blinked open. He was incandescent, glowing, his eyes swirling with a look I'd never seen in them. He stood back to remove his coat, holding my gaze as he unbuckled his jeans and took them off. He was just as I'd pictured him, pale and ethereal, lean and strong. Gorgeous. Every nerve ending on my body was electric and alive, and when he touched me in the same place again, I let out a gasp, my knees buckling.

His gaze held mine as he readied me for what was to come, my breath panting as he continued. When I felt I might faint from wanting him, he took my face in his hands. When he kissed me, my mouth opened to his tongue and the feel of him against me. I moaned when he pressed closer still, ready and willing for whatever he had to offer.

But instead he pulled back to look at me. "And this too?" he asked, poised to do what I longed for.

I wanted to scream yes, to pull him down on top of me, but instead I met his gaze. "Yes."

He took me standing up, our bodies fitting together perfectly. We were nearly the same height. His fingers worked through my hair, his mouth on mine as he entered me. And once he was inside, I felt his light move through, his radiance informing every pore, every cell, every hidden part. I was filled with it, filled with him, incandescent, an overflowing spring bubbling up and over as we entered another realm. His arms and hands held me securely as the intensity increased. His lambent radiance was everywhere, inside me and all around us. I was made of it, my body turning insubstantial as we moved as one ever upward into whatever realm he'd taken me to. I breathed in and out but I was no longer of the earth, my heart beating against the chest that held me. His lips were hot when they touched mine, and he took my breath as he kissed me. I was molten, lost, my need for him taking me to a place where I'd never been.

I WOKE SOMETIME LATER, still naked and lying on the rocks surrounding the pool. There was no sign of Lucifer aside from the ache from where he'd been. I felt hollow, lightless, a dark being in a dark world. Tears streamed from my eyes as I remembered what he'd done to me and what I'd given in return. But the *memory* of Lucifer's light and what had happened between us was not the same. Nor was it enough to stop the cold emptiness. The word love came to me, a word I had always balked at, positive that it had nothing to do with me. At this moment I wasn't so sure.

It was growing dark by the time I dressed and headed down, my thighs shaking as I took each step. I couldn't think, couldn't reason through what had happened, Why had he come there? What did it mean? He wasn't of the Earth—he was a light-being, not human at all.

As the night took me into its velvet embrace, I focused on the group and how to explain my absence. I had the mosses and the herbs, and I had obviously bathed, but I knew that if anyone looked closely, they would notice. Something had changed. And this was even more overwhelming than discovering my power.

15

Animals began to appear in the weeks following my encounter with Lucifer. I shot a wild pig, its eyes accepting as it drew its last breath. I cried as I gave thanks, something inside twisting as the realization hit; we had to kill to eat. We had no real greens or vegetables and lizards would not ultimately sustain us. But why were they suddenly offering themselves up?

We moved, settling into the new caves; everyone took turns in the pool. It was a water source, a bathing source and a spiritual place of solace, all in one. I set out one morning, determined to find others to bring into the fold. They were out there crying for my help. I could hear them. And with the extra caves we had the room.

Sam wasn't feeling well enough, so Joe came with me, saying that I needed him in case there were those too weak to walk. "I'm stronger than you are," he insisted.

I wasn't so sure about that, but I agreed.

We were several miles away from our mountain when Joe suddenly asked,

"You got some magic or something? You look kind of different lately, like you're all lit up."

"I do?" I glanced down at my arm which looked its normal dust color.

"Ever since the day you found the spring there's been a look about you. Can't put my finger on it. Did something happen that day?"

"Other than having my first bath in probably six months? No."

He gazed at me quizzically for a moment before squinting into the distance.

I still felt the effects of that day. Lucifer and I had connected not only sexually but in a way I'd never experienced. When I thought of him, I felt a glow, a warmth all over. And my gifts were enhanced, as though he'd imbued me with a part of himself. Is this what love felt like?

WE WERE fifty feet out when the shooting began. A bullet whizzed by my ear, another headed straight for Joe. When I put my hand up it seemed that time slowed down, the bullet slowing with it. I waved my hand and diverted its trajectory, hoping like hell that Joe wasn't watching. But when I glanced his way, he had his gun out and was focused on the group of people firing on us from within the rough tin enclosure.

Behind the fence were several ramshackle houses built out of tin and wood. And along the wall I saw at least twenty people, all of them holding guns. I grabbed Joe's arm. "We need to get out of here. There's too many of them."

He nodded and we hurried out of range, but not before several more bullets were fired. I turned to see them coming, all six of them. I put my hand up to slow them before I threw Joe onto the ground, allowing them to pass over us.

"What are you doing?" he asked, struggling to get up.

"Bullets, Joe. They would have hit us."

"And how in hell could you see that?"

I was on my feet and tugging his arm. "We need to get out of here before they reload."

He didn't question as we ran as fast as we could away from the settlement.

We rested in the shade of a spindly tree, both out of breath. "So much for needing our help," Joe muttered. "Those dudes are loaded for bear."

"I heard someone calling."

Joe turned, his brows rising. "Here?"

Too late I realized what I'd said. "I thought so, but I must have imagined it."

"This is what I'm talking about. You've gone all ethereal on us."

I laughed nervously. "Ethereal? What's ethereal about hearing someone calling for help?"

"No one was calling for help out there, Fee. If you heard anyone it has to be miles from here and that just isn't possible."

"You're right."

He ran his fingers through his dark hair, and cleaned his goggles on his filthy T-shirt. "So, what now? Do we head back or keep going?"

I cocked my head and held up my hand. I heard it again, faint but it sounded like a child crying. "There's something in that direction," I said, pointing toward the open desert.

"Really? I don't see one fucking thing. What do you see?"

"Nothing, but it's out there."

He let out a groan. "Let's go back. It's close to dark. I'm hungry and thirsty. We can start again early tomorrow."

I glanced around, aware that the sun was close to setting. I had to give it up, at least for today. Maybe tomorrow things would become clearer. I pushed myself to standing and let out a sigh, following Joe back the way we'd come.

By the time we reached the cave the meat was roasting, everyone seated around the firepit. A pile of recently collected dry dung sat next to it. With the absence of wood, it was our only source of fuel. The noisy chatter and the laughter was a nice change. After we ate and people began to bed down inside the cave, I headed off alone. The sky was alive with starlight that blinked on and off like fireflies. They reminded me of Lucifer and the light I still carried. I felt him, as though his essence had merged with mine. Maybe I was meant to reflect his light.

When I got back from my walk Sam was already standing watch. "I'll spell you," I told him, settling on the ground.

He stood gratefully, reaching for a boulder to steady himself. "Ted's due for the next watch. Don't sit out here all night."

I stayed for three hours watching the stars wheel across the sky, and listening to the scrabble of rodents and the distant yips of coyotes. Peace washed over me, my thoughts taking flight as I stared into the darkness. I cherished any time to myself, but somehow the nights felt especially important.

When I heard Ted's heavy tread, I rose from where I'd been sitting cross-legged. "Nothing to report," I told him as I walked past, heading into the cave.

THAT NIGHT I dreamed Lucifer was making love to me. His dark eyes stared into mine from where he was poised above me naked in the moonlight. Instead of asking if I wanted him, he murmured, "I want you." He was just about to complete the act when I woke up, a scream of frustration rising from my mouth before I could stop it.

"Are you all right?" Elena whispered from beside me.

"No...yes. It was just a dream."

She chuckled. "Sounded intense."

"It was."

I stayed awake the rest of the night thinking about Lucifer and realizing that my mission was coming clear. I was supposed to be rounding up groups to form one large one. But in order to do that I had to create a persona for myself that embodied the strengths I'd recently gained. The catch was that the people had to want my protection; they had to search me out. And that led back to the creation of a mystique. My bad-ass reputation had to travel and raise alarms. It was time to cultivate what I'd managed when I was in jail. Peyton called it teleportation. Whatever it was, it would help with my plan, that is if I could do it again.

The next step in this process had not been revealed, but I knew there was something in there about empowering women. Aside from our group, all I'd seen so far were weapon wielding thuggish men who used women for bargaining or to satisfy an itch they had. No couples, no families, no female fighters. Except me. Aside from Elena, the few women in our group clung to their boyfriends, letting them make the decisions. They seemed afraid of me and avoided my gaze. Even Maisie had given up, her attention on the man she was currently sleeping with.

I thought of the women in Jeremy's group who were unwilling to be shoved into a little box. Most were strong and had a mind of their own. Where were they now? I had to find Jeremy and his sister.

And as my thoughts cascaded into the past, I remembered what Mirabelle had told me. Her baby was surely born by now and in the hands of some wealthy couple who lived in Uptown. Those bastards were keeping the women to use as breeders in order to sell their babies to the highest bidder. I sincerely hoped that the strong exotic women in Jeremy's group were out here and not locked into some cell. Was Mirabelle still there or had she been turned out in this desert wilderness like a used-up cow? Both scenarios were equally horrible. Maybe it was *her* voice I kept hearing.

I fell into an uneasy sleep around dawn, my dreams filled with gun fights, women being raped and hysterical screaming. I was lost in a dust storm, unable to help anyone.

I WOKE SLEEP-DEPRIVED AND CRANKY. Joe arrived outside where I sat hunched over my warm cup of herbal tea. He looked rested with a pack slung over his shoulder. "Ready to go?"

I slanted a glance up at him, one eye closed against the brightness. "I will be, but give me a minute."

He grinned. "Not enough beauty sleep, milady?"

"Fuck off," I muttered.

"I'm coming with you today," Elena announced, arriving next to me.

"The hell you are."

Her eyes narrowed dangerously as she pulled her loose peasant blouse into place and tied it in front. It was faded and unraveling at the bottom, her cleavage showing where it drooped. "Because I'm a woman I can't go?"

I stared up out of my bleary eyes. "No. I just thought you were needed here."

"For what? Sam has the big weapon and he and Ted can stand lookout, Maria can tend to the needs of the sick, and I've already enlisted several people to collect dried dung..."

"Fine," I muttered, wondering why I'd turned her down. Here I was having some lofty idea about empowering women and at the same time barring Elena from participating. "Bring a knife or a pistol. Yesterday we were shot at."

"I already have it. Ted lent me the Walther. And before you ask, I know how to shoot a gun. My *abuela* taught me when I was ten."

I saw her as if for the first time. Tough, wiry and not to be dismissed. "Sorry, Elena. I didn't get enough sleep, and..."

"You're grumpy because you were dreaming about a man."

I stared at her. "What?"

She laughed. "Anyone who cries out like you did was either dreaming about sex or in the midst of it and got interrupted."

I laughed. "I admit it."

"One of these guys?" she whispered, glancing around.

I glanced from Ted to Sam to Joe and the other men who wandered shirtless in the early morning light. "No."

"I thought not." Her eyes twinkled. "One of these days we need to talk."

WE WERE several miles out when we heard shouting and gunshots. I figured this was as good a time as any to attempt teleportation. It came with need. And I *needed* to see what was going on. I closed my eyes and imagined what I'd heard. A second later I was standing in a dusty courtyard in the midst of a bunch of ramshackle houses made out of scrap wood and corrugated metal. A fight was taking place, a dark-skinned woman held tight against a white man holding a gun. There were others holding guns and a man lay dead on the ground.

When they saw me there, all eyes went wide. "Where did *you* come from?" the man holding the woman asked.

"I'm your conscience," I muttered, the words coming out garbled as they had before.

He leaned forward. "What was that?"

"She said she's your conscience," the woman told him, trying to twist out of his grasp.

"Fuck that!" he said, pointing the gun at me.

Even though I was not corporeal I felt the impact as the bullet passed through me.

"What the fuck!" the man screamed. "You're a ghost!"

The woman screamed too and pulled away, running for the shelter. A second later the man was running after her. The others took off, guns abandoned on the ground. But on remained, his sad brown eyes on me. "Please help us," he murmured. He knelt next to the man on the ground, feeling for a pulse, tears in his eyes.

"Fee? Fee!!"

Joe's voice dragged me back. I opened my eyes, my mind still cloudy.

"Where were you? It's like you went into a trance."

"I was imagining what's going on out there."

"A woman is being raped," Elena hissed. "I'd know that scream anywhere."

I could hear it too. My appearance had made him act on his impulses, his fear driving him on. I'd made things worse. "There's a man lying dead out there," I muttered, "and another man who asked for our help. The rapist is a bully and has taken over their settlement."

Both Elena and Joe stared at me. "How do you know that?" Joe asked.

I took in a deep breath and let it out. "I have psychic abilities."

Joe shook his head. "I said it, didn't I? Something happened to you a while back."

"Instead of talking we need to help that poor woman." I headed in the direction of where'd I'd been only a few moments before.

Elena caught up to me. "You are a *bruja*," she whispered.

I turned. "What does that mean?"

"You're a witch."

"I'm not a witch."

"Then what are you? You have a strange aura that shimmers."

I stopped, glancing behind me. Joe was still twenty feet away, his gaze down as he shuffled behind us, puzzling over things. "I'm the dark goddess," I told her. "I come from another time."

Elena laughed until she saw that I was serious. "What?"

"Don't believe me. It doesn't matter. But I'd appreciate it if you didn't pass it around."

"Pass what around?" Joe asked, catching up.

"Fee was telling me about an experience she had—for women's ears only," Elena lied.

A frown formed between his brows. "How far are we, Ms. Psychic?"

"Very funny. I'm not sure, but I think another mile or so. It's just over that ridge." I pointed toward the slight rise in the distance.

Instead of being flat as it seemed, the landscape undulated like snow drifts, distant settlements often hidden from view. The desert was deceptive in many ways, hiding its secrets like a woman behind a veil. When I glanced at Elena, giving her a quick nod of thanks, she winked, but I could tell she was troubled.

. . .

By the time we reached the settlement all was quiet. We skirted around the perimeter, me giving signals to Elena and Joe, each of us heading toward certain sections of the enclosure. It was my intention to go directly to the shack, but as I was climbing the fence the rapist appeared from within. "You!" he shouted, pulling a gun from his belt. When I moved my fingers and waved my hands, the gun was yanked from his grip, landing on the ground ten feet away. Before he had the chance to reach it, I was pointing it at him. "What did you do to that woman?"

His bloodshot eyes met mine. "Only what she deserved."

"Show me," I hissed, gesturing with the gun. He stared at me for a moment before he sighed and turned toward the shelter.

It was one room that held a filthy pad to sleep on, an iron pot, and a small smoldering firepit. The woman was curled up in the corner, her arms covering her face. When I touched her shoulder she flinched away, letting out a cry. "I won't hurt you. I came to help," I whispered.

She opened bleary brown eyes, but when she saw the man behind me, she flinched. I glanced at where he hovered. "Get out of here."

"This is my place and this woman is my property."

"Is that right? Since when can you own human beings?"

"Since living out here, you stupid cunt."

I waved my hand and threw him across the small space. The tin wall shuddered when he hit it and landed on his back. I reached for the woman's hand. "You're coming with us."

She let me haul her to her feet, her frightened eyes never leaving the man on the ground. "Is he dead?"

"No, but he'll have a headache." She let out a disappointed huff.

We were almost to the door when Joe burst in, his gaze

going to us and then to the guy on the ground. "Guess you didn't need back-up," he muttered.

The woman's glance darted toward the back of the shelter. "There's another..."

Before she could finish her sentence, a blast split the air, fired through one of many holes in the wall. Joe stumbled backward and fell heavily, his gun slipping from his grasp. When I saw Elena heading toward the shelter, I yelled for her to stay back. But before I could reach her, the shooter had raced around and grabbed her, the shotgun pointed directly at me.

Behind me the man I'd thrown was stirring. "Let her go!" I yelled.

"And why would I do that?"

"Watch out, she's a *bruja*!" the guy behind me yelled.

The moment of startle gave me the opportunity to rush the shooter. And when

the blast came toward me I slowed the lead shot with my mind and ducked out of the way.

"Holy mother of God!" the man from inside yelled.

The guy holding Elena was white-faced and staring. When his grip on Elena wavered, she pulled away and ran, the woman racing after her. In the chaos I was able to grab the gun out of his hands, before hurrying to check on Joe.

Joe was moaning and attempting to get up, blood spatters across his chest and belly, his T-shirt bright red. "Can you walk?"

He glanced up at me and nodded, holding out a hand. I tugged him to his feet and he put an arm around me, hobbling toward the door. In the courtyard surrounding the shelter there was no sign of either man. The dead one from the day before still lay on his back, flies buzzing around him.

Once we were outside the fence, the man who'd asked for help the day before appeared, holding up his hands to signal surrender. The woman we saved ran toward him sobbing. "This is my husband," she said, turning her tear-streaked face to mine.

"These bastards came a week ago," the man muttered. "The rest of our women ran away, but they caught Maria."

"What did they want?" I asked.

"Our shelter, our food, the spring behind. Six of our group were killed right off. The rest got away. But I couldn't leave my wife. They raped her every day." He let out a sob, pulling her close.

"You couldn't stop them?"

"We are peaceful and we had no guns. We relied on God to keep us safe."

Elena scoffed. "I used to believe in God."

I frowned at the man. "You were a fool to think this wouldn't happen."

He bowed his head and nodded. "I know that now."

Joe suddenly sagged against me, his coppery skin turning gray. "Can you help me carry him?" I asked the man.

He nodded. "My name is Mateo."

I gave him a nod, unable to smile after what we'd just been through. Joe was a mess, blood everywhere.

Maria and Elena walked ahead as Mateo and I carried Joe, me holding him under the shoulders and Mateo holding up his legs. I thought about the two men still out there somewhere, hoping they would spread the rumor about the *bruja* who could stop bullets and appear out of nowhere like a ghost.

16

Joe was unconscious by the time we got back. He'd lost a lot of blood and I feared for him as we carried him up the mountain and found a spot in the cave where Elena could treat him. She had some yarrow left over from Ted, but Joe's injuries required picking many fragments out of his body, and some were deeply imbedded. Maria was a *curandero* and helped her, the two of them setting to work as soon as they had him settled.

Sam wanted to hear all about what happened, taking me outside so I could brief him. "And you say the other two men are gone now? What about Mateo's compadres?"

"I don't know."

He ran agitated fingers through his gray hair. "I hate being useless."

"Sam, you aren't useless, you're sick. And I value your opinions and your insights."

He stared into the hazy distance, his brows pulling together. "What aren't you telling me?"

I started. "What do you mean?"

He turned his rheumy eyes to mine. "I know you, Fee. And I know when you're holding back. Something happened out there."

I let out a sigh. "Do you believe in the supernatural?"

He chuckled. "I've had some experiences, yes."

I glanced back to see if anyone was within earshot before taking his arm to move to the side of the cave. "I can do things that aren't normal."

His brows rose. "What kind of things?"

I wondered if it was wise to tell him, but at the same time I wanted him to know. He felt like a father to me. "I can be two places at once."

"Like astral projection?"

"I don't know what that is. I can send myself somewhere else, but when I get there, I'm a ghost."

Sam didn't even blink. "Can people see you?"

I nodded. "I can also slow time, or at least slow bullets. That's how I managed to keep from being shot."

He let out a huff and rubbed his hand over his stubbly face. "Have you always had these abilities?"

I shook my head. "I...someone told me I came from three-hundred years in the past--that I'm here in this time to do a job."

"Someone...here?"

I hesitated, wondering if I should mention Lucifer, finally deciding that I'd gone this far, I might as well. "You know the man they call Lucifer? He told me."

Sam shook his head. "Lucifer isn't a man, Fee. It's a myth."

"If he isn't real who did I have sex with?"

Sam's eyes widened. You're saying you had sex with Lucifer?"

"Yes, and to tell you the truth it was mythic."

Sam chuckled and shook his head. "You are some amazing

lady, Fee. I'm not sure whether to believe you, but it seems you think you're telling the truth. When did this happen?"

I questioned why in the world I'd chosen to reveal all this to Sam, but I kept going, knowing that I could trust him to keep a secret. "It was close to two months ago now. I haven't seen him since."

"And that was it? The one time and the sex? What did this guy look like?"

I smiled and stared into the distance. "Dark hair, pale skin. Ethereal and gorgeous."

"Sounds like it may have been a dream."

"We met several times before that...he was the one who told me where I come from."

"This is sounding more and more implausible. I can't see some guy appearing out of nowhere, having sex with you and then disappearing. If I were young and you and I had sex, I would not be doing a disappearing act."

My eyes met his. "He's not human, Sam. He's a light-being."

Sam let out a roar of laughter. "Now you've gone too far. Let's just leave it there, okay?"

"Next time I see him I'll make sure to introduce you," I muttered.

"You do that. Now as far as this other stuff you told me, I can wrap my mind around some of it because I've had a few mystical experiences myself."

"Fee!"

I turned to see Elena, her eyes wide with distress. "What is it?"

"Joe...he's..."

I glanced at Sam before I jumped up and hurried toward her. "What happened?" I asked, following her inside the cave. But as soon as I saw him, I knew. Joe was gone.

137

"We tried," Maria said, tears in her eyes. "Too much metal, too many wounds."

I kneeled next to him, my eyes welling. He was one of the good ones. "I didn't get a chance to say goodbye."

"Nobody did," Elena answered. "He never regained consciousness."

Something about Joe's death infected me with discouragement. With all my talents I hadn't kept him safe. I thought of Lucifer, angry that I hadn't seen him in so long, and the knowledge that he could have healed Joe. What was the point in having an ability if you didn't use it?

"We have to bury him. I can't stand the idea of him being eaten by crows."

After dark we carried his body down the hill, every one of our group coming along to say goodbye. We used the knife to dig, that and a few gardening tools Joe had kept hidden in his pack. It wasn't a deep hole but it was enough to cover him, with several inches to spare. I cried through the entire process, giving up on trying to stay strong. Once he was under the dirt we circled around the mound and put our hands together. "May you find peace wherever it is you end up," I murmured. I heard sniffling, several people sobbing openly. Joe had made a lot of friends.

THE FOLLOWING morning Elena and I headed out together to search for herbs and do some hunting. "Did you notice how well Sam's doing?" I asked her, remembering that he hadn't coughed once the day I'd poured my heart out.

Elena glanced at me as she pulled the dark hair away from her face. "He has a stash of pills that he was keeping for emergencies."

"Pills that...what?"

"They suppress the symptoms but they don't cure."

I frowned, thinking. "If he was saving them for an emergency, is this it? Is he bad enough to need them?"

Elena gazed into the distance, trying to keep me from noticing the tears that welled. "He's dying, Fee. Once the pills are gone the pain will overwhelm him."

I suppressed the gasp that lodged in my throat. I was unable to breathe for a moment as I adjusted to the news. I'd known he was sick and I thought I'd faced his encroaching death, but I was wrong. "We need a healer," I muttered.

"A miracle is what we need," Elena replied.

BUT THE DAY was not finished throwing curve balls. As we came across the valley floor, heading for another temple mountain, I saw them for the first time. The Natives. There were probably eight or ten men. They carried spears and wore animal skins around their waists and nothing else. When they spied us, they trotted off in the other direction like a herd of antelope, disappearing into a haze of dust.

Elena and I looked at each other. "Wow," she said.

"They seem like they belong in some bygone time when game was plentiful," I whispered. There was something awe-inspiring about the way they carried themselves, straight dark hair chopped short, small wiry bodies and the ability to just vanish.

"From what Sam says, they've lived here for thousands of years."

"Watching the white man take over and wipe out every living thing," I muttered.

Elena nodded her agreement. "Pretty much. I'm proud to have brown skin."

"I wish I did."

She glanced at me, smiling. "You're one of us."

I laughed. "In my heart I am." I turned to face her. "I told Sam about my abilities."

Elena looked down. "He said you'd confided some crazy stuff that he felt was a fantasy that lived inside your mind."

I squinted into the distance. "I shared a lot more than I did with you."

She glanced at me, pausing for a second before she said, "We should go. It's too hot to stand out here chatting."

"You're right." We headed off toward the small upright mountain in the distance. "Hope that isn't where the Natives went. I wouldn't want to get in the way of those spears."

"I expect you to tell me all of it once we find some shade," she murmured, ignoring my comment.

ONCE WE REACHED the hill we climbed until we found the herbs Elena was searching for. A tiny spring dripped into a crevasse where several plants managed to eke out an exis-tence. As she picked, Elena told me what they were and their uses, knowledge from my past seeming to click in as she talked. But the herbs I was familiar with were not these. Besides Yarrow, there was Feverfew, good for migraines, Snakeroot for fever, intestinal problems and liver ailments, plus Yellow Bells to get rid of worms and Coneflower, a painkiller used for toothache, coughs, colds and sore throats. They weren't flourishing so Elena was careful to pick only small amounts, making sure to leave the roots intact.

Once she had what she needed she sat back on her heels and turned to me. "Time to share, Fee. It hurts that you would tell Sam first."

"I didn't mean to tell him; it just came pouring out. I love that man—he feels like a father."

Elena smiled. "He loves you too."

I let out a heavy sigh. "You've seen some of the stuff, like the slowing down of time and being able to move things with my hands."

"No. When would I have seen that?"

"When Joe got shot? I was in the line of fire right after that. I could see the bullets coming and I moved to avoid them. I thought you saw it."

Elena's eyes widened. "I was too busy wriggling out of that bastard's grasp."

My gaze went to the trickle of water and I reached to cup my hand under to get a drink. When I glanced at Elena again, she was frowning. "I'm sure this is hard for a person who once believed in God," I said.

She shook her head. "I still believe that Jesus was a miracle worker. Is there more?"

"You know the mythical Lucifer? I ran into him early on. He knew all about me, Elena. He said I came to the future because I was needed here."

"Now you have my attention. Is he the one you were dreaming about?"

"You believe me?"

She shrugged. "I can tell when people are lying. I've had a lot of practice."

I smiled. "Thanks for that. It means a lot."

"Tell me the dream."

"My dream came because of what happened between Lucifer and myself. It was the day I discovered the pool. He found me there and we made love."

Her eyebrows rose. "Ooh. This is getting interesting."

"Not much more to tell. I haven't seen him since."

"But that was like two months ago."

I took in a deep breath and let it out. "Tell me about it. I figure he was saying goodbye, but the sex was like nothing I've ever experienced."

"So, this Lucifer, who is he?"

I gazed at her. "This is the part you won't believe. He told me he's a light-being. He isn't of the earth at all. And judging from the light I've had inside me since our one time, I believe him."

Elena's eyes widened in alarm. "Are you pregnant?"

"You know I'm not. We've gathered the moss together. And I have a device that prevents it."

"Prevents a magical being from impregnating you? I doubt it."

"Even so, I've had two moon periods since then."

"You're in love with him, Fee."

"Why do you say that?"

"Your eyes go soft and shiny when you talk about him, and that aura I mentioned before? It gets stronger when you mention his name."

"It doesn't matter. He's gone."

Elena gathered the herbs together, her eyebrows pinched in thought. "Why would he make you fall in love with him and then leave?"

"He didn't *make me* do anything. How would he know what I would feel afterward?"

"If he's an entity from another dimension and knows all about you and who you are, he's got to be aware of your feelings. He knows, Fee, and he's choosing not to do anything about it."

I thought about that for a moment, an ache of wanting him making itself known in my lower belly. I hadn't allowed my thoughts to stray this far for several weeks. "He told me he's acting under certain laws. Perhaps one of them is not to get entangled with humans."

"You're making excuses for him. At the very least he should have explained before disappearing. I'd be furious if I were you. Did you initiate the sex?"

I shook my head. "He appeared when I got out of the pool. He was the one who started it."

"That bastard."

"Come on, Elena. What if an angel came down to earth and made love to you? Would you be mad when you found yourself in love?"

"With an angel it would be inevitable, wouldn't it?"

"Lucifer says he's not an angel, but he's definitely not of this world. He took me somewhere...I can't even explain it."

Elena stood and tied the bunch of herbs around her waist. "I hope he does the right thing and comes back to explain. An angel would do as much. They're kind and good, aren't they?"

I laughed. "I have no idea. This is the first time I've encountered a being from another realm."

On the way back we saw the Natives again. They had an animal suspended on a pole and they were trotting along together in a sort of formation. "I think we were in their territory," Elena whispered. "I hope they don't notice the herbs I took."

We watched them move toward the temple mountains and waited until they disappeared up the trail.

"Glad they weren't there when we were," I muttered. "Those spears looked sharp."

"Says the woman who can dodge bullets and send people flying with a flick of her hand."

"And I can project myself. Forgot to mention that."

Elena glanced at me. "Sam told me about the projection."

"Anyone else know?"

"No. He confided in me because I'm an herbalist and we've been talking about ways to lesson his pain."

"Did he believe it?"

"He did. He said he's had too many strange experiences to be dismissive."

"I can read thoughts too, but out here it seems that people mean what they say. I haven't heard any conflicting thoughts from anyone in our group since Adam."

The heat had risen, the humidity with it. Charcoal clouds hovered on the horizon. My skin prickled with the electricity in the air, the humidity bringing sweat to the surface to my skin. It was the first possibility of a storm I'd seen. I breathed in the scent of rain, feeling a little lift in the region of my heart. As we walked the last mile together my thoughts went to Lucifer. He could heal Sam. And this time I was willing to pursue it.

17

"You were gone for all that time and you didn't bring any meat back?" Ted shouted. "If I'd known I would have gone hunting myself."

"Elena and I were talking, and..."

"And we saw a group of natives and got kind of spooked," Elena finished.

"Where were they? Did they seem dangerous?"

"They were carrying spears," I said. "But they saw us and they didn't pay much attention."

Ted let out a huff. "Wondered when they'd show themselves. Sam says once they get used to you, they just go about their business. But if you encroach on their territory, watch out."

"We were on their mountain," Elena said. "That's where I found the herbs I needed. I imagine we won't be going there again."

The clouds had massed above us by now, a smattering of rain pattering down. Thunder rumbled in the distance. And then the wind came up, violent and wild. "Everyone inside!" I yelled, running for the cave. A second later the sky opened up, rain slanting sideways as lightning speared down.

We all moved into the back of the cave as the storm intensified. The temperature dropped a good twenty degrees in the space of a few minutes.

"Monsoon rains," Sam muttered from next to me. "It's rare these days but they still can happen. This will bring all sorts of plants that have gone dormant to the surface."

I glanced at him, noticing how puffy his face looked, the bags under his eyes. "Elena told me about your stash. How much do you have left?"

He made a sound in the back of his throat. "I swore her to secrecy."

"It's payback for you sharing my secrets."

He laughed and then coughed, the hacking deep and disturbing. "I didn't tell her everything, Fee. She knew some of it already."

"Yeah. Now she knows all of it, and unlike you, she believes me. You look like shit, you know?"

"What's your point? I feel like shit so it stands to reason I'd look like it."

I put my hand on his arm. "Don't you dare die on me."

He grimaced. "Not much choice when it comes to the grim reaper. He's on his way."

"Damn it, Sam. I need you."

His bloodshot eyes met mine. "You are perfectly capable of leading this group without my input. I've never met a stronger woman. If I were twenty years younger, I would have pursued you. But as it is, I've had to be content with being a father figure."

I stared toward the cave entrance watching the water stream down, turning the dirt to mud. I swiveled away to hide to hide my tears.

THE SUN WAS out the next morning but the air was at least ten degrees cooler. I needed time to myself, so when Elena approached, ready for another trip, I told her no. "I'm hunting alone today."

She nodded, seeming to get what was going on with me. "I have to deal with the herbs. Some are dry enough to grind and others need to be hung up to dry out."

"Take care of Sam while I'm gone," I whispered, glancing into the back where he slept.

She nodded.

I FELT heaviness as I walked across the damp ground, my mind on Sam. I barely noticed the large puddles and the other places where the sand was completely dry. I knew in my heart that Sam had only days to live. I'd awakened in the night with this knowledge and also the certainty that I would do everything in my power to save him. And that included finding Lucifer.

A small domed temple mountain in the distance called to me. I'd seen traces of human habitation from an earlier time, but no natives. I headed in that direction, hoping this one wasn't on their hunting route. I needed solitude, a place to let down my guard.

The path was overgrown, the rocks undisturbed as I climbed. There were several small pools but none as deep and wide as the one on the mountain where we lived now. I was sure we'd found the best spot for us, and especially since it retained the magic of that special day with Lucifer. The rain had the springs bubbling, the water singing as I moved from rock to rock, climbing to a shady spot where I'd been once before. Shadows raced across the rocks and boulders, as though hurrying to find somewhere to rest.

"Lucifer, I know you can hear me," I began as I lowered to a flat rock and unwound my scarf and removed the goggles. "I haven't asked you for anything, but now I am--I need your healing ability. Not for me, but for Sam, who is dying." I thought of other things to say, reasons why he owed me, but in the end, I left it there. I imagined him in my mind, remembering his swirling eyes the day he made love to me. I was tearing up when I felt a stir in the ether.

"You revealed my identity," he said in a low growl.

I stared into his frowning face, afraid for a second. He did not resemble the naked man who'd loved me with such intensity. This one was angry, and there was hurt behind his eyes. His long dark coat was closed today, buttoned all the way to the top.

"Why did you do that, Feirin? I told you early on that you could not reveal my identity."

"I don't remember you saying that. You did say..."

He bent toward me, his frown deepening. "What you have done has put me into a precarious position. I am not allowed to do what I did."

"Do you mean make love to me, or help me?"

"My task was to come here, reveal your mission and leave. What happened between us is not permitted."

I rose to my feet, anger coursing through me. "And how is this my fault? Was the seduction part of revealing my mission?"

"What seduction?"

"What you did to me, Lucifer. Did you think it was nothing, that I wouldn't have feelings for you as a result? Why haven't you contacted me?"

His eyes softened. "Feirin, I am not human. You knew that.

I thought it best to leave it the way it was." He looked away before his gaze met mine again. "I am not allowed to feel, nor am I allowed to become attached."

"Technically, I'm not human either. And not being allowed doesn't change the fact that you felt something, Lucifer. I don't know why you're pretending you didn't." I touched his cold hand, wanting contact. His light came into me, snaking up my arm.

When I met his gaze, he looked wooden, as though he was trying to suppress any reaction to my touch. "Feirin, I can't."

"Why not? You did it once."

He let out a long sigh. "It will not serve you. And that is my only purpose here. And now I have overstayed. I should have left your realm after I conveyed my message."

"I'm in love with you. Was that part of your plan?"

He frowned. "What happened was spontaneous. I could not help myself and now I have hurt you and destroyed my status."

"You're telling me that you spontaneously arrived at the moment I happened to be naked, and then seduced me in the most erotic manner possible?"

Lucifer looked away before he faced me again. "I admit I did see you here. I...I wanted to know what it was like."

"Sex—you wanted to know what sex was like. From what you did to me I would have thought you were an expert. But if you want to understand it better you will need more practice."

"Now who's doing the seducing?" he asked, a small smile turning up the corners of his mouth.

I let go of his hand and focused on the distance, remembering why I'd summoned him. "I called to you because I need your healing abilities. My friend Sam is dying."

He shook his head and took a step back. "It is against the rules."

"And apparently so was making love. Please, Lucifer. I love this man, he's like a father to me. I can't lose him."

He stared at me for a long time before he let out a sigh. "One healing, Feirin, and then I will leave this realm."

I nodded. We set up a time and place to meet and then he vanished, leaving me feeling hollow and alone. As soon as he completed this one task he'd be gone and I'd never see him again. I let out a scream of frustration, the sound echoing as it ricocheted off the rocks.

ON THE WAY back I made sure to catch a few lizards. It wouldn't do to arrive with nothing to show for my hours away. As I left the temple mountain behind, an old Javelina presented himself. Lucifer had to be responsible for this. He'd heard my pleas for food. This was his way of providing it.

I met the old boar's eyes, an understanding passing between us before I fired. I tied my shirt around his neck and dragged him behind me as I sobbed, my tears in response to his death, but even more because of Lucifer's imminent departure. At least he'd promised to heal Sam.

AFTER OUR MEAL of roasted lizard, I headed into the back of the cave to talk with Sam. He hadn't come out to eat with us and I had the feeling he'd run out of pills.

He had his eyes closed when I reached him, but as soon as he heard me, he opened them. "Back's bothering me," he muttered.

"Are you out of pills?"

"Took the last one an hour ago. Sorry, Fee, but I can't hang on for you."

I put my hand on his. "Lucifer is going to heal you, Sam. I spoke with him today."

He let out a laugh and began to cough. When the spell was over, he looked up at me, his eyes watering. "You live in a dreamworld."

"I'm serious. Tomorrow very early you will have to summon the energy to come with me to the designated meeting spot."

He shook his head. "Are you trying to kill me?"

I squeezed his hand. "Trust me, Sam. Please. You know I don't lie. The effort will be worth it."

WHEN I HEADED to where I slept next to Elena, she was awake and watching me. "I heard what you told Sam. Is it true? You saw Lucifer today?"

I nodded. "He agreed to heal Sam. I'm meeting him around the back of the mountain at dawn."

She let out a sigh. "Without the pills I figure he has a day, maybe two..."

"Lucifer will save him," I interrupted.

Her dark eyes met mine. "I hope you're right. Did you talk to Lucifer about anything else?"

"We argued. His excuse for not contacting me was that he isn't allowed to get involved."

"And yet he's still here."

I nodded, my eyes welling. "He's leaving right after the healing."

When Elena put her hand on my arm I pulled away, curling up into a ball to face the wall. When I finally fell into an uneasy sleep I dreamed about Sam and Lucifer, both of them leaving me to live my life alone in a dark world.

· · ·

I WAS UP and rousing Sam way before dawn. He was deeply asleep and for a moment I was afraid he'd left us in the night. When he finally opened his eyes, I breathed a sigh of relief. "Time to go," I whispered, helping him to his feet.

I waited for him at the cave entrance gazing out on the dawn sky streaked with the pale colors that heralded the day to come. The rains had left clouds behind, their existence indicating the possibility of more. When I heard Sam, I turned. "You up to this?"

He grimaced, his expression clouded. "I wouldn't be standing here if I wasn't."

He didn't look up to much of anything, his face gray with pain, his eyes drooping and bloodshot. He was hunched, his arms around his middle as though it was too painful to stand up straight. I had a momentary panic attack, hoping that Lucifer would keep his word. I had no reason to doubt him, but after our argument and his insistence that he wasn't allowed to have feelings, I wondered.

I let Sam go ahead of me down the narrow path, ready to grab him if he stumbled. By the time we reached the ground he was bathed in a sheen of sweat and breathing hard. "What is it that you have?" I asked, taking hold of his arm when he lurched sideways.

"Cancer."

"I know that, but what kind?"

"The kind that kills, Fee. It's metastasized to all my organs."

I took his arm to support him as we walked slowly along the edge of the mountain, heading toward the sheer wall of rock on the far side. I saw Lucifer waiting in the distance, a slim figure in the shadows. "He's here," I told Sam, pointing.

Sam stopped to look, his expression going from disbelief to awe. "He's glowing."

"I told you he's a light-being."

Sam made a funny sound that seemed like a chuckle but turned into a cough. I waited until it was over before tugging him forward. We had forty feet to go when Lucifer materialized in front of us, his dark eyes grave as he studied Sam. "You are very near death."

Sam huffed. "I am aware of that and I'm glad to be going."

"Don't say that, Sam," I muttered, looking at Lucifer. "Lucifer is here to heal you."

Sam did not look hopeful, his aura as dark as I'd seen it.

"Well?" I asked Lucifer.

"He's worse than I expected. There is very little life force to work with here."

"But you can do it, right?"

Lucifer met my gaze and what I saw in his was not encouraging. "Since I promised, I will do what I can. But do not hold me responsible if he doesn't make it. He needs to want it, Feirin, and this man does not have the will."

"Sam? Did you hear that? You have to want to live to have the healing work."

Sam glanced at me, a grimace of pain crossing his features. "It's hard for me to want anything right now. I'm old, in pain, and I've resigned myself to dying. It hurts to live, Fee."

"But it won't hurt after he heals you. Please, Sam. Do it for me."

Sam lowered to the ground to rest against the wall of rock. He put his head back, his breath labored.

"Remember when we first met and you told me how this place works? You've been my rock through every situation. I rely on your wisdom. I love you, Sam. Please." I was crying now, sitting on my heels next to him.

Sam gazed at me, a tiny spark coming into his eyes. "You're

the best thing that's happened to me in a long time, lady. But you don't need me."

"Yes, I do. There's not one other person in our group who's been through what you have." I heard Lucifer sigh and when I looked up at him, he shook his head. "Lucifer, you promised."

Lucifer sat on his heels in front of Sam and put a hand on his arm. "Feel this? If you have faith and trust, that same feeling will infuse your entire body. But you have to want it."

Sam's eyes widened as he stared down at his arm. He glanced at me and then back at Lucifer. He nodded, the hint of a smile hovering.

Lucifer reached down and lifted Sam to standing before taking him into his arms. I watched in shock as Lucifer turned incandescent, Sam disappearing inside the brightness. A minute later I couldn't see either one of them as Lucifer turned into a pillar of blinding whirling luminance. I backed away to a safe distance, afraid I might be caught up in whatever was happening and turn to ash.

It was many minutes before Lucifer re-emerged and released Sam. "Thank you," I murmured through the tears streaming down my face. When I looked up at him, his dark eyes were filled with an emotion I couldn't identify. He was about to leave. I needed to say good-bye. But before I was able to say anything Sam began to laugh and grabbed me to twirl me around. "I feel forty again!" he shouted.

When I looked back Lucifer was gone.

SAM WAS GIDDY as we walked the distance back to the cave. The sun had come up, and the sky was a pellucid blue with a few mauve streaks along the eastern horizon.

"You did it!" Sam yelled, waving his arms as he circled around me.

"Lucifer did it, Sam. I was only the catalyst."

He grabbed me up in a bear hug. "Thank you, Fee. I'll never be able to repay you."

"Having you here like this is all I need. But listen, we need to have a plausible story when we get back."

He stopped his antics to gaze at me. "Oh yeah. I guess I'd better cool it a bit."

"Let's assume for a minute that Elena found some special herbs that cured the cancer. She's been giving them to you and it seems that they've worked. All you have to do is tone it down for a while."

Sam ran his hands through his tangled and filthy gray hair. "Sounds plausible enough. I'm still in shock. I didn't believe this Lucifer guy existed. Even when we met up with him, I figured he was just some regular dude you had sex with."

"He's definitely not a regular dude. When I begged him to heal you, he told me he'd do this one thing and then he was out of here."

Sam turned serious. "You love him, don't you?"

"Yup, I guess I do."

Sam sighed. "He must have feelings for you. Who the fuck wouldn't?"

I scoffed. "Lots of people. But this particular being is not allowed to consort with the likes of me." I headed toward the path, turning to Sam as I started up the trail. "Act like you still have some pain. These herbs Elena's been giving you would take a while to work."

Sam grinned and put a hand on his side as he hunched over. "Will this do?"

I laughed. "Perfect."

18

The weeks flew by. We had light rain and more wind, and a sky filled with dark fast-moving cloud. When no one was around I stared upward, something stilling inside as I watched the wind tear the clouds apart and shred them into so many wisps. The desert bloomed and then bloomed again, herbs that Elena hadn't ever seen here busy raising their heads toward the sun. She gathered and dried them, her stash growing.

Sam got better, his health returning as Elena pretended to ply him with herbal formulas. He began coming with me on my raiding parties, his awareness of what I could do making it less stressful when I dodged bullets, turned into a ghost or sent men flying. He also knew where to go and what to expect, his familiarity of how things worked in the desert, invaluable. And he had lots of good ideas for how to spread gossip, sending men on their way with outlandish tales to tell others.

My reputation was growing, the people I encountered aware of me from the crazy stories they'd heard. Several had given themselves up as soon as they saw me, joining us instead of chancing another encounter with the woman who could kill them with a flick of her hand. I didn't trust many of the men, but the women were a different story, most of them ecstatic to be free from their duties as sex slaves and bargaining chips.

Our little group had grown to thirty, with several more women than before, a boy around ten and girl of five along with them. In the wee hours I taught the women how to fight, instructing them in kickboxing and how to use their fists. Some had knife experience already, quick with a blade and not averse to using them. I enjoyed our little band of women fighters, something in me reveling in the strength we had over the men, who seemed reluctant to trust me and disinclined to engage in our skirmishes. We had children with us now, and a young woman named Becky and Maria were both pregnant. It felt more and more like my initial vision.

A month had gone by since Sam's healing and the last time I'd seen Lucifer. I'd hoped for a while that he was still hanging around, but when he didn't show himself, I figured he was gone for good. I tried to ignore the constant ache, steeling myself against it, and concentrating on what I had to do.

"IT'S TIME TO MOVE ON," I announced one morning when everyone was eating the left-over pork from the night before. "We don't have enough room, and besides, it's time to explore further afield."

The two pregnant women protested immediately, and when I glanced their way, I realized we would have to wait. They were both enormous, close to their due dates.

"We will leave two weeks after Becky and Maria give birth, barring any unforeseen problems. Anyone object to that?"

"The babies will be tiny," Elena murmured.

I glanced at Becky and Maria. "Is two weeks enough?"

"Yes," Maria said, glancing at Mateo sitting beside her. "It's easy to deal with newborns. All they do is eat and sleep."

Becky nodded, smiling as she took her man's hand in hers. Jack was a decent guy who seemed devoted to her. For a second I envied them, almost wishing I carried Lucifer's child. I shook myself, dispelling the vision I'd conjured of Lucifer smiling down at me where I sat holding a tiny glowing baby. "So, when will these babes be born?" I asked.

Maria laughed. "When they decide it's time." Her hands cupped her enormous belly. "It won't be more than a few days."

"And yours?" I asked, glancing at Becky.

Becky looked frightened for a second, her young face filled with doubt. "I have no idea."

"Hers will come before mine. Look at her," Maria said.

I did, and what I saw was a red-faced woman who seemed ready to pop. Becky was already a month gone when Maria and Mateo arrived. Her baby should have been born by now. I frowned, staring at her for a moment before she noticed me watching her. This was an area that frightened me too. I had no idea what to expect or how women managed such a thing. I was counting on Elena to be there when the time came.

It was that night when Becky's labor began, her screams waking everyone. I cleared the cave and asked Elena what to do. "Boil water and find clean rags," she told me. "The herbs I need are ready."

I did as she asked, my nerves shattering every time I heard the shouts and the terrified screams. How could such a natural process cause this much pain? Hours went by, the screams continuing. Our group meandered, some gathering around the fire and others heading away down the path. Most of the men had disappeared. Jack was there though, at her side to help her through it. I was sitting on a rock staring into the distance when Sam appeared next to me. "She may need some help."

I frowned. "What kind of help?"

"The baby could be turned the wrong way. It's been hours, Fee, and according to Elena she hasn't gotten anywhere."

"What does that mean?"

He stared at me in exasperation. "It means that the labor hasn't progressed. She's not dilating, which means the opening to the birth canal is still closed."

"Oh. Um...can you do anything?"

"I can try. I've helped several women give birth."

"Better you than me," I muttered, giving him a little shove.

Sam frowned at me before he hurried into the cave. The screams increased, close together and piercing. I held my hands over my ears, afraid of what was to come. When Sam came out with bloody hands I nearly fainted. He wiped them on a rag and headed toward me. "It's progressing, but it could happen too fast. I got him turned."

"She's bleeding?"

He scoffed. "You know nothing, do you? Yes, there's blood. The pressure split her open. If we had a doctor, he or she would have to stitch her up. As it is Elena will have to pack her with yarrow after the birth."

I swallowed. "Will she be all right?"

He shrugged. "I hope so. Nothing to do now but wait."

The screams turned into moans, growing weaker. I sat with my arms around my middle, terrified. When I heard Elena calling my name I got up and hurried inside.

"I need your help," Elena said, brown eyes focused between Becky's legs. "The baby's coming and I need you to catch him while I try and stop the bleeding."

"Catch him?"

She turned to look at me. "Yes. Do you see his head there? In a few moments his shoulders will emerge and then he will slide out. You need to wrap him in a clean cloth, clean him with the water you boiled, and cut the umbilical."

I stared at her with my mouth open. "Can't Sam do it?"

She motioned for me to kneel, and pointed to the dark head. "Sam has already done his bit. Use your instincts, Fee. It isn't that hard."

But to me it felt alien and terrifying as I leaned closer, seeing how much blood had pooled on the pad under Becky and the strain on her face. "Where's Jack?"

"I had to send him away." Elena's hands were full of moss, her gaze on Becky. "Push," she urged. "He's almost here."

"I can't," Becky muttered.

Elena glanced at me. "Take hold of his head and pull ever so gently. Becky's too weak."

"Elena, I..."

"Do it!"

I reached for the head, wrapping my fingers around the slick wetness and trying not to squeeze too hard as I tugged. There was a whoosh of fluids and then he slid into my hands. Elena was immediately there with the moss, stuffing it inside Becky who was bleeding profusely. I reached for a rag and wrapped it around the baby, jumping when he let out a strangled cry.

"Is he breathing? Clean him and then hold him level, Fee. Wait a couple of minutes before you cut the umbilical."

I did as she asked, holding the baby in my two hands to keep him level. I could
see his little chest rising and falling. "Now?" I asked, watching Elena work on
Becky.

She nodded. "As close to the body as you can."

I held the baby in one hand and reached for the knife on my hip, staring down at the bloody stringy cord that stretched from the baby's middle into Becky. I was light-headed as I took hold of the cord. It was slick with fluids and blood, but luckily my knife was sharp. The wound began to bleed, scaring me even more. I pressed the rag against it and held it there. "Now what?"

Elena looked up. "Is he clean? If so, place him at her breast."

Becky had not made a sound in several minutes. Her skin was bleached of color, her eyes closed. I had a moment of panic, but I concentrated on the mewling baby, wiping him again and cleaning his face. He was beautiful, with olive skin and black hair. "Is Becky alive?" I whispered.

"She's unconscious—she lost a lot of blood. I'm doing my best to save her."

"Save..." I was suddenly dizzy, spots in front of my eyes.

"Fee! The baby! Place him at her breast and help him latch on."

I stared at her, unable to understand a word she said. I moved forward, the baby in my arms. Becky's breasts were exposed and I placed the baby next to one of them.

"Help him find the nipple."

I looked down at the baby, calculating the distance between his mouth and the nipple. I tugged him upward and moved him into position, hoping he'd figure it out. When he didn't, I put my little finger in his tiny mouth and tugged Becky's nipple to where my finger had been. When he finally began to suck my knees buckled with relief.

"I'm fine now," Elena said, glancing at me. "You better get out of here before you faint."

Outside I sat heavily, wiping the sweat from my forehead.

"You look like a ghost," Sam said, sitting beside me. "I have a spot of whiskey I've been saving. I think you need it." He reached into his hip pocket and produced a flask and handed it over.

I unscrewed the lid and took a long swig, feeling the liquid burn all the way down my throat. It had been months since I'd had an alcoholic drink. "You've had this booze all this time?"

"I was saving it for emergencies--figured I'd need it at the end."

When I swayed, he took hold of my arm, holding me steady. "Finally, something that scares you, warrior woman?"

I laughed shakily. "That is the most terrifying experience I've ever been through."

"Wait till you have one of your own."

My stomach did a flip-flop. "Not happening, Sam. Not ever."

He laughed. "That's what they all say."

"When Maria has hers, I plan to be as far away from here as I can get."

ELENA APPEARED A WHILE LATER, blood on her shirt and up her arms. Her dull eyes met mine. "She's okay for now."

I shook my head. "I had no idea it would be like that."

"Becky has narrow hips and the baby was a boy with a big head. And he was breach. If Sam hadn't turned him neither one would have made it."

"Is Jack with her?"

She nodded. "The baby's doing fine."

I let out a sigh, sagging with relief. "I can't do that again," I muttered.

"You will if I need you," Elena said, her eyes narrowing. "Maria's next."

"And I'm scouting tomorrow and I'll be gone a full week."

"I hope you're not planning to take Sam."

"As a matter-of-fact I am."

Elena scowled. "He could be needed here."

"Again? Do you think Maria's baby is turned around too?"

"I suppose Sam can check her before you leave. He'll know if it's turned, won't you, Sam?"

Sam nodded. "I'll check her tonight."

AS IT HAPPENED Maria was already five centimeters dilated, terms I was just coming to understand. The baby was dropped and in position. "Can Sam come with me?" I begged.

"I asked the two mothers who just joined if they could help and both said yes. But please, don't get yourselves killed out there."

"I'd rather be shot dead than deal with another birth."

Elena laughed.

19

Sam and I left before dawn, heading in a direction we'd never gone before. "Did you say there's a city out here somewhere?" I asked after we'd been walking for a couple of hours.

"Not sure I mentioned it, but yes, there is. I've only been there once—similar to Elysian City, but not as big."

"Same demographic?"

"If you mean ratio of rich to poor, yeah."

"I want to go there."

Sam glanced at the rocky landscape, the clouds on the horizon. "With perfect traveling conditions it could take us more than a month, Fee."

"I meant I want to lead our group there. I have a feeling that's where Jeremy and his sister went."

Sam squinted into the distance. "There's a storm coming. I suggest we find a cave in that mountain range ahead."

. . .

THE NIGHT PASSED MOSTLY in silence as the storm raged. Conversation was impossible with the howl of the wind and the rain lashing against the stone. The cave we sheltered in was deep and low, the entrance narrow. We chewed on the dried meat we brought along, and drank water from the jugs in our packs. I worried about those we left behind, wondering about the weather and the baby about to be born and Elena's ability to cope in my absence.

"Baby's often come during a storm," Sam announced, glancing at me. "You feeling indispensable?"

I grimaced. "Arrogant, isn't it?"

Sam grinned. "A bit, but also true. You're a born leader, Fee. But Elena has learned from you and she's wiser than you give her credit for."

"She surprises me."

At some point we both fell asleep. I woke before Sam did to see several natives standing around us holding spears. I let out a strangled scream which woke Sam. He sat up, bleary eyed. "What the hell?"

There were two men naked to the waist and a woman wearing an animal skin skirt and nothing else. They were all young, the woman's breasts small and rounded. Her eyes were big in her oval face, her cheekbones high just like the men. Her hair hung to her waist, but the men's hair was shorter and tied back. It looked blue-black in the early dawn light. I stared and they stared back until one of the men prodded me with the spear, motioning to the entrance. When I stood, they gestured to Sam to do the same. We left the cave ahead of them, and were marched down the muddy hill to the desert floor. "What do you want?" I asked as they herded us along. When they didn't answer I held my hands out in the symbol of confusion.

When Sam uttered a few guttural sounds, I glanced at him

in surprise. "I had a few run-ins with them in the past," he admitted sheepishly.

I wondered why he'd failed to mention this the many times I'd brought up the natives in conversation. While I was pondering this, one of the men responded in staccato sentences that sounded vaguely angry. "What did he say?"

"Basically, he said we're trespassing." Sam waved his hands around indicating the desert around us plus several temple mountains in the distance and the one we'd just left.

"This is all their territory?"

"So it seems."

"What now?"

"We will be escorted to their perceived border."

"No punishment?"

Sam made a sound in the back of his throat. "Not this time, but if we happen upon their land again the punishment is death." He glanced at me. "This particular tribe are cannibals, Fee."

I imagined an enormous cauldron filled with boiling water and herbs. "How do we know where their borders are?"

"That's a good question."

"Can you ask them? I do not want to be a meal."

Sam spoke for some time, the words seeming to come from some place deep in his throat. The men replied, their hands waving in the air.

"The boundaries are within the temple mountain that looks like broken teeth at the top, the one that has a rock formation that looks like a deer head, and two others that resemble maidens."

"Maidens?"

"Their tops are rolling and look like sleeping women with hips and breasts and long hair hanging down."

I glanced into the distance, squinting. "I've seen one of those. But that means a huge section of land, Sam."

He nodded. "They are the original inhabitants here. Just be glad they share at all."

"What kind of dealings have you had with them?"

Sam hesitated for a moment, his gaze going into the distance. "I was with a native woman for a while. Not this tribe but another."

I stared at him. "You mean like...?"

"That's what I mean. She was pregnant with my baby when I left the last time."

"Sam! You have a child out here somewhere? How old?"

"Ten years or so."

"Can you ask these people about your woman?"

"I already did. They aren't familiar with her tribe."

"Why didn't you tell me?"

"Why would I? That was another life. In the meantime, I nearly died."

"And now you're healed. Did you love her?"

Sam looked down and nodded. "Very much. Sika taught me their language."

"We have to search for her. You could meet your child."

His gaze met mine. "Why do you think I wanted to come along?"

It was another forty minutes of walking before the tribe members pointed into the hazy distance and mumbled some words. Sam nodded and made some symbol with his fingers before turning to walk ahead of me. There were no temple mountains out here, nothing but a flat expanse of empty desert with little to no vegetation. "Is Sika out there?" I asked, pointing.

Sam shrugged. "I asked them where her tribe lived but they had nothing to say. It's too long ago to remember where I came upon her. There was water back then, a lot of smaller streams and a river where she washed clothes and bathed. There were small huts alongside the river and trees that they'd planted, gardens. The ocean was a day's walk. I stayed with her and her tribe for several years before my health deteriorated."

"Any idea where we should look?"

Sam scanned the area, a frown appearing. "Maybe Lucifer can help."

I felt a pang in my middle at the mention of his name. "He's gone, Sam. I told you that."

Sam scowled, turning to look at me. "Are you sure?"

I shrugged. "He hasn't contacted me since he healed you. He said he was leaving."

"What does your intuition say? You two are linked. You love him."

"My intuition says nothing in regards to him. I have tried hard to put him out of my mind. Asking him to heal you was one thing, but looking for Sika? Even if he were still around, he'd be angry if I asked."

Sam sighed. "I think we should head West since that's the direction to the ocean. Maybe we'll come upon some familiar landmark or settlement and you can do your thing."

I stared at him. "My thing? You mean my astral travel? How is that going to help us?"

"I thought we were out here to gather together converts."

"And after your admission about Sika, I thought our priority was to find her." We stared at each other.

"We can do both," Sam finally said. "If memory serves there were many

settlements out here. The cities have been throwing people out for decades."

168

"I promised Elena we wouldn't be gone longer than a week. And how in hell we'll get back without entering native territory is beyond me. We've been all over their land. Why did they wait until now to complain?"

Sam headed off, looking over his shoulder. "If we don't get a move on, we'll be standing here after dark without any shelter."

I hurried after him, adjusting my goggles as the dust rose and spiraled toward us in a cloud. "Put your scarf over your mouth and nose!" I yelled.

The dust was thick and acrid, the feel of the grit on my bare skin like sandpaper. I put my head down and kept going as Sam disappeared inside the haze of whirling sand, his head bent and his hands held over his eyes. "Get your friend to leave me some goggles!" he shouted, plowing forward.

My friend. What a joke. I let out a scream of frustration.

LUCIFER WATCHED *the woman and the man she professed to love, struggling through the dust storm. Like a father. He wasn't sure what that meant, but he knew it was not how Feirin felt about him. Sam's face was wrinkled, his hair was gray. Feirin's skin was smooth and her hair...her hair was thick and dark. And that alone seemed to be a reason why humans either did or did not have sex with one another. Lucifer's kind had no sex, no relations that evoked emotions. Emotions were not only not allowed, they were punishable by banishment. But despite trying to tell himself that he stayed because she was in danger, he knew that what had happened between them was influencing his behavior.*

He'd already watched over her in the city, had seen what she and the man did together. It aroused his curiosity, this body to body act that seemed to cause so much pleasure. He'd appeared to her during one of those times, had felt her for the split second before he was pulled away. Was that the reason he'd appeared to her at the pool—to complete that one exquisite moment?

He'd thought what he was doing was testing her, testing to see if his clumsy methods would be accepted. He wanted to know what this coupling was all about. But when he really touched her skin, ran his fingers through her hair, felt her mouth with his own, something changed, as though her skin and his were the same somehow. He was already in trouble, his lingering here putting him on some kind of list that he was sure would prove devastating to his life, if that word even applied to the existence in his realm. He felt her thoughts inside him, her hurt and anger causing pain in the body he inhabited. And in the weeks that had passed by since the healing, he'd begun to separate out her feelings from his, his own pain and longing coming clear. Was this love? Since he'd never felt it and since it was not permitted, he couldn't really say. But whatever it was, refused to let him out of its clutches.

Feirin was in danger. That was undeniable. Something dark was on the way. But she was strong, her powers would keep her from being hurt. Then why was he still here? He asked himself that question every day and every day the answer was the same. He did not know or understand the strange pull she had on him. When he was summoned, he transformed into pure light, heeding the call.

"WHAT WAS THAT?" Sam called out.

"What?" I asked, catching up to him.

"A flash of light. I thought it was lightning at first but it went up instead of down."

"I didn't see it." I glanced into the distance where some low hills had shown themselves. I pointed. "A place to spend the night."

Sam nodded. "I recognize those hills. They undulate like the lush body of a woman."

I laughed. "I see that Sika is on your mind."

He chuckled. "Since the healing I've had all sorts of lustful thoughts." He glanced at me.

"Not about me!"

"No, Fee. You're too much like a daughter. I just meant in general. I haven't felt like this for many years."

"How old are you anyway?"

"Sixty-five last I checked. I met Sika when I was fifty-two."

"How old was she?"

"The natives don't pay any attention to age. Her breasts were upright and firm, her stomach was flat, her hips were wide enough for child-bearing, so I figured she was around fifteen."

"Sam! Oh my god!"

"She wanted me. I didn't push myself on her."

I glanced at him and shook my head. "I guess it doesn't really matter—at least not out here. But you're old enough to be her grandfather."

He looked wistful for a moment. "I wonder if she's with another man. She's got to be in her late twenties. She could have a passel of children by now."

"Maybe so, but you do need to meet your child."

We spent the night in a shallow cave, talking together about Sam's past and the woman he'd loved and had a child with. There was so much about this man that I didn't know. But when he asked me about my life in the city, I found that I didn't want to discuss it. I thought about Peyton and what we had together—it wasn't even remotely like what I felt for Lucifer. And yet I felt a pang of guilt when his face appeared in my mind. He loved me. I was sure of it. But I didn't love him.

· · ·

W E WERE U P and out early, Sam's enthusiasm infectious as we hunted for his woman and her tribe. Sam was ahead of me when I heard his whoop. He turned to me and held up a pair of googles before slipping them on. I hurried toward him, surprised to see the goggles. "They must have been here for a while," I said, examining them.

"Your angel is still around," Sam announced.

"He's not an angel and he isn't mine," I muttered.

"Then what would you call him? He leaves things that are needed and he healed me."

"I've told you, he's a being of light."

"And what's the difference? If I remember my catholic upbringing, I think that's what angels are called."

"Lucifer is older than religion, Sam. They took his name and bastardized it—made *Lucifer* into the devil's name."

Sam snorted. "Apples and oranges. I'm just grateful to have these goggles."

I SAW the shimmering before Sam did, the mirage in the distance that looked like an oasis of trees and water.

"Don't get your hopes up," Sam muttered. "The mind plays tricks out here."

"It's right by the hills you said looked like a woman's body. Is that where you last saw Sika?"

Sam nodded, frowning. "She can't still be here."

"Why not? These native people keep to their own territories, don't they? Was her tribe nomadic?"

He shook his head, staring into the distance. "They had animals and planted since they had the river. Jesus. I feel like a kid again. What if she's here..."

I grabbed his arm. "I'm sending my ghost self ahead. Watch over my body while I'm gone." Before he could protest, I was projecting across the expanse of sand, my body still standing next to him.

The little village was indeed an oasis, a small pool of water at the base of the hill fed by a spring and surrounded with small huts seemingly made of mud. There were probably thirty men, women and children living here, all of them dressed as the others we'd encountered. I saw old, young and pregnant women going about their business, men cleaning their spears and children playing in the dirt. But when they saw me all stopped what they were doing to stare.

Before I could figure out a plan of action I was surrounded with men, spears pointed. My voice was garbled when I spoke, but it made no difference since they couldn't understand me anyway. I felt Sam's agitation in the distance, my attention pulled away. A second later I was in my body, sagging against Sam.

He held my forearms, staring at me. "Jesus! What the hell? That was way too long."

"Long? I was gone less than five minutes."

He shook his head. "More like a half hour the way I see it."

There was a time distortion with this ability of mine. I had to remember that for the next time. "It's a native village. Since I have no idea what Sika looks like I couldn't tell you if she's there."

Sam sighed. "Friendly?"

"Not exactly, but they didn't try to kill me. With your knowledge of the language and my sudden mystical disappearance, I think we'll be okay."

20

We approached carefully, not wanting spear-wielding men to run us through before we let them know that we came in peace. Sam let me go first, his excuse being that men were quicker to incite fear than women. He was right. And besides that, I'd already been there.

When they saw me, I held up my hand and signaled to Sam to yell out a greeting, waiting until they put their spears down before heading closer. Sam jabbered in their language as we walked, his hands waving about to emphasize whatever he was saying. I merely watched and noted facial expressions. That is until I saw one woman staring at Sam. In the next instant she hurtled toward him and threw herself into his arms. His expression went from surprise to the realization of who this was, his eyes welling as his arms wrapped around her. She spoke in soft sounds, his head bent to hers, listening. In the meantime, the rest of the village surrounded us, frowns of confusion on faces as they watched Sam and Sika. They'd all but forgotten me in their curiosity.

It was several minutes before Sika took Sam by the hand and said something to the others before tugging him away. We all watched her take him to a group of children playing in the mud and tap a boy on the shoulder. When the boy rose, I noticed Sam's thick curly mop of hair and the face shape that set him apart from his playmates. He looked to be about ten years old. I was still watching them when I felt a spear tip press against my ribs. Two men took hold of my arms and dragged me away toward the mountain that rose up behind their huts. "Sam!" I yelled, but it was too late. I was forced through a small opening and a large stone was rolled into place, sealing me inside a windowless space.

IT WAS an hour before I heard Sam's voice calling to me. "They think you're a witch!" Sam called out.

"They used the word witch?"

"No. Their term means more like sorceress—someone evil, possessed."

"Did you explain who I am?"

There was a moment of silence before Sam said, "How do I explain that you're a dark goddess who comes from the past and has the power to be in two places at once? It would only corroborate what they already think."

"What about Sika--maybe she can help."

"Sika's a woman, Fee. Women are not the leaders here."

"And is she with another man? What about that boy—he has to be your son—he looks just like you."

"She still loves me," Sam murmured softly. "I can't believe it after all this time. Our son, on the other hand, wants nothing to do with me. He's prejudiced against the white man."

"For good reason," I muttered.

A second later I heard the whir of some kind of motorized

something and then the shouts of the natives. "What's happening?"

"There's a gyrocopter flying overhead and it's dropping shit."

"Supplies?"

"No. Looks like trash. The people are covering their mouths and noses, like this has happened before."

"Can you please get me out of here?"

"There's a huge rock barring the entrance. It would take me and at least one other strong man to move it. Apparently, you're in their prison."

"Ask Sika. It's black as pitch and the air isn't good. It smells like something died in here."

"Maybe if you project yourself again..."

"If they think I'm an evil sorceress that would only make matters worse. But please do something before I suffocate."

"Lucifer's still around—he left the goggles. He could get you out."

"That was a coincidence, Sam. Those goggles were left a long time ago. Lucifer's gone."

"I'll talk to Sika. Stay strong. I'll figure something out."

I heard the whirring again followed by screams and shouting from the natives. The smell permeated inside the cave—rotten things, decayed things, dead things and toxic chemicals mixed together, giving me a roaring headache and making me gag. Running feet, shouting, the sound of wheels being dragged across sand, children crying. And above it all the whirring and the miasma of rot. I fell against the rock, my head pounding from lack of oxygen and the stench. I lowered to the ground and covered my mouth and nose with my shirt.

· · ·

It must have been night, because even the tiny sliver of light from before was gone. Sam had not been back. I projected myself outside to see what was going on, shocked to discover the entire village deserted, including Sam. The smells assaulted me, making me cough as I stumbled around the huts that were now destroyed. Things had burned, leaving piles of toxic ash that still sizzled, wires and metal parts scattered everywhere. Moonlight lit up the pond which was now filled with scum and smelled just as bad as everything else. Before I could think about it, I was back in my body inside the closed in space. My coughing continued, the poisonous toxins in my throat, my lungs and on my tongue. I vomited, coughing up what little was left in my stomach. My eyes watered, the seal around the stone so tight that the air was nearly gone. I was struggling for breath when I fell, my hands reaching for a wall that wasn't there. My head hit the stone and everything went black.

"How do you manage to get yourself into these situations, Feirin?"

I opened my eyes to see Lucifer staring down at me. We were in a small cave lit up with candles. Drying herbs hung on strings connected to roots protruding from the dirt and stone ceiling, a firepit smoldered, and a pile of blankets lay in one corner. "Have you been staying here?"

"In my bodily state I need a place to rest from time to time."

"You told me you had to leave. Why are you still here?"

"I saw danger around you. It is my duty to keep you safe."

"Was my being stuck in that prison the only danger you saw?"

He kneeled to light the fire, merely blowing on it to start it burning again.

When he shook his head, dark hair fell across his pale cheek. I longed to touch him, to push the hair off his cheek, to kiss him.

"You would have died here, Feirin. Your friend Sam and the tribe are long gone."

"Why would Sam leave me in that place?"

"He had no choice. What was dropped is poison. Leaving was the only option."

He left the fire and kneeled next to where I lay, dipping a rag into a hollowed-out gourd of water beside me. He lifted the hair off my forehead and wiped it gently across my face and my neck. It was cool and smelled of rosewater. He reached for another gourd cup, waving his fingers over it. "Drink this. It will help with the nausea and work on the poison you breathed in."

I put the cup to my lips and drank the noxious liquid, afraid I would vomit again, but instead my stomach acid quelled.

He handed me another cup. "Rinse with this."

I took the cup and tipped the strong concoction into my mouth, allowing the sting of it to take the last remnants of sickness away. I rinsed and rinsed and then turned to spit. My mouth felt as if I'd brushed with toothpaste. Maybe cleaner. "Sam left me for dead."

"No one had time to let you out, especially once you revealed yourself as a sorceress. These natives are superstitious. And Sam is not strong enough to manage that stone on his own. From the thoughts of his I could see, he assumed you were already dead."

"He probably called to me after I fell and hit my head."

"Correct. Now what shall we do? It is night and I have taken you out of the toxic zone, but not sure following the tribe is the best option. Your Sam has decided to remain with Sika and his son."

"He did? How do you know?"

"I heard him tell her. If you wish it, I can take you back to the rest of your people."

I focused on him for the first time, his beautiful face reflected in the silver moonlight that stretched like a ribbon across the opening to the cave. "Where are we?"

"We are safe here for the night."

"Will you stay?"

He hesitated, dark eyes meeting mine. "I will," he finally said, "but I must leave by morning."

"Lucifer, I..."

He turned. "I have been unable to leave you, Feirin. I am already in trouble for this. I am not sure what is happening to me."

I pushed up to sit beside him. "You're experiencing human emotions. You..." Before I could finish the sentence, he'd taken my face in his hands. He stared into my eyes for a long moment before he pressed his mouth to mine.

When he pulled me down next to him it was the end of any coherent thought. I was wrapped inside his essence as he plied his magic, drawing me with him into his world. Our eyes locked as we undressed each other, shaking fingers on warm skin. When I pressed my hand to his chest to feel his steady heartbeat, he did the same to me. His light flowed into me, spreading like a warm balm. I was wholly his, any plan to save the world or even lead a group of people to safety lost in his kiss, the feel of him, the texture of his skin and the rhythm of his breath. I wrapped myself around him, my breathing synching, my heartbeat matching his, my entire being opening like a flower to receive him.

· · ·

I SLEPT, but when I reached for him later, no one was there, my eyes opening on a cold and empty cave. If my clothes hadn't been scattered haphazardly, I would have thought I dreamed the entire experience. "You can't keep doing this to me, Lucifer!" I shouted. "You love me, you bastard! Even if you don't know what that is," I added softly, tears filling my eyes.

I dressed and drank the water he'd left and picked up the pieces of dried meat, stuffing them into my pockets. The idea of food right now made me feel physically ill. How long would it be before he showed up again and took me on another wild ride only to disappear into thin air? I'd rather not see him at all than be whipsawed every few months. The fucker had to know what he was doing to me.

If his job was to keep me safe, he wasn't handling it very well...he distracted me every time I was with him, my mind and body soaring with our connection only to be left hollow and wanting. I was angry with myself and furious with him.

I waited until dawn before I left the cave, scanning for a landmark. I wasn't far from where I'd been sealed up and left for dead. I knew my way back.

21

Peyton drove the Harley across the many acres of land used for agriculture, noticing the dried-up crops and the lack of anything resembling workers. The river was nearly dry. Before he left Elysian City he'd heard from his father, who begged Peyton to forgive him. As he talked on, Peyton realized that the people living in Uptown were in trouble. They'd sent too many people out of the city and now there were too few workers in the restaurants and in the shops. Robots could only do so much. The virus had taken its toll on those left, as well as spreading into the wealthier segments of society. No vaccine was on the way. The water and electricity that serviced the many buildings was kept going by human hands, and humans were the ones who alerted the higher-ups when there was trouble.

"Please, son. Your mother needs you. I need you. Martina is gone. We cannot cope without her."

"And how did that come about?"

"She...we had to let her go. It was the council's decision to send all the browns and the blacks out of the city. Too many of them, son. They've been breeding. Six mulatto children have been born up here in just the past few months. You can imagine the uproar when the servants were suddenly giving birth to half-white babies."

"And how do you think that came about, Dad? Men who are supposed to keep it in their pants forcing themselves on the women who clean the houses and cook the food? You expect me to believe that the mothers of those babies seduced the rich bastards who run things up there?"

"Be that as it may, you have to help us. Your mother is useless for even the simplest chores."

"After you burned down my bar? Are you kidding?"

"I was not responsible for your bar. It was probably an angry dissident who torched your place. They seem bent on destroying the city. The council has tried to help them, but they refuse to take steps to improve their lives!"

"The guard from your building was on the security footage outside the bar. And FYI, he's white."

"The guard? Which guard? I have nothing to do with them. If he..."

"Fuck you," Peyton said, disconnecting the call.

Above him in the dusty sky, planes circled, their silver sides gleaming and the letters EC in red letters alerting anyone to where they came from. They were bringing supplies in from other cities and other countries. But without workers to distribute, Elysian City was doomed. He had no sympathy for his father or for anyone who lived in Uptown. The bigotry had gone too far, and now they were paying the price. The burning of his bar only cemented his resolve.

. . .

W<small>HEN HE REACHED</small> the gate two of the guards eyed the bike, coming out to examine it. "You want to sell this thing?" one of them asked.

"I do. But what I need are items to help me survive in there." Peyton pointed to the looming desert behind them. "And also, any information you can give me regarding a woman who came through here a few months ago. Her name is Fee and she's..."

"A sexy blonde with a body that won't quit?"

Peyton's eyes narrowed but he kept his temper. "Long dyed blonde hair and..."

"And a smart-ass mouth that could get her killed," the other guard said.

Peyton grinned. "That's the one."

"Last I saw she was headed southeast--leading a group of mostly sick folks. She could be anywhere by now, if she's still alive. It ain't easy for a woman out there."

"I need matches, a good sharp knife, a gun, two days' worth of water and food and a sleeping bag. If you have those, I'll give you the bike."

The guard's eyes widened. "That bike's worth..."

"I know what it's worth—it belongs to the woman I need to find."

The guards glanced at each other. "We got those things, all but the gun. Don't want you turning around and shooting us."

"Fine."

Cat gave a meow from inside his jacket and he pulled him out.

The guards glanced at the cat and back at him. "You taking that in with you?"

"Yeah."

"That cat won't survive the first night."

Peyton shrugged. "He wasn't going to survive back in the city, either."

AN HOUR later Peyton was inside the gate loaded down with a water skin, a packet of dehydrated meat, a seven-inch hunting knife, and a bedroll that had seen better days. He had a hat with him already, plus a change of clothes and a good pair of boots. "Thanks. And take good care of her. Fee won't like it if you fuck up her bike."

One of the guards laughed while the other stared stony-faced. "Good luck out there. Just had a trash dump so be careful of the toxins. They can be deadly. And don't forget about the virus."

"People out here have it too?"

"Oh yeah, unless they've died. New people coming through all the time, half of them sick. Not sure what the city's doing for workers these days."

Peyton pressed his lips together. "They're running out."

He consulted his compass and headed off, wondering if there was any way he'd find Fee in this god-forsaken wilderness. It would surely be a miracle if he did. Even with the dust blowing around him, and the feeling that he was utterly alone in a harsh landscape, he felt better than he had for many days. He had nothing to lose but his life. "It's just you and me now," he muttered, looking down at the cat peeking out of his jacket.

He and Cat dined on dried meat that night, sharing a small amount of the water. When he went to sleep Peyton made sure the cat was secured inside his jacket.

IN THE MORNING the cat was gone, no sign of footprints to indicate what had taken him in the night. Peyton was mad at himself for bringing the animal along. "I hope your death was swift," he muttered, tears welling. He'd grown more attached to the creature than he realized.

HE WAS two days out when he saw a shape in the distance, a man materializing out of the haze. "Where the fuck did you come from?" the guy asked, looking Peyton over.

"I came from the gate," Peyton answered. "Name's Peyton. I'm looking for a woman—strong, beautiful. Her name's Fee."

He let out a humorless laugh. "You're looking for that bitch? She nearly killed me."

"What did you do to deserve that? Fee doesn't normally..."

The guy chuckled. "Tried to get her to suck my dick but she wasn't having it. You know how this shit happens, man."

Peyton eyed him, checking out the size of his shoulders and arms. "Actually I've never forced myself on a woman, so I *don't* know how this shit happens."

The guy frowned. "She your woman?"

"Used to be. Haven't seen her in a couple of months."

"Last I saw she was leading a group of sick people in that direction," he said, pointing. "They're probably all dead by now."

"Thanks for the tip," Peyton said, checking his compass again. "What's your name?"

"Adam. If you find her, tell her I said hello. I was hoping to fuck her, but it wasn't in the cards."

Peyton wanted to punch him in the worst way, but he held himself back, pretty sure the guy could take him. And Adam had a gun strapped to his leg. "See you around," he said, heading off in the direction Adam had pointed.

22

It took me three days to get back from the cave where Lucifer had taken me. On day two it began storming and the storms kept getting stronger as I pushed onward. Not much rain, but plenty of wind and dust that kept visibility down. Instead of veering around the enormous swath of native land, I walked straight across the middle of it, afraid I would lose myself in the sand storm if I didn't have the familiar landmarks. If something happened, Lucifer would be there to save me; it was my only hope of seeing him again. But when I skirted the last landmark and headed East, I knew there was no chance.

ONCE OUR MOUNTAIN temple came into view, I counted up the days we'd been gone, realizing that instead of one week it had been over two. I hoped nothing dire had occurred in my absence. With Sam off on his own adventure it would take me a while to explain why I hadn't done what I'd promised, which was gathering others to our cause. Aside from numbers, what our mission was all about had yet to be determined. Right now, it was keeping people safe, which meant I couldn't be gone this long again. Unfortunately, the distraction of nearly dying and being taken over by my Lucifer obsession had wasted the time when I could have been planning. Falling in love was the worst thing that could have happened.

I saw Elena before I reached the path up the hill, her eyes widening when she noticed me. "Where in hell have you been?" she asked, her brows pulling together. "And where's Sam?"

After I told her the story, including my latest encounter with Lucifer, her gaze softened. "I'm sorry, Fee. Lucifer is using you. Apparently, he's just like every other man I've ever known —in it for what he can get."

I let out a sigh, trying not to think of him that way. "It isn't good for me to be distracted like this. But every time I see him, he…"

"He seduces you and then takes off. What woman enjoys waking up alone after having a man make mad passionate love to her?"

"He loses his nerve."

Elena laughed. "An all-powerful being loses his nerve?" She glanced around and took hold of my arm. "Come on. The others have been worried about you. A black cat wandered in the other day which caused a lot of superstitious nonsense. You need to reassure them."

"Black? I had a black cat when I lived in the city. Where is it?"

"It hangs around outside the cave catching lizards." She glanced toward the boulders lining the area beyond the entrance. "There it is."

I turned to see Cat wandering toward me with his tail in

the air. "Cat!" I cried out, running to pick him up. He endured being held for approximately thirty seconds before wriggling out of my arms. I stared into his savvy green eyes. "Last time I saw him he was with Peyton in the city. How did he get here?"

Elena scoffed. "Came all the way from the city? That's impossible."

"I'm as mystified as you are."

"Maybe this Lucifer had a hand in it."

"No. That's not his style."

"It could be your familiar."

"My familiar? I'm not a witch, Elena."

She raised her eyebrows. "Really? Then what are you?"

"A goddess."

"You have witchy powers, Fee. It's pretty much the same thing."

I shrugged. "Guess I'll go tell everyone that the cat belongs to me."

Elena watched the cat warily and walked into the cave behind me. "Before you get too comfortable, we need meat."

After I made sure everyone was okay with Cat, I headed off again, determined to fulfill my obligations. No one else had the luck I had when it came to finding animals.

I was on the other side of our temple mountain when the deer appeared out of nowhere, a mirage that seemed to come into existence just because of my need. I hated doing it, hated the thought of killing anything. It waited, watching me. I wanted to stop eating meat and wished that everyone could, but there was no way we could survive without it.

It was a few days after this that Peyton arrived, wandering in from the desert as though I'd summoned him. When I noticed him walking up the path, I let out a cry of surprise. A second later he'd crossed the distance between us, his arms going tight around me. I pulled away and crossed my arms over my chest. "How in the world did you find me?"

"Why are you so sure I was looking for you?"

My cheeks flushed. "Weren't you?"

Peyton snorted. "There are a lot of people out there who know of you, Fee. They pointed me in the right direction. A guy named Adam is one of them."

"You saw Adam? That guy, he..."

"Yeah, he's a major asshole. I almost had it out with him but had a feeling he might kill me if I started anything."

I laughed. "Cat's here."

His eyebrows shot up. "I thought he'd been eaten."

"He was with you?"

"I couldn't leave him. My bar burned and he..."

"Your bar burned?"

His eyes darkened. "Torched by one of the guards from my father's apartment. But honestly, I feel lighter. And seeing you, I..." His eyes welled and he wiped at them. "I didn't know if I'd ever find you."

This time I initiated the hug and I didn't pull away. Afterward we stared at each other for a while until I headed up to the pool to bathe. Peyton followed, the cat trailing after him.

"You bathe here?" he asked, disgusted. The pool was down to two inches of murky water.

"This is it until we find another place to live. Are you going? I need to bathe."

Peyton frowned. "I've seen you naked, Fee."

"That isn't what I'm worried about. We aren't together now."

"We could be," Peyton said, watching me warily. "That is unless you've been screwing someone else."

I let out a sigh. "I don't want to pick up where we left off. I don't have time for that."

Peyton's eyes narrowed. "Who are you screwing? I know you and you wouldn't go this long without sex."

I turned away, trying to decide how to answer. "I just can't be involved like that right now. What I'm doing here is too important."

"Bullshit. You're screwing someone. Just spit it out."

"It's complicated. He's..."

"Is it Ted?"

I shook my head. "Not anyone in the group, Peyton. He's... he's a being from another realm."

Peyton laughed. "What? Give me a break."

"Just go away, please."

He stared at me for a full minute before stomping off down the hill.

Peyton being here was a complication I didn't need. He would never accept being rejected and I was already feeling guilty about it.

THE NEXT MORNING, I was up before dawn ready to go hunting again. One deer was all well and good, but our group was growing and we needed to dry the meat and keep it for when game was scarce.

I was down the hill and walking purposely along the well-worn path on the desert floor when I felt him behind me. I turned, plastering a smile on my face. "Sorry about yesterday. I'm glad you're here, but I'm not the same person you knew back in the city. I have a lot of responsibilities and I've discovered who I really am. I have powers--I can be in two places at once, and I can throw people just by waving my hands, and I can..."

Peyton grinned and lifted his hand to interrupt me. "I knew you were special, but...has the sun altered your brain in some way?"

I did a slight wave with my hand, sending him stumbling backward. He nearly fell, catching himself just in time. "What the..."

"Want another demonstration?"

"When did this come about?"

"A month ago? It's been manifesting for a while. There may be more stuff, but I have to wait to talk to..." I stopped before I blurted out Lucifer's name.

"Talk to, who?"

"Remember when I had those dreams and couldn't remember where I came from? I just found out I'm from the distant past and that I have some mission I'm supposed to accomplish. But I'm not sure what it is."

Peyton stared at me. "This is sounding very weird. Who told you this?"

"I remembered." I left him standing there looking thoroughly confused and hurried on.

A few seconds later he caught up to walk beside me. "Tell me what you remember."

I let out a sigh, realizing that this conversation was not going to end well. "I'm a goddess, sent from the past to reclaim what's mine."

Peyton frowned. "What's that supposed to mean?"

I took in a deep breath, ready to dig myself in deeper. There was nothing else to do. At least Peyton knew me and knew I wouldn't lie. "All right, if you must know I met this being from another world. He was sent here to help me discover my identity. The reclaiming has to be about the past, but he hasn't revealed that part yet."

"A being from another world...and what world might that be?"

"He's a light being. I don't know where he comes from."

"Jesus, Fee. I'm seriously worried now."

I shrugged. "You were the one who kept talking about mystical nonsense. Now that it's happening you dismiss it? His name is Lucifer and he's helping me discover who I am."

Peyton's eyes narrowed. "And what else is this *Lucifer* helping you discover? From my understanding Lucifer's the fucking devil."

"That's religious crap," I muttered, striding away. When I looked back Peyton was walking in the other direction with his head down.

I watched him, wondering if I shouldn't catch him up and explain things further. He was angry and confused. I had to tell him the rest, but watching his slow-gaited amble, I decided to wait.

When I returned two hours later a baby was shrieking, the sound grating and annoying. "Can someone please do something about the baby?" I shouted.

Elena met me at the entrance and grabbed my arm. "What is with you? And where's the meat you promised?"

I pulled the dead lizards out of my pockets and handed them over. "I couldn't find any animals today."

Her lips pressed together "And would this vague look in your eyes have something to do with Peyton?"

"He's just an old friend. I told him about Lucifer and my powers."

She glared at me. "He's a normal guy who's obviously in

love with you, but you prefer the nonhuman one who leaves you high and dry?"

I ignored her and moved deeper into the cave, looking over the people huddled in groups, checking for rashes, flushing skin and sweating. More had fallen sick while Sam and I were away. "We should separate the sick from the healthy," I said, turning to Ted who'd come up behind me. "Sam's fine but he isn't coming back," I said, addressing the others. "And this morning I had no luck finding meat. We need a new water supply and new hunting grounds. I hate to do this to you, since so many of you are ill, but it's time to move on."

"Where's Sam?" Becky asked, her baby held tight in her arms.

"He found the mother of his child and decided to stay. She's a native woman he knew years ago." I turned to address the rest of them. "Who else is new here?" I asked as Peyton ducked through the cave opening. A young blond-haired woman and an older man raised their hands. "How did you find us?" I asked.

"There were water bottles set out every mile or so, with arrows drawn with small rocks," the woman answered. "They led us straight here."

I smiled to myself. "Welcome. Okay everyone. We're packing up and moving on. We need a better water source."

I headed for the back of the cave, steering clear of where Peyton sat against the wall studiously ignoring me. I found a spot where I could rest, trying to untangle the emotions winding around my heart. I closed my eyes and fell into an uneasy sleep.

Storms will hit in two days. Walk due South and when you see the line of hills where I first took you to find your herbs, head toward them. You will find shelter and water there, at least for now. When

the storms hit, do not leave until they are past. The rain will be filled
with toxic particles. There will be more dangers to come.

I woke with a start, not sure where I was for a moment. I
rose to my feet, not sure how long I'd been asleep. The people
around me were busy gathering their things together. "South,"
I muttered. "We have to head south."

"What's that?" Ted asked.

"We need to head south."

He nodded, not even questioning my reasoning. We left an
hour later, the sick ones helped by the ones who hadn't yet
caught the virus. The healthy wore rags or bandanas over
mouths and noses, but I had the sense that many of the group
would succumb. The virus was very contagious.

The sky was pale and filled with a haze of heat. Peyton was
behind me helping the sick and Ted walked beside me. When I
felt the presence of an animal, I held up my hand. "Rest here
for a moment. I'll be back in a few minutes." I hurried into the
swirling dust, sensing the deer who seemed to be waiting for
me. I had already killed it when Ted appeared behind me.

"How'd you do that?"

I straightened from where I was securing the deer onto the
make-shift pallet. "Do what?"

"Get that animal to just stand there while you threw the
knife that killed it?"

I shrugged, turning back to the deer. "It wanted to die, Ted.
It was old."

"And you know this, how? I'm a hunter and I've never seen
anything like that."

"There are always new experiences," I muttered.

As we walked back, I asked him, "In the city were the ones
in power always against those with darker skin?"

Ted let out a humorous huff. "Are you blind? Yes, Fee.
Uptown is white and they don't take kindly to mixed blood of

any kind. They call themselves Purists, but in reality, they are white supremacists, a term from hundreds of years ago when there were riots and uprisings to stop racism."

"But why? I don't get it. Skin color has nothing to do with anything. We're all the same."

"True, but in their eyes the whites are the master race. You haven't read any history, have you? Years ago, there were wars fought over this very same thing. Millions have been killed in the name of religion and skin color. World War 111 was fought because of immigrants who were considered 'the other.' No one considered immigrants important until they realized that the privileged weren't interested in doing the jobs they did. This is what began the robot industry, and you've seen how well that's going."

I thought of Jeremy and Isabelle and their people. "Would the non-whites try and get to the other city or would they feel safer out here?"

"Probably. I heard that it was an egalitarian place, with a council that listened to its people. Why do you ask?"

"Remember months ago, when I asked about Jeremy? I'm surprised we haven't come upon him and his sister, or the rest of his people."

"This desert is huge, with many gates that lead to it. He could have left from another gate, or he might have contracted the virus. He could be dead. But if he's still alive the city is probably where you'll find him. A lot of the homeless have set out for Sanctuary. It's a nearly mythic place at this point. Hope it lives up to its reputation."

"Maybe that's where we should go—especially if it's run in a way that takes the poorer among us into account."

Ted shrugged. "So, tell me about this Peyton guy. How do you know him?"

"He owned a bar where I used to go. He's a friend."

Ted let out a humorless laugh. "A friend? I've seen the way he looks at you."

"I slept with him from time to time, that's all."

Ted shook his head. "Whatever, Fee. It's your business. But I suggest you clear things up before he causes trouble."

"He won't cause trouble."

"A jilted lover who sees his woman leading a group and who doesn't want anything to do with him? He'll lose it if you don't deal with it."

Ted was right. But I had no idea what to say to him. I saw the destination in the distance, the mountain where Lucifer had taken me to find the herbs. Instead of heading south as he'd instructed in my dream, I'd taken the group on a short cut through native land. Adrenaline raced through me as I realized the folly of what I'd done. By the look of the sky up ahead and the sudden wind, a storm would be here in moments. "We need to get the hell off native land," I muttered, looking back at the trailing group.

23

What I thought were clouds became clearer as we continued on. Within the wind and haze I saw the gray of beasts of the sky, what I'd thought was thunder turning into the drone of engines. There were many of them and they were headed directly toward us. A few seconds later a flood of toxic garbage was released, raining down on us. "Run!" I shouted. My group sprinted in all directions, shouting and screaming as the air filled with chemicals and garbage. The sky was so dark I could barely see.

I felt a hand grip my arm and a second later I was somewhere white and soundless. "I warned you—why are you here?"

I stared into Lucifer's dark and fathomless eyes. "I traveled across here a day ago with no problem. I figured that..."

"You would ignore my warning? I specifically told you to go directly to the mountain and stay there. I know things, Feirin, circumstances you can only guess at. I see the future. Why would you doubt that?"

I pulled out of his claw-like grip. "I don't trust someone who makes love to me and then disappears into thin air, Lucifer."

He frowned. "Why are you talking about what happened between us when your people are being hit with toxins and slaughtered?"

He released me, and a second later I was back in the midst of a shouting chaos, spears whizzing and guns going off. The dust was so thick I couldn't see, my heart pounding as shots split the air in two. "This way!" I yelled, hoping my voice carried enough for people to follow the sound. "We're on Native land!"

I heard crying, screaming, men yelling. A second later Ted appeared from the swirling dirt and dust, his face pale under a layer of grit. "We've lost at least five of our people, Fee. You need to do something!"

I lifted my arms, the image of the indigenous tribes in my mind as I waved my hands. "Get back!" I screamed. I heard the shriek of wind, the air clearing for a second to show the many bodies lying unmoving on the ground. A baby was crying and I ran toward the sound, finding Becky on her back amidst a pool of blood and the baby in the dirt next to her. Becky's eyes were wide open but there was no life there. I picked up the baby and ran. "Follow me!" I screamed at the top of my lungs. I pulled the scarf over my nose and mouth and held the baby close, running in the direction Lucifer pointed. He was ethereal, a luminescent ghost in the air as he showed me the way.

I ran, my throat burning with the poisonous air, my heart pounding. I could see others running behind me. It seemed that somewhere along the way we began to skim across the ground, away from the garbage continuing to spill from the gaping gray shapes in the sky, away from the spear-wielding natives and away from the carnage. I was panting, the baby in my arms limp as I pressed him against my chest, hoping he hadn't suffocated.

When we reached the first rocky outcroppings Lucifer's directions were in my head as though he'd put a map inside it. There was no trail here, only rocks to climb and the knowledge that at the top we would find shelter. I held the baby with one arm and scrambled upward, relieved to see so many other sweaty faces following behind me.

I found the area where I'd discovered the yarrow and kept going, noticing the narrow trail that angled away from where the herbs grew. The cave loomed ahead, its dark maw gaping. I hurried toward it.

Ted reached the cave a few minutes after me, his face red and covered in sweat. "Jesus. What the hell happened back there?" he gasped.

"The city dumps their toxic waste out here. I thought the dumping was random, but it looked like they targeted us."

"And the ones with the spears? We lost a lot of people, Fee."

I let out a sigh, staring down at the baby in my arms. "Becky...she..."

Ted nodded. "Becky and a whole bunch of others. And what happened just now? I was running, but it felt like I was barely touching the ground."

I shook my head, tears welling as I pressed my fingers against the baby's chest. "Not sure this one's alive."

"His name is Carlos." Ted ripped him out of my arms, placed him on his back on the ground and blew into his mouth. When he let out a thin wail, I breathed out, looking up to see the rest of the group limping toward us. Elena was in the lead.

"Where's Becky?" she asked, frowning at the baby.

"Dead," I muttered.

Elena let out a cry as she took the baby from Ted. "What happened, Fee?"

I heard the anguish and the blame in her voice, turning away to hide my tears. "I didn't realize, I..."

"You're supposed to keep us safe! You have mystical powers, for god's sake! You could have stopped them!"

"Mystical powers?" Ted glanced at me.

"I'm usually more intuitive than I was today."

"You can say that again," Elena muttered, greeting the first of our group. She led them inside while I stared into space, unable to reconcile the misjudgment that had caused so much death.

Once everyone was settled inside, I stood, making my way into what I hoped would be our new home. "Anyone want to help me find water?" I asked shakily, looking around for Peyton. There was a grumbling murmur. I could feel the distrust that permeated the group. "Ted?"

Ted grudgingly stood up from where he crouched next to Elena. When he bent to kiss her, I realized that the two of them were more than friends. How had I missed that? I glanced at Maria behind them who was now holding two babies instead of one. She was opening her blouse to feed them. Peyton was beside her, talking to her in low tones. I felt as though I'd been asleep and was just now waking up. I'd blamed my confusion on Lucifer and the sudden appearance of Peyton, but it was all my fault. I should have known better. "Peyton?" I called out.

Peyton rose, worried gray eyes meeting mine. When he reached me, his expression turned from worry to a frown. "What the fuck is going on?" he whispered. "You led us straight into the worst shit I've ever seen."

"Everyone set up camp!" I called out, ignoring him. "And get the fire going. We have deer meat to cook unless it got left back there. Search for dried dung and use any burnable material you can find."

"We have the meat," a male voice called from the back.

"That's good to hear. We're going for water. Bring up all the jugs and containers."

A few moments later I left the cave, Peyton and Ted behind me carrying the remaining containers. I could hear them talking, and when I quieted my mind the words rang clear. "That toxic crap could have been avoided if we hadn't been in the middle of native territory. You know her better than the rest of us. Can you talk to her?"

"She isn't the same person." *This one is a raving lunatic and a fucking bitch.*

"Becky just died out there and Fee acted like she could care less. We need a new leader. You seem as good a choice as any—how about it?" *Fee can't be trusted. We almost died out there because of her.*

"Me? I just got here!"

"You seem strong and capable. Were you in the service?"

"Yeah, a long fucking time ago. I've been running a bar for the last ten years." Peyton turned to stare at me. *And I had a woman who seemed like she loved me.*

"But we're out here now. You know how to shoot, I heard you talking about it. You're charismatic...and..."

I walked toward them, trying hard to control the anger at myself and the disappointment in them. "If you try to replace me, you'll have a fight on your hands. And for your information, I've been holding my emotions back because of the position I'm in. I have to put up a strong front."

Peyton glanced at me and turned away.

"Fee, you have to admit you've been off your game. What gives?"

"Trying to keep you all alive is what gives, Ted. I admit I

made a mistake back there. I took a chance and I lost. I'm sorry, but I'm sure it won't be the last time. If you want to form a council to decide things, it's fine, but ultimately, I'm in charge. Sam was my go-to, but he's not coming back."

"Wasn't that man on death's door?" Ted asked.

"Elena treated him, remember? She's skilled in herbology."

Ted stared into the distance. "She's never talked much about it."

"It's secret knowledge. It's passed down and lies in the realm of the mystical when it's done properly." Where that came from, I didn't know. Was I turning into a pathological liar as well as an uncaring bitch? If I lost control of the group it would negate everything I'd learned in the past months. I'd decided to let it all unfold, but this latest 'mistake' had taken a toll on me and on the group. Lucifer was pissed and I felt pretty much unsure about all of it, my mind wanting to pick over every little detail. And I could not allow myself to go down that rabbit hole of doubt. My only excuse was the distraction caused by a relationship, something I'd told Peyton I couldn't afford.

I shook free of the negative thoughts and scanned the area. "We'll be safe here. And there's water just up there," I said, pointing toward an animal trail zigzagging around boulders. As I climbed, Lucifer's voice rang in my ears, his tone angry and unforgiving. *"I have better things to do than save you from one disaster after another. This is your mission, not mine. As far as what happened between us? It won't happen again. I'm gone, Feirin, so do not call on me the next time you find yourself facing death."*

"You fucker!" I shouted.

"Who are you calling a fucker?" Peyton demanded, his expression pinched and angry.

"It's the voice in my head, the one that says I'm useless and can't do anything right," I whispered.

"Shit, Fee. You're the most capable person I've ever met," Peyton said softly. "Don't let that voice take over, especially now. People need you."

"Despite what I said earlier, I agree," Ted said, catching up. "How did you know there was a spring up here?"

"This is where I found the yarrow to treat your gunshot wound." I pointed to the flowering plants before I bent to look for the spring, finally finding the trickle of water, the ground wet around it. Not big enough for bathing unless we dug it out, but definitely enough for drinking. And the water was clear after having been filtered through the reeds surrounding it.

I tried to smile, but my heart twisted in grief. Lucifer was leaving for good. I was heartbroken and furious at the same time. Loving me wasn't enough to keep him in a plane of existence where he didn't belong.

Lucifer watched Feirin's reaction to the message he put into her mind. He had not meant to be so harsh. Something strange was working inside him. He had left her there after the intense thing that happened between them, unable to explain to himself why he felt it necessary to be gone when she woke up. He relived the sensations and the ravenous hunger with which he explored her. Not only her body but all parts of her. He could feel the obsession within him to do it again and again.

He was a fifth element being. Of the ether, not of the earth. He wasn't suited to the earth, nor was he allowed to linger here. He was already feeling the weakening effects of the atmosphere. He'd known Feirin was coming long before she arrived. It had been his duty to help her. But he was expected to put the thoughts into her mind, not meet with her in bodily form. What had propelled him down to Earth and why had he felt compelled to touch her? As soon as his fingers felt the softness of her skin, the heavy weight of her dark hair, something shifted.

He could see the bright tendrils of energy that passed between

Feirin and the man who called himself Peyton. They were connected in ways he could never be connected with her. But she still called out to him, keeping him hovering at the brink between here and there. He had to go. If he remained here his usefulness would be consumed. She would consume him. She'd named it: love. He felt the pull of her, his beingness stretching toward her even as he made plans to go.

"What exactly is your end game, Fee?"

I glanced at Peyton next to me, both our arms covered in mud up to the elbows. The more dirt we removed the more the spring filled with water. "I don't know if I have one."

"So, just wander around from place to place in an environment that is virtually uninhabitable?"

I sat back on my heels, pushing away the strands of hair hanging in my face. "We've all been ousted from our homes. I would like to find a permanent place to live or to tackle the city and topple the system, but right now there aren't enough of us to accomplish something that lofty."

Peyton nodded, settling on his heels to stare at me. "I came out here to find you. I traded your Harley for the supplies to keep me alive."

"My bike? You could have sold it for thousands of credits."

"I know, but after my bar burned down all I could think about was you. I had to find you."

I grimaced and settled back on my knees, scooping out more mud. I had to give

him an explanation for why I was keeping him at arm's length, but this was not the time or place for it. A second later I heard Ted shouting my name. I stood and wiped the mud off on my pants as Ted appeared, huffing from the exertion. He pointed into the distance where a plume of dust had risen. A caravan of vehicles was crossing the desert.

"Who is it?"

Ted glanced from me to Peyton. "The city has finally collapsed. Those are its residents."

24

I gazed at the dust, the whine of motors finally reaching my ears. This must be the danger Lucifer warned me about. "Collapsed? How do you know that?"

He grimaced, his eyes narrowing. "While you two have been up here, a couple in their twenties and three other people wandered in. They lived in Uptown. The residents of Elysian City have abandoned ship. According to them the food and water ran out a week ago, supply chains cut off. IRIS went down right after that and Uptown is currently on fire. And let me be perfectly plain—these people are entitled, terrified, utterly selfish and morally corrupt. No one can reason with them. They expect to be taken care of and they're raising holy hell down there."

"Shit," Peyton muttered. "I had a feeling this was coming. My parents could be
among them."

I glanced at him before turning to Ted. "I hope I can settle them down, but I doubt I can."

Ted stared hard at me. "You know that merciless fierceness you have lurking just under the surface?"

"Christ, Fee. What if my parents end up here?"

"That would certainly be ironic," I said, turning to where he stood behind me with a bemused expression.

I heard Ted chuckle before he pointed toward the path, stepping aside so I could go ahead of him. But what I faced a few minutes later was not at all funny. More people had arrived, some of them very sick judging by the spots and lesions on their skin. And everyone was shouting.

"We need food and water!" a young woman with bruises on her face screamed.

"Why aren't you with them?" I asked, pointing toward the caravan of swerving cars. "I assume they're headed to Sanctuary?"

"Our car's automatic driving system went belly up. We bailed before it killed us. We saw the smoke from your fire and smelled the meat cooking. We're hungry and thirsty. Who are you people, anyway?" she asked, looking me over with undisguised revulsion.

I knew how I looked with mud all over me, dreads, and wearing rags. I barely held back the urge to slap her. She was wearing a sky-blue silk dress that was now torn, her hair once secured in some kind of braided configuration, hanging all around her face like limp snakes. "We're the ones you threw out of the city. We will share our food, but do not expect special treatment."

"How dare you!" the man with her exclaimed, perfectly styled blonde hair falling across his forehead. He pushed it back with the heel of his hand and let out a huff of annoyance. "My name is Arnold Havemeyer. Do you have any idea who we are?"

"Who you are makes no difference to me," I said, gazing at

him blandly. His beautifully ironed shirt was dirty and untucked from his perfectly creased trousers, a smear of dirt on his cheek. "We are equals in this new world. If you and the others you brought with you don't like it, you can leave."

"Don't throw us out," another woman murmured, blue eyes wide with terror. A white silk shift clung to her curves, a gold torque hung around her neck and her thin arms were covered in gold bracelets.

"Where did *you* come from, a party?" I asked, eyeing her.

"Well, yes, I suppose it was a party," she admitted, her gaze moving to the man hovering in the shadows. "We were celebrating the..."

"Shut-up, Eliza," the man hissed, moving quickly to her side.

I was sure I'd seen him before, but I couldn't place where. "It doesn't matter where you were or what you were doing," I told him, holding his gaze. "If you want to stay with us you will have to adhere to our rules. I am the leader here. If you have any questions or complaints you will address them to me."

"There are sick among us," he muttered.

"Yes, I can see that. You will all be quarantined until we know you are no longer contagious."

"Quarantine? Is there a doctor here?" he demanded. "Surely you can't expect us to stay with the ones infected!"

"That's exactly what I expect."

Elena moved to stand beside me. "I'm the closest to a doctor you're going to get."

He frowned. "You? You're...you're..."

"Brown-skinned? A woman?" she asked sweetly. "Get used to it." With that she called out to Ted, giving directions on where to take them.

I turned to her, smiling gratefully. "Thanks."

"You won't be thanking me in a few days. Those people are going to be nothing but trouble."

I glanced at the plume of dust in the distance, wondering if I was up to the task. There would be more of them. It was only a matter of time before cars ran out of fuel and the occupants found their way here. Was this part of my mission as well? And that was the moment I noticed Peyton's parents stumbling up the path. His mother's hair was hanging in limp tendrils around her pale face, her dress filthy and ripped. And his father's smug expression had turned into fear. Behind them came a man who had to be Peyton's brother, his face shape nearly identical.

They smiled awkwardly. "Glad to see a friendly face," Peyton's father mumbled, glancing from me to Peyton behind me.

Peyton moved next to me, glaring at them. "There is nothing friendly in my face or Fee's. You are not welcome here." He glanced at Blair coming up behind them. "And that includes you."

I turned to stare at him. "Of course, they're welcome, Peyton. But they'll need to abide by my rules."

Peyton's father frowned. "Rules? *You're* in charge? Where are the leaders from Elysian City? I was told Uptown's residents were out here taking people in. I expected housing, running water and bathroom facilities."

I laughed.

"Not bloody likely," Peyton muttered, turning away.

"You three will need to fit in just like everyone else," I told him. "Follow the others and you will be shown where to sleep." I pointed to where Elena led the new arrivals to an upper cave.

Peyton's mother glared at me, lifting her torn skirt as she stepped over the rocks. "I certainly hope you have a proper spot for us. We are not used to…"

"You'd best get used to it," I said, turning away to talk with Peyton. Out of the corner of my eye I watched the three of them stumble upward, a feeling of sympathy rushing through before I noticed the haughty look Peyton's mother gave me.

Once they headed up the path Peyton reached into his back pocket and pulled out a flask. "You look like you could use a drink," he said, holding it out.

I grabbed it out of his hand and tipped it up, glad of the burn as the whiskey ran into my throat. I coughed and gave it back. "Where did this come from?"

He grinned. "I salvaged three bottles from the fire."

THE REAL TROUBLE began three days later. I'd checked on the group, making sure they had food and water. With Maria occupied with two babies to feed, Elena was treating the sick ones and keeping me up on what was going on. "Arnold is an ass," she told me the morning of the day it happened. "He thinks he's god's gift to women."

"I've met his type before," I said.

But what happened later was worse than anything I could have imagined.

I WAS out hunting when I heard a scuffling sound, following the noise toward the strewn boulders at the base of our temple hill. I saw a man with his back to me, his pants around his ankles and the grunting thrusts making it obvious what he was engaged in. I would have turned away except for the muffled screams. When I moved closer, I saw that it was Arnold, and his hand was pressed over a woman's mouth as he thrust into her. She struggled against him but she was small and no match for his bulk. Rage washed over me as I waved my hand and threw him backward where he landed on his knees. And when he rose and stumbled toward me, I kicked him in the balls. He doubled over, sprawling amongst the rocks as I checked on the young woman whose name I didn't know. "Are you all right?"

Her face was streaked with tears and dirt, her blouse ripped to expose her small breasts. She was naked from the waist down, blood on her thighs from what he'd done. She shook her head, trying to cover herself.

"What's your name?"

"Rose," she muttered.

I pulled off the long shirt I wore and handed it to her. When she looked up at me, I saw the pain and hurt in her eyes. "How old are you?"

"Nearly fifteen."

"Go back to the cave, Rose. I'll deal with him."

She stared at Arnold on the ground. "He followed me. I was collecting herbs for Elena. He..."

I reached for her hand. "Go find Elena. Arnold is about to get what he deserves."

She ran then, my shirt billowing around her bare legs. I picked up her skirt that was ripped in two and lying in the dirt and turned to Arnold. "You will not come back here. If you do, I will kill you."

Arnold looked up, managing a glare of hatred. *This bitch does not control me.* "Eliza's there—you can't separate us."

"I can hear your thoughts, you piece of shit. And I *do* control you since you are on my territory. You just raped a four-teen-year-old girl. How do you think Eliza will feel when I tell her?"

What the fuck? Who is this woman? "She came onto me. She's nothing but a whore."

I moved closer, my anger erupting. "Who I am is the dark

211

goddess, asshole." A second later a hail of rocks swirled up from the ground and headed straight for him. He was screaming when I left, his face bleeding and hands held up to protect his face.

Elena met me at the top of the hill. "Rose is in shock. I gave her a tea to calm her down."

"Arnold is banned from here. If he comes back tell me."

Elena nodded. "Rose was a virgin, Fee."

I nodded, tears welling. "She's only fourteen years old. I'm glad I found them before he..."

"Before he what? He did what he planned to do and now a young girl is traumatized, probably for the rest of her life." Elena grimaced. "These people don't belong here."

I nodded, knowing she was right. "I'm heading up there to tell Eliza what her boyfriend just did."

"She won't care. They screw whoever they want. I've seen it."

"What? What do you mean?"

"Figure it out," she said, turning away.

I worked my way up the steep path to where Elena had found them a place to quarantine. The obviously sick ones were outside, lying on the blankets Elena had provided. I heard the rest of them laughing inside the small cave. Peyton's parents and Brian were with them, smoking some hallucinogenic herbs someone had brought along. It seemed that Peyton's father had taken charge, his booming voice announcing that they all deserved better than this and that he held sway with officials in Sanctuary.

"IRIS doesn't work out here but the car we had must have a communication system intact. And if anyone is an expert on these self-driving machines, we can get the hell out of here."

I am," I heard a man's voice say. "I worked for the company that sold them a few years back. Where'd you leave yours?"

"It's a mile or so south of here. The sooner we get away from these indigents the better. "

I stopped to check on the sick before I entered the cave and spoke to them. "I suggest the ones who wish to leave do it sooner rather than later. We have the sick to take care of and you're trying my patience."

"You do not run my life," Peyton's father growled, stabbing a finger into my chest. "I have friends in high places."

"Really? Where are they now? I don't see any high places here, aside from this mountain."

Peyton's mother came forward, her eyes red-rimmed, her dress torn. "You *will* provide for us. We're on the council."

I glanced around and raised my eyebrows. "What council is that?"

"Very funny," Brian said scornfully. "Peyton really knows how to pick 'em, doesn't he?" he asked, glancing at his father.

I ignored him, turning to Eliza who was watching me suspiciously. "Your boyfriend just raped a young girl named Rose. He will not be coming back."

She frowned. "Are you saying you killed him?"

I shook my head. "Would have liked to, but no, I did not kill him."

"He could die out there."

"Yes, he could, Eliza. He should have thought of that before he forced himself on a fourteen-year-old."

She looked around at Peyton's father and mother, her gaze landing on Brian. "Can't you do something? Arnold is a higher-up too. We own several apartments."

"What can I do?" Brian asked. "You heard her. Our credits mean nothing out here."

"It will once we reach Sanctuary," she said, stalking off. I watched her gathering her things. "You," she said, pointing a finger at the man who'd spoken up about engines. "You need to come with me. I'm going to find Philip and find that car and get to Sanctuary. Anyone who wants to come along, feel free."

I left them to it, listening to the engine guy argue with her about the possibilities she might be up against. "There's no place to charge it out here. And if it's run out of battery or fluids, or if there's sand damage, I won't be..."

"I don't care!" she shrieked. "This is madness—my boyfriend left to die? For raping some little girl whose skin was probably brown? What a bitch that woman is!"

The voices faded as I picked my way carefully down the path, breathing my anger away as I went. I was on the edge, ready to send a hailstorm of rocks flying right at them.

It was late the next day that Elena alerted me that Peyton's parents, Brian and Eliza and the engine guy were gone. We stared at each other. "Good luck to them," I finally muttered.

Ted and Peyton and I were hunting two weeks later when we came upon the bodies. An abandoned car was nearby, tires gone and the glass had been carefully removed as well as the innards from the engine compartment. What remained of the bodies were riddled with bullets and had been partially eaten by coyotes and crows. Remnants of the silk remained, incongruous pastel colors against the coarse sand and the bits of skin and bone and hair still remaining. I counted four, identifying Eliza, Peyton's mother and father and another man who no longer had a face.

"Got what they deserved," Ted mumbled.

I glanced at Peyton. "But who shot them?"

Peyton and Ted exchanged a look, neither saying a word.

"All of them?" I whispered, staring hard at Ted.

"We didn't do it," Ted answered darkly. "Would have liked to, but this was someone else's work."

I let out a heavy sigh, glad that my suspicions were wrong, but when I glanced at the two men again, I wasn't so sure. "Bury?"

Ted shook his head. "Let the vultures have the rest."

25

It was a terrible two months before the sick ones succumbed. The labored breathing had gone on and on, keeping me awake at night as the virus filled their lungs with mucous until they could no longer drag in breath. We managed to bury them under rocks in shallow graves, marking them with the small cairns we built.

The only remaining couple, Silvia and Daryl, were attempting to fit in, trying hard not to suffer the same fate as their friends. I could barely look at them, my anger flaring every time I thought of Rose. The formerly bright and light-hearted girl had sunk into herself, becoming withdrawn and depressed. The rape had resulted in pregnancy. She was small-hipped and way too young to be bearing a child.

"She'll be okay," Elena assured me every time I brought it up. "But I do wish we had Sam."

"Shall I go get him when the time comes?"

"Thought you told me the tribe nearly killed you."

"That's true, but if I handle it right, I hope to avoid another run-in with them. I'll do my projection to find Sam first. He'll protect me."

Elena glanced at me. "Will you contact Lucifer?"

"Lucifer's gone, Elena."

"Then how is it that we find water bottles whenever we're out?"

"*Empty* water bottles. They're old. He's been gone for probably three months." But the mention of him made the memories rush back, his absence like a wound that never healed. I still dreamed about him, but the dreams were different now, my own longing mixed up with the feeling of having been deserted. An emptiness that couldn't be filled.

"And what about you and Peyton? He should go with you. Maybe you two could rekindle what you had."

I turned to see Peyton wandering down the path toward the desert floor, a knife in his hand. We'd killed a deer the day before and he was heading out to deal with skinning and dressing it. "I don't love him, Elena."

"Who gives a crap about love? Having a man's body next to me is all I care about. And it's obvious how he feels about you."

"It wouldn't be fair to him."

"From what you've told me you and Peyton were together in the city...he..."

"I don't want Peyton, I want Lucifer." Before I could stop myself, I was crying, turning away to hide my tears.

I felt Elena's hand on my shoulder. "It's hard not to feel sorry for the guy. Peyton loves you. He's like a lost puppy."

I jerked away. "That's his problem, not mine."

I left her standing there and went about my business, making the rounds to check on everyone, talking with those who needed to talk and visiting with Rose.

The girl was pale as ash, her skin pinched. Because of how thin she was, her belly already protruded. "I asked Elena how to get rid of it but she wouldn't tell me."

I sat next to her. "Elena believes in saving life, not destroying it."

"But he forced me. How am I expected to take care of it or love it?"

"You'll feel differently once it's born."

"Will I?"

I sighed. "I don't know, Rose, but I hope so. If not then maybe one of the more maternal in our group will raise it."

"How about you?"

"Me? No way. I'm the least maternal woman here."

"Maybe it will die before it's born," she said darkly.

I stood and glanced down at where she huddled. "I understand how you feel, but the baby can feel it too. It's not the baby's fault it was conceived this way."

Rose placed her hands on her belly. "I hate it," she muttered.

I left her and stopped to speak with Maria next, the two babies still thriving from the milk she'd managed to produce. Mateo was with her. "The babies are doing well?"

Maria nodded, smiling. "Yes. You do know that I am a *curandero*? I can help Rose with the birth."

"Thanks, Maria. Rose doesn't want it."

Maria frowned. "A baby is a gift from God. I will speak with her."

A few minutes later I headed for the cave entrance, knowing that I would feel exactly as Rose did. But I would have done something to get rid of it before it began to move around in my womb. There were herbs for that, herbs that had been used since the dawn of time. I was angry with Elena for not helping her. I felt the girl's anger and grief as though it was my own, the memory of seeing that man forcing himself on her bringing waves of red-hot fury. A second later I was back with Lucifer, my fury at his absence leaving me breathless.

The anger bubbled up then, my hands clenching. Elena's lack of understanding regarding Lucifer, Peyton and his feelings for me, the sick we'd had to bury, the responsibility to keep these people alive, my own inadequacies...I emerged from the cave in a black rage. A split second later I heard a crack and an earth-shaking rumble as two huge boulders crashed by, slamming into other rocks as they hurtled past. I looked up to see others teetering just before plunging toward the desert floor. People were screaming and running to avoid being taken along with them.

"What is happening?" Elena shouted, rushing out of the cave. "The cave ceiling is cracking!"

I put up my hands and calmed my mind just before another boulder loosened and came to rest in front of the cave.

Elena watched me, her lips going white where they pressed together.

"Are you responsible for this?"

"I was angry and..."

Elena glared at me. "You were *angry*? You could have killed us all!" she shouted.

"It wasn't intentional, Elena."

"You'd better learn how to control your temper, Fee."

The anger was all-consuming, a red-hot fire that burned until there was only ash, suffocating everything in its wake. I no longer trusted myself or the job I was supposed to be doing. Taking care of people and keeping them safe did not tally with the raw emotion building inside me. I felt like a bomb about to explode. Why was this happening?

But I knew why. I was in love with a light-being who was gone for good, I was faced with a job that was becoming increasingly difficult with no end in sight, and I had a man mooning around me wanting me to love him. I had to have some quiet time to reflect. And if I didn't get it, I was a danger, not only to myself, but to everyone around me. I felt brittle, like glass that was splintering into a million pieces.

"I need to be alone," I muttered before rushing past Elena. I had to dodge around the large rocks and boulders that now littered the path, amazed by the damage I'd caused.

"Wait!" Elena called. "How long will you be gone?"

"As long as it takes!" I shouted back.

She frowned and shook her head before turning back toward the cave and the people staring wide-eyed at the mess.

SWEAT RAN down my face as I ran, trickling between my breasts. I was half-crazed, sick inside, unable to reconcile my erratic behavior with the role of leader. People had died because of me and this latest craziness could have caused even more death.

Tears flowed non-stop, dripping down my nose to mix with the sweat. When I couldn't run anymore, I lowered to the dirt, my hiccupping sobs loud in the silence. The tears finally released the pressure on my chest, my ability to take in a deep breath returning. Without Sam I was lost to myself and to the ones I was supposed to be protecting. And Lucifer's silence made it even worse.

I stared into the far distance toward the line of cars, an unfurling snake that wove in and out of the swirling dust. They were still very far, but too close for comfort.

I THOUGHT back to life in the city. I longed for the surety of my construction job, the simple sex with Peyton. Lucifer had changed everything, my love for him an all- consuming fire that refused to let me go. "Lucifer, you must know my purpose here. I need help," I whispered. But what I was really asking was to see him again, to have him tell me he loved me too and to feel his mouth against mine.

When I rose to my feet, I could see the far-off hills, the boulders that could provide shade. The sun beat down, the heat and the agony of my thoughts coalescing as I jogged in that direction.

The boulders lifted up from the desert floor like recumbent beasts. I put my hand on one, feeling the lingering warmth but also savoring the blessed shade. I felt a murmur, like a purr. "Are you alive?" I whispered. Of course, they were. Everything was alive, just in differing vibrations. The boulders were slow, ponderous even.

I lay in the shade with my back against the rock, feeling it give a little as though molding to my shape. My mind was a blank now, an empty screen that showed me nothing but my own reflection. The sun lowered and disappeared beyond the horizon in a blaze of glory, and as the light slipped away, stars appeared, blinking into existence one by one. The rock cooled as the sky turned dark blue, the color reminding me of my moon tattoo. My fingers went there to feel it, hoping for some memory of how it came to be, but there was nothing, not even a slight echo of the moment when the tattoo had been stippled onto my skin. As night deepened my worries scattered like the trillions of stars that now peppered the sky.

THE SHADOW STARTLED me at first, but then Lucifer's deep voice drifted in the air, my name on his lips. I was up and rushing toward him before I could stop myself, knocking him over where we tumbled to the ground in a heap. I held him and cried, the wool of his coat chafing my cheek.

His fingers traced my tears, my heaving sobs causing him to hold me more tightly. "Feirin," he murmured, his lips brushing mine. "I did what was asked. But I cannot stay away."

When I pulled away to gaze into his eyes, the stars reflected back at me. "You didn't know you'd have feelings for me."

His forehead creased. "It is forbidden."

"And yet the heart knows what it wants."

"I heard you call. I will always hear you no matter where I am."

A few minutes went by before I pulled out his arms. "I can't do it, Lucifer."

Lucifer's face was in shadow, his hand in mine. "Have you determined what *it* is?"

"I hoped you could tell me, because right now I'm floundering. I don't trust myself."

"I was given the message and sent here to convey it, not in bodily form but in thoughts. I was there in the city when you and Peyton, when..."

I stared at him. "That was you? Yes, now I can see it—your face—it was your face that came through."

"Because of what I've done they have forbidden any more interaction between us."

"You saw what Peyton and I did together."

He nodded. "I not only saw it, I felt it—I felt you. The experience was over-powering."

"You've never..."

"Light-beings are not corporeal. We exist on another plane."

I began to undo the buttons of his long black coat, slipping them out of the buttonholes one by one, before I pushed his coat back to expose his lean chest. The moon rose, enormous and bright, revealing the supernatural radiance in his eyes.

I put my hand on his chest. "You're real, though. You have a body, a heart."

"Feirin," he murmured. "I am lost when I'm with you."

"You love me. It isn't a normal feeling for your kind. If we make love you must promise me you will stay."

But there was no *if* about it. His hands were already exploring, tugging at my top, pulling it down to kiss my breasts. I felt his urgency, his hunger, my hunger rising to meet it as we removed the rest of our clothing. For a moment he held me still in the moonlight, exploring every inch with his eyes before he followed with his mouth. I moaned, arching up to press against him, the exquisite sensations pulsing, an intensity I could barely stand. I wanted him inside me, and when he accommodated my wish, we created a rhythm between us, lost to everything but each other. And then there were no more thoughts, nothing but his light filling me up, my pendant blazing between us.

I woke with a start, my heart hammering. When I felt next to me there was no one there, but then I noticed his silhouette in the opening of the shallow cave. His back was to me as he stared into the darkness. I moved to sit next to him. "You didn't leave," I whispered.

He turned to look at me and took off his coat, placing it around my shoulders. "I couldn't leave now even if I wanted to. I am yours."

I took his hand, twining my fingers through his. "What will happen?"

He shrugged and looked away. "It is a breach of trust, an offense that will not be tolerated."

"You can't just be with me?"

"I am not of this earth. To stay would kill me."

"Then how can we be together?"

His dark eyes met mine. "We will steal the time and make the most of it."

"Steal the time. Like now." I stared into the night. "They must know that I'm still confused about my mission here. Isn't that a reason to be together?"

"We were never authorized to be together like this. They have told me what happens to those who break the rules between humans and our kind."

"It's happened before--love between light-beings and humans?"

He nodded. "I will spare you the details of how it ended."

I clutched his fingers. "But I love you. Doesn't that count for anything?"

He smiled. "It is hard not to love an ethereal being. We are mystical and carry light within us. Humans cannot resist this."

I snorted. "I love you because of who you are, not because of *what* you are.

Being with you has given me hope again. I was lost."

"I know this. It is why I came."

"If that's true, why won't they let you help me? I need you now more than ever."

"I have done all that I am allowed. It is now up to you."

"But why, Lucifer? Why are the gods gone from this time?"

"Lack of belief, the violence that lies hidden inside the human heart? We tried to rid the world of all that, but the human realm turned their back on us a long time ago."

"How can one person change anything?"

Lucifer smiled. "History shows that it is possible. Think of Jesus, the Buddha, Gandhi."

"And yet Jesus was crucified and his teachings have been twisted to suit the ones who run things."

"But the Eastern teachings remain in certain parts of your

world. Many still believe in the avatars. You are the dark goddess—you must embrace what you are."

"All I've done lately is cause pain and nearly kill everyone with my anger. I'm powerful but I don't know how to control it. We have people coming to us who are fleeing the city—they are spoiled, arrogant, entitled."

"And yet you see the folly of who they are. You are saving the ones who would otherwise be persecuted, and turning the thoughts of the others."

I shook my head. "I haven't turned anyone's thoughts. They leave before I have a chance."

"You will find your way. Do not despair."

I leaned into him. "How can I despair when you're sitting next to me?"

He gazed at me, his eyes swirling with light. "You consume me," he murmured. "I am not whole without you."

"Are you sure it isn't the novelty of sex?" I asked, teasing him.

He lay back and tugged me down next to him. "It is not only the bodily connection. You have changed me."

"Changed you...how?"

He kneeled over me, his forearms bracketing my head. "What do you want, Feirin?"

"I want you."

"I am yours," he whispered.

I cried then, tears streaming down my face as we connected, his luminance consuming everything I was or had ever been. I was lost to myself, tangled up with him so completely that nothing could pull us apart. I wasn't sure anymore where I ended and he began.

· · ·

I WAS SLEEPING when it happened, for once at peace with the knowledge that he was with me, my head on his shoulder, his arm holding me against him. I woke with a start as Lucifer was dragged away, his light dimming until I could no longer see him. A second later I was surrounded with shadowy beings, unable to keep myself from their greedy grasp. I screamed and fought, but it was no use. Blackness descended, blinding and complete, my ability to breathe lost within it.

26

"Fee!"

I opened my eyes to see Elena peering down at me. "Where...where am I?"

"You're here, with me, with all of us. Where did you think you were?"

A headache pounded against my temples. "But...I was with Lucifer, and then..."

She shook her head, frowning. "You wouldn't wake up. You must have been dreaming."

The group watched warily, Peyton lurking behind her. "But I went off to be alone. I was..."

Elena shook her head. "You came into the cave two hours ago, fell into your bed and dropped into a deep sleep."

I held my head, the pain making my eyes water. "The last thing I remember is being with Lucifer. And then... they took him away."

"Who is Lucifer?" Peyton asked. "He can't be what you told me he is. Are you fucking him?"

I frowned and shook my head. "*Fucking* is not a word I associate with Lucifer," I muttered.

"Lucifer is a mythical angel who helps people in the desert, but no one has ever seen him. Isn't that right, Fee?"

"But Fee's seen him," Peyton said. "She told me he's from another dimension. I didn't believe her."

Elena and I exchanged a glance.

"He's real," I whispered. "And the shadowy ones with him are keeping us apart."

There was a murmur from the group. "Are they evil?" someone asked. "Will they come for *us*?" another person asked. "Lucifer is the devil," someone muttered, causing a collective gasp.

I didn't answer as Peyton helped me up. "You need to tell me the truth," he mumbled.

"I love him," I said simply.

"You love a creature that that isn't human? I'm here and I'm flesh and blood. Why won't you let me in? I was really worried about you."

Instead of answering, I walked out of the cave, trying to sort out how I ended up here and if indeed it had all been a dream. I could feel Peyton's confusion, his thoughts circling. *I love her and she prefers a figment of her imagination? I won't believe it until I actually see this dude.*

I took Peyton's hand. "I'm sorry, Peyton. I truly am. I didn't mean for this to happen. You were my best friend back in the city."

"And you liked my body," he mumbled.

"Yes. I enjoyed our sexual relationship."

"Then why can't we resume what we had?" *I swear you're dreaming this guy.*

Tears welled and I wiped them away. "Because I can't do that to you. It wouldn't be fair."

Peyton stared at me. "I'm sorry too. I'm sorry that you've chosen this screwed up way to break up with me. I put my life at risk to find you, Fee. I've loved you for years and now I find out you've never loved me?"

"I never said I loved you, Peyton. I liked what we had but I can't resume it as though nothing's changed. Something *has* changed and I can't ignore it."

He shook his head and walked away.

I WAS OUTSIDE LATER STARING up at the haze of heat, alone in my musings. I'd hurt Peyton but I had no choice. There was no doubt that I'd been with Lucifer, and the light-beings, like angry parents, had separated us. He loved me and I loved him. But now what? Did they have the power to keep us apart?

When Elena joined me, I turned to her. "Lucifer and I were definitely together. I don't know how the creatures did what they did, but they were the ones who brought me back."

Her gaze narrowed. "How are you so sure it wasn't a dream?"

I made a face. "How do you think?"

"Oh."

"They didn't like it that Lucifer pledged himself to me."

Elena looked skeptical. "They must be incredibly powerful to pull that off. And why would they care?"

"What happened between us is not allowed. Now I'm afraid they've taken control of him. What if they stop us from being together?"

Elena shrugged. "Why don't you think more about your charges and less about this elusive love affair you have going? I don't have patience for this now that Rose is getting close to term. Not to mention the new people who are seeking our help every day."

"Rose? She's not even close to due yet."

"She's close to six months. Where in hell have you been?"

Strangers walked past, their curious gazes making it obvious they'd never seen me before. "Rose was only a couple of months pregnant when I left. It felt like I was gone one night."

"As I recall you promised to fetch Sam. This baby could come early."

I felt disoriented, dizzy, the headache returning. "Should I go now?"

She gazed at me worriedly. "You just went very pale. Maybe you better take Peyton or Ted along."

"I'll be fine."

She gave me a withering look. "No more fooling around with Lucifer and disappearing. I mean it, Fee. If you screw this up that girl could die."

I nodded and went to get my pack, my head spinning. I gathered a water skin, deer jerky, and a blanket, and stuffed them into my pack before heading down the rocky path toward the desert.

"Hey! Are you the one who can get boulders to come loose and project your body like a ghost?"

I turned to the young girl with the blue eyes and sandy hair. I'd never seen her before. "I'm Fee. Who are you?"

"I'm Liza," she smiled. "And I want to be just like you."

I laughed. "Well, once I'm back maybe I can teach you how to defend yourself."

"And stop bullets with my mind?"

I shrugged and walked past her. "Maybe!" I called out.

I WAS WELL on my way when I noticed the seedlings. They'd recently sprouted, bright green diploids along the path I'd taken on my last trip. When I stopped to examine them, I couldn't identify what they were. But without water and the blistering sun shining down, they would soon die.

Cat joined me along the way, twining around my legs as I walked. "How are you here?" I asked him. He only stared at me out his knowing green eyes and trotted ahead, as though he knew the way. If he hadn't led me on a circuitous trail that did not cross native land, I would have put myself in danger yet again, my distraction keeping me off balance. I watched him up ahead of me, wondering if he was in touch with Lucifer. Someone was attempting to keep me safe.

I skirted around the abandoned cars with their doors flung open, bodies lying here and there in various states of decay. Some had died of thirst and starvation, others had spears and knives still sticking out of them or bloody gaping wounds from gunshots. I said prayers for them before carefully removing jewelry and clothing. Boots, wool cloaks and jackets made their way into my bulging pack, the jewelry tucked into my pockets. I still believed in barter.

I slept in the open with the cat nestled against me. In the morning I went on, leaving before dawn. I passed by the prison where I'd been left for dead, following the trail of prints still left from Sam and the tribe. They were indistinct, covered over with sand, but with the cat's help I found them. He was off ahead of me, looking back to see if I followed.

IT WAS another week before I found them. Sika's tribe had formed a camp in the shade of a few spindly trees that grew next to a small rocky outcropping. I heard laughter, my spirits rising when I recognized Sam's deep baritone.

"Sam!" I called out, knowing that if I didn't alert them to my arrival I might be attacked.

He appeared from within a small shelter built out of mud and twig, his face breaking into a wide smile when he saw me. Behind him I saw Sika, her belly already swollen with his baby. I felt a pang of longing as I watched him turn to her, reassuring and protective. He strode toward me like a much younger man, lean from work, his skin dark from the sun. I was folded into his arms a moment later.

"I thought you were dead, Fee. I am very happy I was wrong."

"Lucifer saved me. He said you were calling for me. I was passed out for a while. I thought you left me there."

"I did leave you there, but by that time I figured you were a goner. That poison killed four of our people." He pushed the long hair off his forehead. "Why have you come?"

I laughed. "Does there have to be a reason?"

"Out here? Yes, there does." He glanced down at the cat standing beside me.

"We have a situation."

After I explained it all he nodded. "I will come. But I can't stay long. Sika carries twins."

I glanced at her watching me. "When is she due?"

"Should be plenty of time, but I wouldn't want to chance it." He smiled and put an arm loosely around my shoulders. "How are you, Fee? Have you seen Lucifer?"

I told him the latest, my heart in my throat as I voiced my worry.

"You're right to be worried. If what you say is true, those beings manipulated time. This means they're serious about keeping you two apart."

"What can I do?"

"Until Lucifer finds his way back to you? Nothing. I'd say

concentrate on what your ultimate mission is, and try to forget him."

I glanced at Sika, their son standing next to her. "And how did that work out for you?"

He laughed. "You love him. And he loves you. A bond like that can travel across time and space." He stared at the cat. "This one knows, don't you?" he asked, reaching to scratch Cat behind the ears.

"It does seem that Cat has special powers."

"He's a protection spirit, Fee. Sent here to keep you safe."

"I already have one of those," I said, lifting my stone to show him.

He stared at it. "Judging from the light pouring out of that thing I'd say it's a link between you and Lucifer. This cat is something else."

"Sent from where?"

"Now that's the question, isn't it?"

We talked late into the night, catching up with the news of our very different lives. Sika sat with us next to the fire, her questions soft as she asked him to translate.

But the next day when he packed up to come with me, Sika spoke to him in staccato tones. He held her shoulders and talked to her, finally turning and heading to where I waited.

"What did she say?"

"She's worried I won't come back."

"Did you reassure her?"

"I told her that I wouldn't miss this birth for all the gold in the world."

"Gold is important to them?"

"They know gold's value. They trade with things of this nature."

"I have some in my pockets," I said, pulling out a bracelet.

Sam took it, his eyes narrowing in wonder. "Where did you

get that? It's probably worth at least five-thousand, maybe more."

"Worn by a woman along the way—one of the Uptowners who died in the desert."

"Can Sika have it? It might help with her nerves."

I shrugged and nodded, watching him run back to give it to her. It was a circlet and he worked it over her hand, pushing it up until it encircled her upper arm. When she saw me watching she smiled and waved like a child just learning, fingers closing and opening in a gesture she must have learned from Sam.

WE TRAVELED for several days before we came upon the seedlings.

"What is this?" Sam asked, bending to look at the little tree that had emerged from the dry ground.

"I don't know. I assumed they would die. They're all along the path I took before Lucifer found me."

Sam straightened, frowning. "What thoughts were you having?"

"I was angry and then I was sad. I cried for nearly the entire trip. I hardly ever cry."

Sam grimaced. "I do know that about you. Your tears watered the ground enough to sprout seeds that have been dormant for a very long time."

I bent to look closer. "But what are they? Trees don't grow in a desert."

"They did once. This entire basin was a fertile valley."

"But they can't last, Sam. They haven't been watered since the day I cried."

"And yet they're growing."

I scanned, noticing the muzz of green. The plants were now a foot high. "How?"

Sam chuckled. "Is that a real question, dark goddess?"

BY THE TIME we arrived at the cave Rose had gone into premature labor. Elena was frantic, grabbing Sam to drag him inside the moment she saw us. What were the chances of this baby surviving? I remembered the look on her face when she said she hated it. Maybe it was for the best.

When the screams began, I raced down the hill to the desert floor. I felt sick with nerves and afraid for the baby and for Rose, and I did not want to be called to help. She was so young, barely a child herself. I wandered around the scattered rocks, letting my light flow out to encircle Rose.

It was later and I was resting against a boulder when I heard Lucifer, wondering if I was making it up until I realized what he was telling me.

They have forbidden me from returning to Earth.

A second later his pain wrapped around my heart, connecting with my own. I let out a sob, feeling him reach out in tendrils of light. I reached back, touching him through the ether. Silver light wafted from my fingers, traveling in waves. His was gold, meeting mine and pulsating back. I felt us connect, the gold and silver twining together, a shimmering cord of brightness. "Lucifer," I whispered, feeling him wrap around me.

I was nearly asleep when I heard Sam call, the sense of being held in Lucifer's arms dissolving. I was up and running a moment later. Sam stood at the top of the hill waiting for me as I rushed toward him, fearing the worst.

But Sam was smiling. He took me by the hand and led me

toward the cave. "She's tiny but alive. Thought I'd lost them both, but Rose is a fighter."

"She didn't want the baby."

Sam grinned. "She does now. She's already feeding her."

I let out a sigh of relief. "Funny what carrying a baby inside your body will do."

"I wouldn't know."

"Neither do I, but I've heard." When he tugged me inside I pulled away.

"You're not coming in to see her?" he asked, turning.

"Not my thing."

Sam made a face. "The girl who's afraid of nothing is afraid of a tiny baby?"

"I'm not afraid, I'm..."

Sam gazed at me, the corners of his mouth turning up in a smile. "Right."

I watched him head inside, heard the light sound of Rose's voice and Sam's deeper reply followed by the tiny cry of the newborn. I shivered, wondering why I felt so cold. The sun had not set, there was no wind. *I want Lucifer's baby.* The thought was gone a second later, hardly making an impression as I walked steadily up the hill to the water source. A bath was all I wanted.

27

I was out hunting a week later when I spied the plants. They'd grown another foot and now I could identify what they were. Trees of all kinds--conifers with tiny needles on their spindly branches, oaks and maples and others with leaves. The sky was white with heat, mirages shimmering across the ocean of sand. And yet these trees were growing and thriving. I heard a whisper as I bent to examine them, indistinguishable as wind through grass.

I carried the deer over my shoulder, my gaze on the trees waving in a non-existent breeze. They were whispering again. "I can't understand you," I muttered. But there was something, a message that haunted. When I stopped to look at them, they stilled, as though keeping watch. They formed a meandering green wave that disappeared into the distance. Had I shed that many tears?

I left the trees and hurried across the baked desert sand, the dust getting into my nose and lungs as I ran. There was something uncanny and disturbing about the trees, something that called to me that I didn't want to look at.

. . .

BACK IN THE cave I took a deeper look at our growing group. There was so much diversity now. Skin color ranged from ivory to ebony. Eyes the palest blue like the sky at dawn, dark like the stormy sea, green like a forest pool, brown like warm wood, and every shade in between. Cultures were represented in the colorful rags worn and turbans wrapped about heads. Some women like Elena wore loose blouses decorated with bright threads in intricate patterns, some wore short tight tops like mine and low hanging skirts, revealing pierced belly buttons with gold and silver rings, some wore robes that crossed in front with belts to hold them closed—older women had gray hair tied back or pushed into loose knots on their heads, and held with sticks. Some were dressed in long tunics over loose pants or skirts, anklets with bells that tinkled, and rough boots. But despite the former colors and styles represented, all clothing was torn and dirty now, and some were merely rags barely held together. A few had needles and thread but it was running out quickly.

These people had lived in Uptown before being kicked out for their skin color, or put to work in the bowels beneath. Others had been wandering the desert for a long time, living on their own and barely surviving until they found their way to us. News had spread of the woman who could throw a man forty feet using her hands and project herself from one place to another.

The men wore camouflage or filthy ripped jeans, with knives hooked onto belts and guns strapped to chests. Their clothing was rough, dirty and tattered. Many carried animal skin pouches filled with beads and trinkets to trade, as well as the dried herbs they pressed into pipes and smoked that made them silly. Some had earrings in one ear or both. Many had tattoos either recently done in a haphazard manner or older with intricate designs done in color.

And then there were those like me who wore whatever I could find, whether camouflage, khakis, or filthy skirts and tank tops, wide belts and jackets that had seen better days, my hair knotted and unkempt. We were as different as we could possibly be, and yet many of these diverse men and women were hooking up. Women's bellies swelled with new life. We were one hundred strong with new people arriving every day. And soon there would be more mouths to feed.

Rose and her baby were thriving, Elena's herbs helping the young girl cope. When I glanced her way, Rose was smiling down at the tiny bundle in her arms. I was amazed by all of it. And yet I knew that this was not enough. People had no real space to themselves. For sex they went off, climbing the hills to find some privacy.

They had no work, no gardens to tend, all eager for something to occupy their time. I worried about the men especially; they were quick to anger, ready to fight. Many went out on their own to hunt, some smoked mind-altering herbs or gathered mushrooms that had hallucinogenic properties and had long mumbling conversations that went nowhere. Others helped Elena or Ted gather dried dung and helped with the cooking. Some gave me sideways glances. I knew they didn't trust a woman to lead. It took all my strength to keep control, to make them understand that I was the one in charge. If it came to fighting over it, I would certainly win considering the powers I had, but I didn't want it to come to that.

Liza had come to me, making me keep my promise. And now I had a class of ten women and girls that I was teaching how to kickbox. I was busy, but the nagging feeling never left. This group of caves was merely a stopgap, a way to stay alive until...until what? That was the question that floated through my thoughts every day. We needed a community of houses, a garden, a place where we could live together in peace and harmony. There were artists among us, farmers too. The men had to be occupied or there would be an uprising. We needed a real Sanctuary.

When I wasn't worrying about how to bring this dream into reality, I was thinking about Lucifer. Missing him was an ache that would not go away. Weeks had gone by since he'd reached out, the strange gold and silver connection between us reminding me that he was not human. I worried, crying sometimes when no one was looking. But mostly I thought and planned, talking to Elena, Ted and Peyton and a few others about my ideas for our little village.

"But how can you create something like that?" Peyton asked. "There's nothing here to build with. Not enough water to grow crops."

"I don't know. I just know it's what I'm supposed to do."

Elena looked at me askance. I knew what she was thinking —did Lucifer play a part in this fantasy future? I wished I knew.

Ted was the only one who seemed enthusiastic, making drawings on rocks using charcoal from the fire. They were simple designs for shelters, organized into blocks that worked aesthetically with the boulder strewn desert and the temple hills. "Were you an architect in a former life?" I asked him, looking over his shoulder.

"No, but I worked for the city doing planning."

When I wasn't consumed with this future I'd conjured in my head, I thought about my family, the gods and goddesses that no longer existed. *Reclaiming what was mine.* The sentence floated in my mind. What did it mean?

. . .

AN OLDER WOMAN named Phrani befriended me. I liked her and looked to her when things got too much for me to handle. She was like Sam in female form—wise and sensible. Phrani had wandered in with the other Uptowners, but she was not of the same mind. She wore long skirts and beads, her olive skin and long gray hair setting off wide sea-green eyes.

"Uptown needed a shakeup. The entire world needed it. We have created a world that is populated by the haves and the have-nots. I am lucky to be one of the have's, but I am not proud of it. I did nothing to deserve it—I inherited what I have. I decided I was meant to make a difference in some way, but the system in place in Elysian City was impossible to change. Now I have the chance to remedy it—here, with you."

She had a tiny ruby set into what she termed her third eye, a spot just above her eyebrows in the center.

"It is the gate that leads into the higher realms of consciousness," she told me when I asked. "It is from the Hindu religion. My spiritual training tells me that the only thing that really counts is what lies hidden within. You are a goddess. You understand what I'm talking about."

"How did you know I'm a goddess?"

She laughed. "Everyone here knows. You are the main topic of conversation. Some fear you, others revere you, but everyone is in awe."

I thought about what she'd said. I had not been paying much attention to what lay hidden within. I'd been too busy dealing with human complaints, procuring food and making sure we were safe. Maybe it was time to search out the hidden —perhaps, as Lucifer had told me, the answers lay in the darkness. But in order to find answers I had to know the questions.

It was a week later when our possible bright future was thrown into the wind, as a caravan of black cars came to a stop right outside the temple hill. The occupants had to be more Uptown residents, but instead of the women and men who lived here already, these were militia carrying weapons. They stormed up the hill with guns pointing. When one of them grabbed me I kicked out, but they had me in handcuffs before I could raise my hands to fight back. They bound my feet as well, throwing me on the ground before they entered the cave. Seconds later I heard screaming, people running by me toward the path down, the sonic blasts of the guns sending shivers up my spine.

The men in my group tried to fight back, but pistols and knives were no match for the weapons the newcomers carried. I saw Ted run by, Elena just behind him. Rose was there, the baby in her arms as she took off after them. I twisted to see them, but the dust and commotion was too thick. Where had they come from? What did they want? And why was I hogtied while they opened fire on the others? I lay there, unable to do one thing, watching my people rush away only to get shot in the back. And when there were no more screams, they carried me down the hill, threw me into the trunk of a car and drove away.

I woke up sometime later with my ankles burning, my wrists sore and my bladder nearly bursting with the need to pee. "Hello?"

"Get the bitch out of the car," I heard one of them say. "But watch her. She's the one they call the dark goddess."

How did they know that? Who were these guys?

The trunk opened and I was dragged out. "I have to pee," I said.

The man looked at me. "Boss? She says she has to pee."

"Let her pee. You can help her, Cliff. Do not under any circumstances undo those fucking cuffs. Her hands are lethal weapons."

Cliff took me by the arm, leading me a short distance away from the car. When he reached to pull down my pants, I managed to shove an elbow into his belly. "You fucking bitch," he muttered, kicking my legs out from under me. "You want to pee, bitch? Pee in your pants."

"Please...you won't like the smell if I do that."

He stared at me, finally pulling me up by my hair. I held back the cry of pain. This time when he undid my pants, I let him, squatting in the dirt right in front of him to do my business. When I was finished, I docilely allowed him to pull my pants back up, glad that he didn't take the opportunity to rape me. I heard the others talking, and smelled the rolled-up tubes they smoked as the guy threw me roughly into the trunk. I projected myself out to hear what was going on, making sure my ethereal self was hidden from view.

"Why haven't you just killed the cunt?"

"We need to take her to the big boss. He's waiting up the way."

"What does he want with her?"

"She's got powers, dipshit. He wants to use her to save the fucking city. How stupid are you?"

"The city's already fallen."

"The other one, idiot. The one they call Sanctuary."

When I saw them turn toward the cars again, I melted back into my body. I had no idea how they'd heard about me or what was going on. All I knew was that I had to get out of the cuffs and find my people. The few who were left.

I was dozing when the car lurched to a stop, my head bumping painfully against the metal. A second later I heard voices. "Do you have her?"

"Yes, boss."

"Good. Get her out of the trunk."

The trunk opened, revealing a star-filled sky, the smell of desert dust tickling my nose. One of the men dragged me out, my legs numb from where they'd been pinned awkwardly beneath me. I heard Adam's voice. He couldn't be the one in charge.

"Yup, that's her," Adam said, pointing a flashlight in my face.

Beside him stood a tall imposing man in his sixties with graying hair, his cruel eyes fixed on me. "The dark goddess," he whispered. "At last."

"Who are you? How do you know me?"

"My son, Adam here, has a good eye. I sent him out months ago to find you. He told us where you were, you and your band of misfits." He laughed nastily. "Took a while to track you down and in the meantime our requirement for your services has grown. All I want is the use of your powers, Feirin. You must quell the unrest in Sanctuary. A lot of dark-skinned monkeys are protesting their lot in life. We need them to stop."

I shook my head. "I won't do it."

His icy eyes narrowed. "You will do it or you will die." He gestured to Adam. "Put her back in the trunk."

Adam smiled and grabbed my arm. "Not so cocky now, right bitch?" he hissed in my ear, squeezing my breast painfully. "Nice," he murmured, moving his hand between my legs. "I *will* have it off with you. But right now, I have to follow my father's orders."

He threw me into the trunk, his laughter growing fainter when the trunk's lid slid into place. I gritted my teeth, seething. Anger took over then, and I was able to wriggle my hands out of the cuffs. I twisted to undo the ones around my ankles, but they were too tight and for some reason I couldn't shuck them off like the others. But as soon as they opened the trunk, they would receive the wrath that I'd gathered around myself.

IT WAS hours before we stopped again. We were on paved roads now, the bumpiness of the desert long gone. I heard them talking and then the trunk opened, daylight blinding me for a second before I moved my hands, sending the two men flying backward where they sprawled. I pulled myself out of the trunk and crawled to one of them, feeling in his pockets. There was nothing there.

"No key?"

Adam's mocking voice rang out in the early dawn. He held up the key, dangling it in front of me. When I raised my hand, he flew through the air and hit the car hard and slid down in an unconscious heap. I crawled to where the key had flown out of his hand and undid the cuffs around my ankles. And then I was up and running.

SANCTUARY WAS VERY similar to Elysian City. But here there were many more people living on the streets. There was a charged feeling brewing, the hair on my arms standing up as I walked. The homeless were angry and hostile, eyeing me warily as I went by. When one of them barred me with his gun, I stopped. "I am not your enemy," I said evenly. "I'm trying to help you."

"Whatcha doing to help *me*, lady?"

"Lady?" I laughed and looked down at my torn camouflage, the dust and dirt that covered every part of me. "I've been living in the desert—that is until a band of goons picked me up and wanted me to quell the unrest here."

"You? They think *you* can stop us?" The guy was burly, his eyes gleaming as he took me in.

"I'm a goddess, dude. I have what you might call a black belt in goddess powers. You want a demonstration?"

His eyes narrowed dangerously. "And I have an assault rifle."

I knocked the gun out of his hands and picked it up before he had a chance to register what I'd done. I threw it into the street where it clattered. I stared at him defiantly until he shrugged and let out a little laugh. "Okay. I'll bite. What are these fucking powers you supposedly have?"

"I just showed you. Do you know a guy named Jeremy? He has a sister, Isabelle."

"Fuck, yeah. He's a buddy."

"He's a good friend of mine."

His hostile expression turned into a grin. "I'm Laurence," he said, holding out his hand.

"I'm Fee. Can you lead me to Jeremy? I may need his assistance."

THE CITY LOOMED up around us, the buildings dark and imposing. They blocked out the light, the windows mirroring the other buildings. I heard shouting as we came around a corner, armed militia wearing gas masks going after protesters.

They were setting off bombs that sent smoke swirling, the protestors gagging and dropping to their knees to vomit. When I saw Jeremy, he was on the ground trying to help his sister who was being beaten by a uniformed man. A second later I was in the air, my hands flailing, my feet kicking. I was a tornado, a whirlwind, filled with fury as I beat them back. They shot at me and I deflected the bullets, my body snakelike and lithe as I eluded what they threw at me.

"She's there!" I heard someone yell, my attention distracted for a second by the voice. It was Adam's father at the head of the line of militia. And in that moment of inattention I was grabbed from behind, my arms pinned.

"Get her out of here!" he shouted. They held a foul-smelling cloth over my mouth and I was carried away, the world going dark.

"You will be an asset."

I opened one eye. I was in a light-filled room filled with antiques and soft

Persian rugs. They'd placed me on a leather couch, my arms and legs trussed up like a pig ready for slaughter. My gaze went to Adam's father sitting in a chair facing me, his arms folded across his chest. His eyes were like chips of ice, pale blue and cold.

I didn't answer.

"Nothing to say? You certainly set things back out there, but we have it under control now. If you hadn't arrived, we wouldn't have had to use lethal force. You got those mother-fuckers mightily worked up, Feirin. Many of them are dead because of you."

I sucked in breath, hoping that Jeremy and his sister were

still alive. When I glanced at my legs, I realized that there were no cuffs or ropes around them, and yet I couldn't move. "What did you do?"

"I have some magic of my own. Now, if you promise to be good, we can get started. "

Magic of his own? "Who are you?"

"No one you've heard of."

The door opened and Adam came in, followed by a woman in her late twenties. She was blonde and very thin aside from her enormous breasts, her body-skimming ice blue top and skirt matching her flat eyes. She looked like a porcelain doll.

"This is Asia. She will take care of you while we ready you for what we have in mind." He nodded to her and rose from the chair. "I will speak with you later, Feirin. I expect you to be amenable by then."

Like hell. When Asia walked toward me, I wanted to kick her, but I couldn't move my arms or my legs. Adam followed her, watching me. "Can I play with her?" he asked Asia. "Just for a little while." He reached for his crotch and pantomimed humping.

"No, Adam. You heard what father said. It's time to get down to work."

Asia was surprisingly strong as she hoisted me up and over her shoulder. I felt like a rag doll as she carried me out of the room and down a long hall. We entered a room filled with electrical devices. "This is the torture chamber," she announced casually. "Father wants me to soften you a little. If you want to save yourself from excruciating pain, I suggest you go along with the program."

I glanced at the tables and the metal devices hanging over them. "I'll do whatever you ask," I murmured.

She stared at me with her cold eyes. "But will you really? I'm afraid I will have to demonstrate our ability to hurt before I believe that." She placed me on a table and lowered a metal circlet to rest around my head, reaching to tighten it. "When I ask a question, you must answer properly. If you don't you will feel pain." She stood back, regarding me impassively, a small black device in her hands. "Will you help us?"

"No." A second later my head lit up like a light bulb, my eyes feeling like they might burst from their sockets. I let out a scream.

"Wrong answer," she said.

I lay back panting, my eyes watering.

"Will you help us?"

"Yes," I gasped. Again, the pain filled me, worse than the first time. My bladder gave way, warm liquid soaking my pants. "Why did you do that? I said yes."

"You didn't mean it. Will you help us?"

I stared at her. I had to help them or they'd either kill me or torture me forever. And I had to get out of these wet pants. "I will help you."

She smiled. "Good." She waved her hand and the magic paralyzing me released.

She helped me up and led me down the hall into another room. "Bathroom there, clean clothes there," she said, pointing to a door and a wardrobe. She left, closing the door and locking it behind her.

I sank onto the floor, my legs shaking. My head still pounded from what she'd done. These people had magic. Who were they?

I took a long shower, letting the hot water stream over my head and loosen my filthy dreadlocks. I shampooed my hair and scrubbed my body with a washcloth until my skin was bright red. In the closet I found underwear and several dresses. Not my style but at least they were clean. I picked the simplest one I could find, cinching it with my leather belt. In the mirror

I saw a face hardened by the sun, glazed eyes that stared back at me with a look I didn't recognize, my clean hair a dark halo around it. I looked like what I was, the dark goddess, strong and implacable. But I was now at their mercy. The dress was blue with long sleeves, a simple linen tunic that reached to my knees.

I rolled the sleeves up to show my tattoos, starting when Cat appeared. "How did you get here?" I whispered. He only stared at me out of his swirling...*swirling?*... eyes. I leaned in closer. "Lucifer?"

Didn't you learn anything from the trees? You must control your anger.

What? What trees? I opened my eyes, taking in the bed, the wardrobe in dark antique wood, the Persian rug, my filthy clothes in a heap. I'd fallen asleep on the floor.

When the door opened and Asia entered, I was dressed and ready. As she led me out, I glanced back, but if the cat had been tere at all, he wasn't there now.

"Come along, Feirin. It is time to get to work." A dark aura shimmered around him, the room shifting and changing. The furniture and rugs were all a mirage. This place we were in was his invention—it wasn't real. "The protestors are getting in the way of what I have planned here. They are taking up valuable space and time with their antics."

Adam and Asia were in the hall when the man steered me through the door, Adam looking up from the device he wore on his wrist. He sneered, glancing from me to the man at my side.

"What are your plans for me?" I asked, looking up at him.

He had to be nearly seven feet tall, and when his eyes met mine, they were colorless and empty. "This city will serve as my headquarters while I'm here. I have much to do, you see. But these rats infesting the streets must be eliminated. They are nothing but scum, bleeding this place dry."

"But what are your plans?"

He frowned. "I just told you. If you want to live, you will do exactly as I say. Do you understand?"

"Do you want me to kill the protestors?"

He smiled again, his lips thinning. "That would be nice, but I'm thinking perhaps something a little more helpful to my cause. I want you to turn them, Feirin. They must be led to believe that I am their savior. Once that happens, they can be put to work."

"Work...like slaves, you mean?"

His eyebrows rose. "These dark bastards belong in the buildings and under the buildings, making sure everything runs smoothly. You surely know this, being of pure blood yourself."

Pure blood. I shook my head, anger building. It was coiling like a spring in my stomach. *You must control your anger.* I took a deep breath and let it out. "So, no death, just enchantment?"

"Now you're catching on. I'm assuming you are capable of such a thing?"

"I've never tried it. But yes, probably so."

"How long do you think it will take?"

"I have no idea. Will you release me once it's accomplished?"

"Why of course, my dear."

"Let me go, I mean. Let me leave this city."

"Adam will escort you to the border, Feirin, where you can rejoin whatever sad people still remain alive. We've been doing some cleansing while you've been gone. It won't do to have others come into Sanctuary and start another uprising."

"I will not be leading anyone back here."

He stared at me with his head cocked, as though listening. "I see that you mean those words. Good." He led me into an elevator and down many floors, the doors opening up on a glass fronted foyer. Outside the wide glass doors, I heard shouting, the rat-a-tat of gunfire, screaming. He pointed. "What you see out there is only a small part of the problem. After you quell them you must search out the rest. Once the entire city is under my control, you may leave."

"But how will you know?"

"Adam and Asia will be watching you. Once they've determined that the ones demonstrating have been tamed, they will let me know."

I nodded, swallowing down panic. What did I know about hypnotism? I headed toward the door, my heart hammering.

I was amongst the chaos when I heard Lucifer. "*Let me come through you*," he said. "*I can help, but only if you allow it.*"

I gave my silent assent with a nod of thanks. As I summoned my strength, I told myself it was for the best—I was saving them. I felt Lucifer's light come into me, his calm resolve quelling the fire that burned in my heart. I held up my hands and waved them in patterns, watching the colors that spiraled from my fingers.

The atmosphere shifted. I was in another dimension and Lucifer was with me, focused on the crowds, his lips moving as he mumbled words. We stood shoulder to shoulder, warriors of the light, my hands moving in patterns that made no sense while his words rang out, their shapes flowing from his mouth to drift over the crazed crowd. I saw their eyes go blank, the sudden confusion that came over them. I shouted, screamed, pushed the ones with the guns and heavy batons back, forcing them to their knees. They sprayed me with tear gas. I thought I was dying as my throat closed up, on my knees vomiting as the toxins took over. I saw Lucifer in the air. Could they see him too? And then he was beside me, pulling me to my feet, his words ringing over the militia and stopping them.

We ended up in an alley, my eyes watering, my insides heaving. But when I turned to say something, Lucifer was gone. Once I felt able to stand, I made my way back to the street, watching as the zombie-like crowd headed away, only to be rounded up and shoved into vans. The streets were cleared, the stench of tear-gas and vomit all that was left. I was still standing there when I felt a hand on my arm.

"There's another uprising three streets over," Adam muttered.

I let him lead me, as though what Lucifer and I had done to those people had penetrated into my own body. I was like a lamb now, a sheep with no will of my own. He shoved me into the midst of an even more lethal situation, where several dark-skinned men lay dead from gunshots.

But instead of waving my hands I stared at them, unable to even lift my arms. A second later Adam shoved me. "Call on your angel, girlie. The sooner this is done the sooner you can go."

When I met Adam's scornful gaze, I knew there was no way he or the man he called Father would let me leave. I tried to summon energy, but I had nothing left, no magic at all. And this time Lucifer did not come to my aid. Adam finally gave a grunt of anger, and grabbed me, dragging me backward by my hair. I didn't remember much until I was standing in front of the man again.

"The fight's gone out of her," Adam told him. "I think she got hypnotized too. That angel was there, the one you've seen in the desert? He helped her. Maybe he did this."

The man frowned. "Lucifer was there? I thought we took care of him."

Adam shrugged, glancing at me.

The man peered at me. "I suggest you gather your strength, because if you don't, you will be working alongside your friends out there."

"Why don't *you* hypnotize the rest?" I asked. "You're obviously strong."

"It is not one of my talents. Perhaps you just need a short rest—is that it?"

"I don't know. I feel drained."

He nodded. "Adam, take her to her room and lock her in. An hour or two should straighten her out."

Adam herded me out, his hands in places I didn't want them to be.

"If you rape me, I swear I'll..."

He laughed. "No fun to rape a woman who can't fight back. I'll have my chance soon enough."

I WAS DEEPLY asleep when I felt a feathery touch on my shoulder. When I opened my eyes, Lucifer was standing next to the bed. When I reached for him his arms came around me. But a moment later he let me go. "The man out there is Surt, the god of chaos. He created all this, but in the end, it doesn't suit his needs. You must recover, Feirin. If you do not, he will destroy you."

"Is he responsible for why you can't stay?"

Lucifer's gaze shifted into the distance. "Partially, yes. We are enemies from long ago. I will imbue you with some of my light and then you must rest. You are in danger of losing everything. He will take it, Feirin. All of it."

"Surt is that powerful?"

Lucifer glanced at the door. "Lie back and close your eyes."

When I did what he asked I felt waves of energy sliding

over me and entering my body. When he touched my eyelids, I fell into a dreamworld, imagining that we were together making love. I drifted in a nebulous cloud, asleep but not.

"ARE YOU RESTORED?"

I opened my eyes to see Surt's tall frame filling the door-way. I sat up. "I think so."

"There's been a resurgence of protestors in a section of the city where my offices lie. Time to use your talents." He held out his hand.

I rose from the bed, shaky, but I could feel Lucifer's energy flowing through me. How long would it last? I walked toward him and placed my hand in his.

He led me out and closed the door. "See? Not so hard, is it?"

I WAS in the streets again, the crowd surging in a mass of shouting, tear gas and hysteria. The militia had gas masks on, guns in hands. Many protestors had already been shot. I waved my hands, letting them form the patterns that my mind didn't comprehend. I watched expressions go blank, the militia marching in to drag the confused out of the crowd. I kept at it until my body felt hollow and empty. I had dropped to my knees, gasping, when Surt appeared. He dragged me to my feet. "Not good enough," he muttered, his glittering eyes meeting mine. "But I do have another use for you."

My knees buckled as images of his machines wafted by my eyes. He would hook me up and suck away my goddess powers to use for himself. How he could do this, I didn't know, but it was as clear to me as the stench of tear gas. Somehow, I managed to wrench free of his grasp. I ran as fast as my shaky legs would carry me, away from the buildings, away from the shouting and away from Surt.

I heard Adam pounding after me, Asia's voice shouting my name. But in my peripheral vision I saw Lucifer next me. He was barely visible, just a shadow. He gave me the strength to keep going. The gate was closing as I ran toward it, my legs pumping. I saw the mechanics twitch, the second's hesitation in the gears that allowed me to get through before it crushed my body. The desert stretched unending, the dust filling up my nose and eyes. I was never so glad to see it or to feel the rocks and sand dig into the heeled boots I wore. The cat appeared a few minutes later, running alongside me.

And as I ran, I saw the sea in the distance, the undulating blue-green waves that rose up, cresting white and foamy and rolling toward the white sand shore. Enormous machinery stood idle, robot arms hanging loose, the many berths for the ships empty. No more supplies were coming. The entire port was a graveyard.

28

It took a month to get within ten miles of our former cave. I wasn't sure why I was heading back there—I supposed it was to check on the few who may have sought shelter after the massacre. I felt dizzy most days, headaches coming and going. On the way I saw more abandoned cars, more dead, and a few people wandering who seemed to have lost their minds. Most were from the city, their wits gone from the scorching sun and the shock of where they were. Trying to explain anything to them did not work. I tried hard to cajole them to come along with me, but they refused. A feeling of futility joined the other disheartening emotions that plagued me. The cat remained by my side, leading me to shelter when I couldn't go on, and finding the tiny springs to slake my thirst. I was hot, feverish, my thoughts rambling and incoherent.

I was within a week of home when I ran into a tribe of natives, spears pointing at me when I woke up from a dreamless sleep. I waved my hands to push them back but nothing happened. I'd been drained in Sanctuary and whatever energy

I'd used to traverse the scorching desert and stay alive had taken the rest. I held up my hands and fell to my knees, giving myself over. They watched me for a long time, finally coming close to take my shoes, my belt and my tunic, leaving me in the bikini briefs and tank top provided by Asia before they jogged away. It felt like a mirage as they disappeared into the swirling dust.

The haboob hit an hour later. I huddled into myself, completely exposed, my skin flayed open from the stinging dirt. And despite the burning hot sun I had chills that shook me to my core. And still the cat stayed, oddly comforting. Sometimes he looked like Lucifer, sometimes like a cat, fever making me hallucinate.

IT WAS dark when I finally made it to the caves, my hopes disappearing when I found them abandoned. I had no way to make a fire, no blanket, no food. But the cat meowed, leading me deeper where a tiny stream burbled. I was sure it had not been there before.

As I scooped up water, I noticed the carvings in the wall behind. Runes. I traced them with my fingers, tears welling. My mother, my father, my family had been here in this cave. I could almost feel them through the ether, the hands that had made these marks over three hundred years before. The story they told was heartbreakingly simple and yet as unattainable as the stars in the sky. My ultimate mission was to open the portal between past and present—to bring the gods into the future. Exactly what Lucifer had told me.

It was deep night when I climbed the hill to the spring, rinsing my blistered skin in the murky water. I was still there when I heard Elena. I stood, trying to see in the darkness.

There was no moon, the sky covered with the cloud of dust left from the haboob. "Elena!" I shouted, pulling on underwear before hurrying down the hill.

She stood with Ted, the two of them staring at me as if they'd seen a ghost. "It's me," I said. "I escaped."

"We thought you were dead. You have cuts and bruises all over. What happened?"

"Dust storm."

Elena turned to Ted. "Give her your extra clothes."

Ted pulled the pack off his back and dug inside it. He handed me a pair of loose- fitting khaki pants and a man's shirt. "Glad you're alive. Most of our group hasn't shown up."

I pulled the khakis on and rolled the legs up, pulling the shirt tight and tying it in front. The shivering subsided once I was dressed. "We'll find them."

Ted made a fire and we huddled together talking, filling each other in on the past two months. "The guy in charge in Sanctuary is Surt, or that's what Lucifer told me."

"The god of chaos," Ted muttered. "Stands to reason."

"He forced me to put a spell on the people resisting him. Jeremy and Isabelle were there."

"The ones you spoke about," Elena muttered, staring into the flames. "Did you get them out?"

I shook my head. "I didn't save anybody. I'm not sure I'm still the dark goddess. I've never felt drained like this."

Ted lifted his eyes to mine. "I studied myths and the gods back when I had a real life, and Surt is evil. You're lucky to be alive. You said he promised to free you if you did his bidding? It never would have happened."

I glanced at him. "You believe in all this now? I was afraid to mention anything."

"Yeah, well, I've seen too much to dismiss it." He glanced at Elena, smiling. "And El convinced me."

Elena met my surprised gaze. "I told Ted all of it, Fee. He had a right to know."

"None of that matters now. I have to start over and I don't know if I have the will for it."

"You're a goddess, right? Goddesses are always goddesses. At least that's what I've read."

"In a book maybe. But..."

Elena put a hand on my arm. "You've been through a lot. Give it a few days."

When I sighed, Cat moved close to my leg. I rubbed him behind the ears absentmindedly as I mused about Surt and what he was up to. But then I remembered the runes. My purpose had morphed. When I told them about the message in the cave, they both stared at me without speaking. "Hard to wrap my mind around gods and goddesses actually walking among us," Elena finally said. "One is enough."

"Two," Ted reminded her.

Elena's shoulders sagged with fatigue. "Time to get some sleep. I think there may be a few blankets left inside the cave. If not, you can cuddle up with us."

I laughed for the first time in two months.

You are correct about Surt. He has power over me. There are certain things I have not told you.

"When are you coming back? I need you, Lucifer. I thought you were sent to protect me."

*I was. I am. But Surt is interfering. There are powers working against...*his voice drifted off.

I waited for more but he was gone.

260

Wʜᴇɴ I ᴡᴏᴋᴇ in the morning Ted and Elena were not where they'd been. I jumped up and ran outside, the idea of their absence freaking me out more than I cared to admit. I found them in front, the fire going, deer meat cooking and the cat begging. "I thought you two were a figment of my imagination."

Elena gazed at me quizzically. "Heard you talking to Lucifer last night. Was he here?"

"No. Did you hear his voice?"

"Just you. You look feverish, Fee." She reached to place a hand on my forehead. "You're hot."

I shrugged and took the meat Ted held out, but ended up giving it to the cat.

"Hey, did you notice all those trees on your way back?" he asked.

I shook my head. "Came another way, but...um. I think they're there because of me."

"There's a fucking forest out there. How could you do that?"

"How big are they?"

"Trees, Fee. Ten, twenty feet tall?"

"Last I saw they were a foot or two high."

Elena glanced up. "How are you responsible for trees in a desert?"

"I...I was crying out there. I wouldn't think it mattered except the trees are on the exact path I took. I figured they would dry up and die."

Elena's eyes widened. "You're saying your tears did it?"

I shrugged. "I think so."

Ted frowned, his gaze in the distance. "Must be a reason for them. Are you connected with trees?"

I shrugged. "My visions of the past are all filled with trees;

we lived within a forest. I heard those plants whispering the last time I came through but I couldn't understand them."

"Tree sprites," Ted mumbled.

Elena laughed. "Since when do you believe in tree sprites?"

"Since I found out we have the dark goddess and the god of chaos in our midst--and I've done a lot of reading—fantasy, sci-fi, mythology."

"Siofra," I whispered as the Gaelic word floated into my consciousness.

"What does *sheefra* mean?" Elena asked.

"Fairy, sprite, elf, magical being," I muttered as echoes of my past life wafted by.

WE SPENT one more night there and the next day set off for the forest. "What happened to everyone?" I asked them.

Ted glanced at Elena before he answered. "A lot of them died that day. We buried as many as we could. Half the group has to be out here somewhere, but with El's condition we haven't wanted to stray too far."

Elena laughed. "I'm not an invalid, Ted."

I frowned, my gaze taking in Elena for the first time. I hadn't noticed because of Ted's oversize shirt that covered her from neck to knees. My expression must have registered my shock because a second later she chuckled.

"Who would have thought it possible at my age and the chaos we've been through?"

"I'm extremely virile," Ted announced, grinning.

"I guess you are," I murmured. "When are you due?"

She glanced at Ted. "I think I'm around six months."

"That means you were pregnant when I was taken to Sanctuary. Why didn't you tell me?"

"She wasn't sure back then. She told me she might be going through menopause and not to get my hopes up."

Elena took his hand, smiling up at him where he walked beside her.

I walked in shocked silence for a while before I asked about Peyton.

"We haven't seen him. And he wasn't among the dead."

"And Rose and the baby?"

"Never saw her. We hope she got away."

"And Maisie, Carl, Liza?"

Elena shook her head.

I pressed my fingers to my welling eyes, afraid to ask about anyone else. "Did I tell you that Adam was in Sanctuary? Apparently, he works for Surt. All that crap I went through with him? Surt sent him to stalk me."

"That's weird," Elena said. "He seemed like a normal asshole to me."

I laughed. "Normal redneck with rape on his mind? Good cover."

Ted glanced at me. "I always wondered about those military goggles he came up with. But I will say that anyone in their right mind would kowtow to Surt. Adam may have been coerced."

"He says Surt's his father, but a god? That can't be true. How is it that Surt is here when no other gods or goddesses can exist in this timeline?"

"You're here, Fee. Maybe he's the dark to your light."

"Possibly," I muttered, thinking.

Ted touched my arm and pointed toward the towering forest in the distance. There were thousands upon thousands of trees. They stretched from one side of the desert to the other, dark green with wide hanging branches. I could hear the chirp of birds, saw a hawk soaring. "Your tears must be pretty fucking potent," Ted muttered.

"*Were* potent. Nothing about me is potent anymore."

"You haven't recovered from what they did to you," Elena said, noticing my expression.

It was cool under the trees, the aroma of loamy earth and mushrooms permeating our senses. I saw a deer rush by, a fawn running after her. I heard snuffling, noticed strewn acorns and other nuts. I heard the whispering again but this time I could understand. *You are safe here,* I heard, picking up their language as though I'd known it forever. "Tree spirits just told me that we're safe here."

Elena laughed. "The energy does feel like it's holding us in an embrace."

I glanced around at the clearing where we'd stopped. Trees surrounded us, leaning in as though protecting us. "I'll search for the missing while you two set up camp. There's a rocky outcropping a mile or two over there," I said, pointing. "It's where I met Lucifer the last time. A few may be sheltering there."

Elena gazed at me worriedly. "You're sick, Fee. You should rest."

"I'll feel even better if I can find a few of our group. I won't be gone long." But it was mostly Phrani who was on my mind. I'd been afraid to ask about her.

I LEFT them and hurried through the thick woods, the cat following at a distance. I was out of the forest, cutting across the desert floor toward the shallow caves when I heard Lucifer. *Surt is after you, Feirin. I will try to hold him off until you feel strong again. Remain in the forest. The trees will revive you.*

I was dizzy for a moment, squinting up at the sky. I began

to sweat, my mouth dry as I walked unsteadily up the path that led toward the caves, every step taking all my concentration. "Anyone here?" I called.

A second later Peyton called back—I would know his voice anywhere. And when I looked up, he was heading toward me, ten bedraggled members of our group behind him. When they saw me, their weary faces lit up with smiles. A second later Peyton grabbed hold of me and buried his head in my neck. "Thought I'd lost you for good," he muttered.

He was very thin, his eyes sunken. "How long have you been here?"

"Since those fuckers took you away in that black car. That's been, what...two or three months now? We scattered and I ended up here with a bunch of our people. But half of us got sick and ten people died of that fucking virus. I had it too."

I thought about my dizziness, Elena's insistence that I was feverish. "What are the symptoms?"

"Fatigue, fever. A feeling of despair."

"Maybe I have it."

He frowned, staring at me. "What's wrong?"

"I'm weak, depressed. No goddess powers."

Peyton felt my forehead. "You're burning up."

"Elena and Ted are waiting for us in the forest."

"What forest?"

"The one right outside your door. Didn't you notice?"

Peyton squinted into the distance. "We've been holed up inside, afraid they'd come for us. How in hell did those plants get so big?"

When he led the way into the cave, I noticed the dried herbs they'd gathered, took in the familiar scents of peppermint, thyme, and the roots Elena used for healing. Several people greeted me, including Rose. I hugged her close. "Your baby?"

She shook her head, tears welling. "The virus took him."

"I'm so sorry," I murmured.

Others came to greet me, faces I recognized. Sylvia, Gabe, Laney, Gates, Sarin, Canada, names I hadn't known but did now. They huddled around asking question after question. But Phrani was not among them. A woman appeared from in the back, her gaze hostile as she looped her arm through Peyton's in a proprietary manner. She was wide shouldered with clear gray eyes and tangled russet hair. I recognized Peyton's type.

"I guess this is the Fee I've been hearing so much about?" she said, glaring at me. She glanced down at Cat. "Your familiar, I presume?"

Peyton looked at the cat. "He's still here? That animal is definitely a survivor." He reached down to pat him before introducing us. "Fee, this is Sally. She's an herbalist. I would have died without her expertise."

I smiled at her. "I'm glad you're here. Where did you come from?"

"Where did any of us come from? The city—Elysian City."

I pushed down my annoyance. "I wondered if you lived in Uptown, or if..."

"Yes, I lived in Uptown. What of it? I'm not a racist bitch, if that's what you think."

"I don't think anything, Sally. A lot of our group came from Uptown. Just getting my bearings." I turned to Peyton. "What about the rest of our group?"

"They took 'em, Fee. When they ran, they shot some and rounded up the rest and drove away."

"They can't all be dead. They must be in Sanctuary. They need bodies to run the city."

Peyton frowned. "If they are, they won't help him. They'll fight."

"Not anymore."

"Why not?"

"Because I stopped them—turned everyone into automatons."

"You...what?"

I waved my hand wearily. "Too long a story to get into right now. I should get back to Elena and Ted. She's pregnant—did you know?"

He shook his head before turning to the hostile woman behind him, reaching for her hand. "You're not leaving until Sally takes a look at you. She knows how to treat this virus. She saved a bunch of us."

I lowered to a rock and allowed the woman to look me over, surprised by the coldness in her eyes. "If you're interested in Peyton, please don't let me stop you," I murmured. "We had a thing a long time ago, but it's over now."

"Not according to him," she whispered, glancing over her shoulder.

"It takes two to make a relationship, Sally." When I tried to rise, she pushed me back down. "You have a fever. If this thing takes hold, you could get very sick. Peyton says you have special abilities? Have you noticed any changes in that area?"

"It's all gone."

She tried to hide her smile as she pulled my lower eyelids down to look into my eyes. "It's got hold of you pretty good. I'll give you herbs, but you have to rest. This virus kills."

"How can I rest when I'm trying to find our people?"

"I've warned you. Now you have to decide." She left me there and hurried into the cave, returning a few moments later. "Take a pinch of these two times a day with water," she ordered, handing me a small muslin bag. "You should start them as soon as you can."

Peyton appeared at her shoulder. "Will you stay here until you get well?"

I shook my head no. "Elena would worry. Why don't all of you come back with me?"

Peyton glanced at Sally. "Not right now. We have issues to clear up before we join others."

"Issues? Like what?"

"We have a life here," Sally said. "We don't need you or your group. Peyton's the leader here and he's taking good care of us."

But Peyton's expression told me something different. He walked me out, leaving Sally behind as we headed down the narrow trail. He stopped by the opening between boulders, glancing back to make sure he wouldn't be overheard. "Is there any chance for us? You know how I feel about you."

"Sally's in love with you."

"I know she is. I just wanted to make sure about us."

"I'm in love with Lucifer, Peyton. I suggest you stay with Sally."

"The mythical Lucifer who I've never seen? Come on, Fee. He doesn't really exist."

Instead of answering I left him standing there with a bemused look on his face. I thought Cat had chosen to stay with Peyton when he appeared next to me, trotting ahead like a dog.

I WAS HALFWAY BACK when I decided to take a pinch of herbs. Like Sally said, better to get the stuff into my system as soon as possible. They were bitter and nasty but I managed to choke them down. It was about ten minutes later when I began to see spots, my vison going in and out. I had fallen to my knees when shadows surrounded me, darkness flowing across my vision like a heavy blanket. "Help me," I muttered.

"Help you? Fat chance. Sally's herbs are a godsend." I was lifted roughly, my head lolling.

"Get her into the bunker. I'll deal with her once she comes back to consciousness."

"And the cat?"

"Don't you know who that cat is? Kill it."

29

"This isn't good. Was she like this when you picked her up?"

"I don't know. She was nearly unconscious."

I heard the voices through a haze. I was suddenly sick, leaning over to retch. I could not open my eyes.

"Get a fucking bucket and clean this mess up. And when you're done with that get her up to the room. You know the one. I'll have to go ahead with the plan. If I don't start now there won't be time."

"But she's barely conscious!"

"I can bring her around. Just do as I ask."

I FELT the tight bands first. They held my head still. I opened my eyes on a cement room that smelled damp. No windows just flat gray and cobwebs. We were underground somewhere. "Where am I?" I muttered hoarsely.

"She's awake." Surt loomed into view, Asia just behind him.

"What are you doing to me?"

Surt smiled. "We are taking what you are, Feirin. You're too close to destroying my plans."

"Plans..."

"Yes. My plans to keep the gods out."

"What gods? I have no idea how to..."

"You will, my dear. It is only a matter of time."

"Lucifer didn't say...he..."

"Lucifer has no say in this. It is between us. You represent the light and I the dark. We cannot exist together."

I put my hand up to the cold band around my head. "But light and dark balance each other out."

"You would think so, but I am chaos and you...you want it all. That will never work."

Asia sneered, coming close to stare down at me, her cold eyes flat and expressionless. I began to think she might be a robot. A second later the door opened and Sally came in. "I see my herbs worked."

Asia turned. "Father brought her back to consciousness so that we can take her power."

Sally gazed into the far distance. "You'd best hurry. I feel something in the ether."

Surt frowned. "Quit dithering and work the controls, one of you. She's prepped and ready."

I was about to say something when my head felt as though it would split apart. I let out a scream as the agony tore through me, something giving way. Memories drifted from my mind, echoes of where I came from and who I was becoming tendrils of shimmering energy that flowed into the glass tube hooked up to my head. "No!"

"Turn it up," Surt ordered.

The next wave of pain was worse. My body shook from it, my mouth open and dribbling, my bladder giving way. My muscles slackened as I screamed and screamed. I could feel the thoughts pulled out of me, ripping the shreds of what I was. My powers were going with them, sliding from me into the glass tube where they swirled like maddened snakes. My screaming turned into a howl, the pain taking my sanity with it.

"Shut her up," Surt said.

A second later a rag was stuffed into my mouth, but the agony continued until I felt blackness take my consciousness.

"She's out cold," I heard Asia say before the pain abruptly stopped.

"Let her rest for fifteen minutes and start again," Surt answered.

"Won't this kill her?"

"Maybe. But once we get what we want, she's not much use to anyone. She'll be a blithering idiot."

I called to Lucifer from where I floated in a shadow world. If they succeeded, I would be empty, a shell. No memories, no powers, no me. They wanted it all. We were deep underground where no one could find us. If Lucifer didn't come, I was as good as dead.

"We have to finish this now," I heard Surt say.

More agony, my entire body contorted as electricity shot through. I couldn't remember my mother, my father. I was too weak to cry out, too exhausted to fight it. "Please, Lucifer..." the words hung in the air, each letter distinct and drifting like smoke as I lost consciousness.

"She's calling him."

"Don't worry about it. We're almost there."

SCREAMING. Shouts. Screeching metal. Hands, soothing, cooling. Whispered words, my hair pushed back from my forehead, a feather light kiss against my lips. I was lost, gone in a white space, my memories only echoes. I let the emptiness take me, not even remembering my name as I was lifted and carried roughly away.

When I opened my eyes Elena and Ted were bending over me with worried eyes. "Are you...do you know us?" Elena asked.

All I could do was nod, my tongue too thick to form words.

Elena exchanged a glance with Ted. "I think what he did worked."

"I hope so," Ted muttered.

I closed my eyes and slept.

All I was aware of for the next few days was Elena holding up my head and pouring bad-tasting liquid down my throat. I gagged and coughed it up but it didn't stop her. I heard her talking to Ted, the anxiety in her voice ringing in my ears. "She's still sick. We need Lucifer."

Why was she expecting Lucifer? Ted's mumbled reply was lost as I fell into a dark pit, losing the struggle against the blackness that came over me.

I saw my body from where I drifted in the air, my face swollen and bright red, sores lining my arms and chest. Elena bent over me, tears in her eyes. "She's nearly gone," I heard her whisper, looking up at Ted.

"How can the dark goddess die? Isn't she immortal?"

Elena shook her head, letting out a sob.

Ted shrugged. "Where is the fucking cat when she needs him?"

"What can the cat do, Ted? It's just an animal."

"It's her familiar, Elena. After what happened out there that cat shouldn't be alive."

Elena scoffed. "You've certainly changed your tune," she murmured before letting out another sob.

Lucifer was around me, I could feel him, but I couldn't see him. I was no longer corporeal, unable to speak. My spirit lifted from my body, pale and ethereal. All that was left was a shell, the skin muscle and bone that held me. I saw Lucifer, his expression desperate. I couldn't speak, could barely see him as he struggled with the shadow beings. I felt heat as he wrapped around me, blinding white light filling every cell, every pore. I sucked in a ragged breath as my essence returned.

Lucifer held me, muttering words I couldn't understand. I returned bit by bit, but by the time I was fully back to consciousness, Lucifer was gone.

Elena pulled me close and sobbed.

"Did you see him?" I asked, my voice a hoarse whisper.

She smiled and pushed the damp hair off my forehead. "He's beautiful."

I sighed and fell back, entering a restorative sleep.

WHEN I WOKE AGAIN, I was lying on a blanket in the forest, Elena fussing over me. "Did you get the tube—the glass tube?" I managed to croak from my parched throat as I tried to sit up.

Elena rearranged the pillow she'd made out a couple of shirts. "Lucifer retrieved it, Fee. Surt cannot enter this forest. All is well."

"My memories...my powers."

She placed her hand on my arm. "It's all been restored. Your angel was here."

"He's not an angel, he's..." I fell back, exhausted.

"Whatever he is, he took care of you. That place where they had you is an ancient military facility used for questioning prisoners."

"Torturing is more like it."

Elena nodded. "All kinds of nasty. Lucifer found you. Without him you'd still be sitting in that chair."

"What happened to Surt, Sally and Asia?"

"All I know is that Lucifer got you away from them and brought you here, to us.

"Did he say when he'd be back?"

Elena shook her head, placing a soothing hand on my brow. "He told us that you need lots of rest--that you are NOT to leave this forest."

I put my hand to my head, feeling the lesions the metal strap had left behind. I felt shaky, weak, and my brain felt sore, if that was even possible. I wanted Lucifer more than ever.

30

A month passed by. I wasn't back to normal yet. We'd begun construction on a few small shelters in the forest, using limbs that had come loose and branches full of needles. Without tools it wasn't an easy task.

"Why can't you do stuff?" Elena asked nearly every day when I tried and failed to make something happen.

"I wish I knew. What did Lucifer say?"

Elena sighed. "He told us to be patient. That what happened to you was on a psychic level as well as physical."

Despite Elena's dire warnings, I stumbled out of the woods and searched in the desert every day. One morning as I was leaving Elena stopped me, her hand on my arm. "If you're determined to put yourself in danger at least find Peyton and the rest of our group. We need to be together now."

I hesitated, thinking about Sally. "Sally was his girlfriend, Elena—she tried to kill me."

"But Peyton knows you and trusts you. If you want to grow our community, we need them."

I nodded and headed out, trying not to hear her shouted warning to be careful. Her worries were well placed. I had no way to defend myself now.

WHEN I RAN into Peyton he was hunting, a crudely made bow in his hands. "Been thinking about you and what you said. Are you set up for more people?" he asked me, a wary expression in his eyes.

"We have room, but you said you didn't want to come."

"Sally's gone. She took off two days after you were here. Said she was tired of loving a man who couldn't love her back."

"Peyton, Sally's involved with Surt. They captured me on my way back from here last time, all because of those herbs Sally gave me. They were drugged. I nearly died."

Peyton's eyes went wide. "What?"

"They took me to some military installation from years ago and removed my memories—and my powers. If it hadn't been for Lucifer..."

"Lucifer again? God, I'm sick of hearing that name."

I glared at him. "That's all you have to say?"

"Removed your memories?" He scoffed. "How do you *remove* someone's

memories?"

I shook my head, angry. "You know me, Peyton. I don't lie."

"And Sally was involved in this? Seems pretty far-fetched to me."

I held my hair back to show the burn marks on my temples. "They tortured me. They sucked what I am into a glass tube. I would have been a zombie when they were finished."

Peyton made a sound in the back of his throat. "I see the

burn marks, but this story is hard to believe. Sally told me you were crazy."

"Sally wanted you to go against me, Peyton. She wanted to recruit you."

He frowned. "Bullshit. All she did was love me, unlike you who love some mystical being who lives in the fucking sky."

"I'm sorry you no longer trust me. I thought our bond was stronger than petty squabbles over lovers."

His lips pressed together. "Have you screwed this being from another realm? Does he even have a penis?"

"Lucifer is flesh and blood when he's here with me. And yes, we've made love. He has no trouble in that department."

He stared at me, his lips thinning. "Fuck you, Fee."

I watched him stride away, his shoulders rigid. I'd hurt him badly and lost a good friend in the process. But he did not believe in me. There was no turning back from this.

Focus Feirin.

Surt had confirmed what I already knew. My ultimate mission was to bring the gods back. My tears and the trees they'd produced were a gift. The forest was a place of refuge where Surt could not reach us. It was time to do what I came for.

ELENA'S EYES narrowed when she saw the expression on my face. "What happened?"

"Can you or Ted come with me in the morning? I have to search a little further—see if we missed anyone."

"Your powers? Anything yet?"

I shook my head.

She let out a heavy sigh. "You look tired, Fee. You're not fully healed."

"Where is Lucifer when I need him?" I quipped.

"Maybe he thinks you should take care of yourself and stop expecting him to do it for you."

"So now you're on his side?"

"There are no sides. You just had your brain drained on top of having a virus. I won't be responsible for you running around when you're not well."

"I know my limits. Will you come with me or not?"

"I suppose I have to. Ted's working on the shelters and he's better at it than I am. Will Peyton and his group be here today?"

"Not coming."

Elena stared at me. "I won't even ask."

"Good, because I'm not willing to discuss it."

THE NEXT MORNING Elena and I were out before dawn, heading in a different direction toward two temple mountains that had springs. If anyone was still hiding out, they'd be there. Cat trotted behind us, his green eyes scanning.

"Are they dead?" I asked while we walked.

"Is who dead?"

"Surt, Sally, Asia."

"How should I know? Lucifer was too busy saving you to tell us much of anything."

I had a momentary adrenaline rush, my head spinning for a few seconds. "So Surt could come after me again."

Elena stopped to face me. "Why do you think I'm worried? Being out here is folly after what happened."

"I have to do it. I'm looking for Phrani."

She stopped, hands on hips. "Phrani? Who the hell is Phrani?"

I frowned. "The older woman who was with us before Surt and his goons picked me up...gray hair, older...beads and long skirts? A red jewel embedded in her third eye?"

Elena shook her head, her hands going to her bulging stomach. "Never heard of her."

My mouth opened and closed. Was the woman a figment of my imagination? She couldn't be. But Elena was still staring at me like I'd lost my mind.

31

S *urt moved through the ether, searching. When he saw her,
*he stopped to watch her movements. He was in the shadow
world now, invisible until he chose to make himself known.
That fucking light-being got away with it once, but he wouldn't
manage it again.*

A COLD WIND hit the back of my neck, but the sun was shining,
hot and bright. "Did you feel something?"

Elena glanced at me. "No. Why?"

"Nothing, I guess." I pointed toward the temple mountain
a half a mile away. "Let's search there. I've been here before. It
has a tiny spring."

"Lead on," Elena murmured, shading her eyes.

We came up the hill single file. Before we reached the top, I
heard voices, looking up to see Mateo and Maria running
toward us. Behind them I saw a woman who looked familiar. A
second later I recognized Mirabelle from the jail. But now her
belly was flat, her eyes sunken and sad.

Maria threw herself into my arms. "We thought we'd never see you again," she sobbed.

"The babies?"

"Only one lives...mine and Mateo's. Sofia. Little Carlos caught the virus."

I nodded, sad for all of it. I turned to Mirabelle. "How did you come to be here?"

"When I didn't get pregnant a second time, they turned me out. I found my way here a few weeks ago."

I put my hand on her thin shoulder. "I'm so sorry. At least you know your child is safe."

She shook her head. "The city is no longer. I have no idea what's happened to my little girl." Her eyes welled.

I had nothing to say after that, no words of comfort. "We're building a home in the forest where we can all stay safe," I told her, watching several other hollow-eyed men and women emerge from inside the cave. "Will you come back with us?"

"Gladly," Maria said, Mateo nodding beside her. "We will gather our things. It's been hard here without your protection. We've had to hide from bandits several times. They come from everywhere now. The ones from the city are desperate and crazy."

"Have you two seen Phrani?"

Maria frowned, glancing at Mateo. "I don't remember anyone by that name. What did she look like?"

"Gray hair, long skirt, red jewel in her forehead?"

Mateo glanced at Maria and then they both shook their heads. "Never saw anyone who looked like that."

I stared into space for a moment. It seemed that I was the only one who had seen her. Maybe she appeared to bring me a message. *The third eye—the gate to higher consciousness*, I thought, my fingers going to the spot in the middle of my forehead. I felt a tingle just before I noticed a strange dark cloud moving toward us, a shape coalescing from within it.

Run!

"Run!" I screamed, echoing Lucifer's warning. But before I could herd them anywhere, I was sucked into a vortex, my breath cut off as Surt grabbed me around the neck and squeezed.

There was a battle going on around me, shadows flailing. I thought I saw Lucifer, but then he was gone, replaced by shadow fighters. Surt's expression contorted in anger just before his hands loosened their grip around my neck. I dropped, hoping for Lucifer, but there was no one to catch me. I let out a scream as pain radiated. I was unable to move as fire rained down, my shirt in flames as I struggled out of it. High above me shadows moved in and out of sight, thunder rumbling as the sky turned black. People were screaming when Mateo appeared at my side. "Can you stand?"

I shook my head, pain making me mute. Mateo lifted me and took off at a run, Maria behind him with a baby in her arms, Mirabelle and the others hurtling behind her. Where was Elena? But then I saw her in the lead, her dark hair like a flag in the wind as she ran, pregnant belly and all.

Fire hailed down, narrowly missing us as we hurtled under the trees. I could do nothing, held tight in Mateo's arms, the pain leaving me breathless. In the distance I saw Ted run toward us. He turned as soon as Elena caught up to him and everyone ran for the clearing. Screeches and the hiss of lightning, thunder booming, flames streaking down. Mateo lowered me gently to the ground. "Are you okay?"

I shook my head, squeezing back tears.

"The fireballs aren't getting through," Elena whispered, staring at me. "Are your powers restored?"

"No," I hissed, my hands on my hip. "You have to stop asking me that."

Maria kneeled to examine me as the rest of the group settled around the firepit, trying to catch their breath. I heard a baby cry, the sound of sobbing. "Nothing is broken," Maria muttered, glancing at Elena for corroboration.

Elena prodded the muscle and bone around my hip. "Not broken but severely bruised. And I don't have the herbs to treat it."

"I think we have more serious issues to deal with than Fee's hip," Ted muttered, pointing.

Shadow beings were flying above the trees, greedy hands stretched to find an opening. They were grotesque, shifting from one shape to another, claws out to grab hold of branches. But whenever they discovered a break in the thick canopy, the trees bent to close it. "The trees are enchanted," Elena whispered, gazing at me in wonder.

"Don't look at me. I have nothing to do with it."

"They grew that way," Ted muttered, glancing at me. "This forest is protected."

Frightened expressions began to soften as everyone huddled around the fire Ted had coaxed into existence. As night came over the forest, the shrieking wind and lightning strikes subsided. "Lucifer and the light beings fought off Surt," I whispered.

"There was definitely a war going on up there," Ted answered, his brows pulled together in a frown. "Did they stop him?"

"I wish I knew."

"Now you have a reason to ask for his help," Elena informed me, winking.

I shook my head. "He just saved my life again—I can deal with a little pain until my hip recovers."

A DAY PASSED, and then two, three. A week, and my hip was nearly healed. Our people were finding spots to call their own, leaving their meager belongings as they hunted in the forests, collecting nuts and berries. With the arrival of Maria, Mateo and their group, something had shifted. Despite Surt and his creatures, it felt as though we were building a community again. And one day I discovered a stream carving a course through the forest. Ted and Mateo dammed up an area to use for bathing, the feel of a real home settling into our hearts and minds. When I drank from its clear waters, I felt stronger, some inkling of the dark goddess returning. But when I waved my hands or tried to move through the ether, nothing happened. Perhaps Surt's efforts had hurt me more than I knew.

I WAS SLOWLY STRETCHING my muscles with the crutch Ted made for me out of a cedar limb when Mirabelle rushed up. "Who are you?" she whispered.

I laughed, surprised that Maria and Mateo hadn't said. "I was the dark goddess, but in Sanctuary it all disappeared. The waters," I said, bending to cup my hands into the cool stream, "seem to be restoring me."

Her face registered fear. "Are you a sorceress?"

"No, Mirabelle. I'm a goddess."

"BUT THERE'S ONLY ONE GOD." She stared with wide eyes before turning and running into the forest.

32

Murmuring water rushed by, leaves like tiny brightly painted boats dropping from the alders, oaks and other deciduous trees. I watched them, imagining a sprite sitting on each one, carried off to a new home. I'd taken to sitting by the stream every day, letting my mind settle. The tree spirits were affecting me, their whispering and the occasional glimpse of iridescent wings, healing my soul. Phrani's words echoed: *the only thing that counts is what lies hidden within.* I was exploring this hidden part, the darkness Lucifer had mentioned, where the secrets were buried. And as I let my mind rest, it opened, revealing things I'd never noticed before—like the language of the murmuring water I was just beginning to understand, or the whir of bright wings that led me to the places where berries grew in profusion. I no longer felt the anger that had consumed me every day.

Maybe it was knowing my ultimate mission. I was still unsure how to accomplish this, but Surt had confirmed it. I was destined to open a portal from the past into the future—to bring the gods into this timeline. I envisioned the goddesses walking sedately through the forest dressed in velvet gowns, the gods in tunics somewhat like Lucifer's coat. I thought of their powers, the magic they would have—healing and protection, magic that made the plants grow tall, animal communication. Mine were limited to fighting off evil; my skills were primarily as a warrior rather than a healer. We needed all of it now. The world needed them.

Most of Peyton's former group had arrived, but Peyton was not among them. When I asked, Sarin filled me in. "He went to find Sally. He told us she was in Sanctuary and invited us along. Canada and Bruce went with him. The rest of us decided we'd had enough of the cities."

As I listened, I felt responsible for this rash act. He hadn't believed me about Sally. It made me sad to know he had so little faith, and also worried that he was out there somewhere. But telling him about Lucifer had freed something in me. Secrets took too much energy, energy that I needed in order to concentrate on what came next, my powers notwithstanding. Surt was still at it, trying to find a way inside the forest. But every day he tried I felt a small wavering of his intent.

No one dared leave the forest. I walked daily, trying to figure out where the trees met sand, but as my treks grew longer, I realized that the edges were expanding. The forest was moving on its own, covering more ground.

THE DAY I decided to take my chances outside the protection of the trees, was the first day my hip was without pain. Two months had gone by since Surt's assault on my powers. I had not seen or heard from Lucifer since then. It hadn't bothered me at first, but as the days turned into weeks and then months,

I began to doubt. If he was truly free, he would have come to me, or at least spoken inside my head.

I followed the stream, surprised to see how much it had widened, and the many ferns and mosses growing along its edges. It was how I envisioned it, wide enough to bathe in, crooked enough to feel like a mountain stream and clear enough to drink. When I reached the edge of the forest the stream turned sharply, heading in another direction. I pulled back the low hanging branches and peered out, feeling like a recluse who had shut herself up inside a tower. The forest was safe and wonderful but I needed to find my own edge, the place where I could test myself. The desert was always on the edge, lives snuffed out with the merest whisper if circumstances weren't just so. The warrior part of me needed that too.

I stepped out, sniffing the dusty air. The heat beat down on my bare head, my neck tingling with the sudden change in temperature. The sun was warm, hot even, but winter was coming. I smelled it on the breeze, observed it in the sun's angles as it slid westward. Nights were colder now. We would need more deer hides for warmth.

A temple mountain rose into the pale shimmering sky, shadows clinging to the boulders at its base. I glanced up and around to make sure there was no sign of Surt before I headed there. Behind me the forest sighed, a message of warning.

I was halfway there when I felt it. The change in atmosphere. And a second later he was there, a long shadow following as he strode toward me.

I waited unafraid.

"You're taking quite a chance out here," Surt said when he reached me.

I stood my ground, holding his gaze. "Yes, well I can't stay in the forest forever."

"I counted on this," he sneered.

"What do you want with me? I have no powers. And I still don't know how to open the portal. I'm useless to you the way I am."

He let out a snort. "You don't know?"

I didn't answer, waiting for him to go on.

Surt looked to the sky before leveling his gaze to mine. "You are changing, Feirin. A change that I knew would come. Your boyfriend knows it too, but I daresay he hasn't mentioned it."

I frowned. "The only change I know about is my inability to do what I could before. Do you have my powers?"

He laughed. "I don't care about your former abilities. They are nothing." When he moved a step toward me a spark of brightness flashed between us. He stopped and nodded. "It is too late. I cannot touch you now."

I looked down at my arm hanging at my side. "I didn't do anything."

"I suggest you talk to your boyfriend. Perhaps you won't be happy with him once you find out what's he's been keeping from you." His thoughts curled and twisted against me. *I know what you are and I will stop you.*

He stared at me for a full minute before a cloud of dust spun around him. When it dissipated, he was no longer there. I stood still for several moments watching the place where he'd been, my mind stirring the pot of my thoughts. "Lucifer!" I shouted.

I was walking up a narrow animal trail when he appeared. "I heard you call. Are you all right, Feirin?"

"I had a run-in with Surt. Why haven't you come? It's been months."

Several emotions ran across his features before he turned

away. "I am not free. I may never be free. Every time I come here, I suffer as a result."

I stepped closer, wanting his arms around me, but instead he stood like a statue, his expression stony. "Why didn't you tell me? I've expected to see you, or at least hear you in my mind."

When his agonized gaze met mine, I took his cold hand and twined my fingers through his. "Surt told me I'm changing. What did he mean?"

"I told you what you were."

"Something's different now. Surt told me you were keeping it from me."

"I have kept nothing from you. It is you who has forgotten."

I huffed impatiently, pulling my hand away. "What did I forget?"

"The dark goddess creates the world—she is the mirror, reflecting all that is or has ever been."

"You never said that."

"I did say that. But you did not hear it."

"It doesn't matter since it's all metaphor anyway. I still don't get what Surt was saying. He wants to stop me, but I don't know why."

Lucifer stared at me without expression. "The dark goddess is not metaphor. Bringing the world into form is your purpose, but your power does not end there. You are transforming; the deeper parts of yourself are rising to the surface. Surt is afraid because you embody both the light and the dark. There will be no place for him in the world you create. The other gods and goddesses will be ushered back, taking away his power."

I frowned, trying to find my lover in the solemn being who stood before me like an avenging angel. "The only change I've noticed is a lack of anger. I'm calm where before everything pissed me off."

"This forest you've brought into existence embodies everything that you will become. It sustains life, it is protective, it is growing and will continue to grow. Haven't you thought about what this means? It is *you* who commands it to grow."

"I don't command anything."

Lucifer watched me out of those dark eyes of his, his beautiful mouth thinning. "Every dream, every picture in your mind has the potential to come into being."

"But what about us? I visualize us together every day. Will this become reality in this new world I'm supposedly creating?"

"I am bound to you. But I am also not of Earth. We cannot make a child together."

"Who said anything about a child? I'm only asking to see you more than once every two months." But I *had* envisioned a child, had seen her in my arms with Lucifer standing beside me. "What happens if you don't go back?"

"I will grow weak and die."

"What if I can...change you?" My question hung in the air between us, a soft mist that radiated gold and silver, the colors of who we were. The mist formed a twisted braid that led from his heart to mine.

SHADOWS GREW LONGER as day moved into night. The dust settled, the sounds of day becoming the echoing yips and the scurry of nocturnal creatures. And still we stood there, locked together with the gold and silver chain. I saw the shadow beings hovering, wanting to break the connection between us. I moved closer, my lips grazing his. His mouth twisted in despair before he took hold of me and pulled me against him, covering my mouth with his own.

"We are bonded," he whispered. "The shadow beings cannot reach us as long as we are connected like this."

"Then that is our answer."

He shook his head, taking a step back and breaking the connection. "It is not strong enough, Feirin."

"Maybe it isn't now, but it will be," I muttered, watching as he succumbed to the amorphous creatures who pulled and tugged. The last thing I could see of him were his swirling onyx eyes staring into mine until there was only silence and the dark of night.

33

Elena glared, her forehead contorting into a frown. Her thick braid hung over her left shoulder, wisps of dark hair escaping. She looked harried, like a mother hen who couldn't keep track of her chicks. "There are people here who won't accept this, Fee. We don't have the numbers that we once did. We can't afford to lose them."

I'd arrived back in the forest with nothing to show for my absence but my story about Surt and being with Lucifer. It was deep night now, the trees whispering again. The firepit burned, our group sitting around it talking and drinking the tea Elena had concocted from the herbs she'd been gathering. I'd taken her aside to tell her what Lucifer had told me about the forest and what was happening to me. "I have the ability to make a real home for us. I don't have to explain anything."

"With the forest expanding and rivers and hills and valleys appearing overnight? Even your former followers worried about sorcery. You know this."

"Most of them know who I am now. They feel protected."

Elena sighed. "If we have a schism in the group it could

spell disaster. Conspiracy theories could develop. The ones you counted on are gone now, possibly taken to Sanctuary to work for Surt. Didn't you say he boasted about cleansing the desert? These people are newcomers—they don't know you as we do."

"I will address the group, Elena. They've all seen Surt and the shadow beings. They know about Lucifer."

Elena shook her head. "Ted and I know about Lucifer. The others do not. You must be realistic about this. These people aren't like sheep—they won't follow blindly."

I frowned and shook my head. "Your negativity is exactly what I don't need right now. Let me work this out, okay?"

It was a few days later that my thoughts returned to our conversation. News of this forest was spreading. People were arriving. And some were from Sanctuary. They wondered about the origins, how trees could grow in a desert. So far, I'd held them off with a story about rainstorms that re-invigorated seeds that had been lying dormant for many years. But I'd begun to notice whispering, hands held over mouths, and furtive glances. When I was around, people talked in hushed whispers. Standing up in front of them and explaining who I was would need to happen before the gossip was allowed to grow and spread.

I dreamed in vivid color. The varying greens of trees, leaves of red, orange and magenta, falling to leave a multi-colored carpet on the forest. The indigo blue of the sea somewhere in the distance, bright blue sky, sunsets of salmon pink, with streaks of deep maroon and gray. Faces, dark and light and everything in between, eyes shaped like almonds and round like marbles. And when I woke the images remained and I embellished them in my mind, painting pictures of how I wanted our world to be.

A mountain formed overnight, streams sending sparkling rivulets downward where they fed into a pool of indigo water. Sunlight sifted from a cerulean sky, giving life to herbs and plants that grew on the mountainside. Deer, wild boar, skunks, badgers, beavers and many others, ran through the underbrush. Birds of every color and size sang songs that echoed like temple bells, their feathers shimmering iridescent in the cool forest light.

Some of our newcomers had seeds with them from gardens they'd grown in the city. We cleared areas and planted. And when I held my hands over them and visualized their tiny diploids, they rose from the ground, reaching for the sun.

"You can't keep doing that," Elena hissed one afternoon. "Some of them are talking, Fee. They see you as a witch, a sorceress, a bruja. They are religious, afraid of the devil."

I gazed at her. "If they don't like it, tell them to leave. This is my spiritual calling—it's what I came to do. I have more pressing matters to worry about, like how to open a portal into the past."

Elena's mouth opened in shock, her eyes widening. "Now?"

"It's what I was called here to do—to bring the gods into the future."

"Isn't it enough to create a forest, rivers and streams, a mountain, a deep valley, and a home where we can live in community and grow food?"

"This is my calling."

She shook her head. "There will be chaos, anarchy, if you do this."

"No need to worry yet—I have no idea how to manage it."

FIVE DAYS after this conversation we had an uprising. I'd just finished erecting a small house with my magic when they came. At first it was two and then it was three and then the unrest spread, people who had recently arrived gathering together to accuse me of being a witch. They grabbed me, tied my hands behind my back and marched me out of the forest, Elena in hot pursuit. "What are you doing? Stop it!" she yelled, but they elbowed her out of the way and kept going. Maria and Mateo hurried behind, only to be shoved aside.

"You aren't so powerful now, are you witch?" one of the men who held me hissed. "That forest is evil, just as you are. I've heard you whispering to the trees. It's unnatural. Only God can make the world."

There was a general murmur of agreement before I noticed the woman who worked her way toward me. It was Sally.

"Her devil power comes from her hands and her words," she told the others. "We must keep her quiet until Surt arrives. He'll know what to do."

We sweated in the sun waiting. They'd managed to grab me because I wasn't expecting it, but Surt couldn't touch me. We were both gods and I could hold him off.

"Why are you doing this?" Elena cried out, trying to get close to me. I saw Ted behind her, shaking his head, his eyes wide with worry. Elena was very pregnant now. The stress of this could bring on premature labor. Next to him were Mirabelle, Sarin, Maria and Mateo, and others from our original group.

"It's okay, Elena. Surt can't touch me now and he knows it."

"But they can, Fee. Don't you see what they're planning?"

And then it hit me. They would do what Surt could not. I saw it in my mind. The bonfire, me tied to a stake. And when I glanced toward the forest, reality struck. They were carrying limbs out, piling them up. A man was hammering in the piece of wood where they would tie me. *Lucifer, if you're watching you might want to come and help.* But I didn't feel him at all. A few moments later Surt arrived, his cold eyes staring into mine. "Told you I'd find a way."

I reached out with my silver cord, sending it into the ether. I watched it travel into the sky, stretching upward until I couldn't see the end anymore. I imagined it connecting with Lucifer's gold cord, the two of them braiding tight together. I closed my eyes and made the images stronger.

My eyes flew open as they shoved me stumbling toward the pole. The men were rough, hurting me as they bent my shoulders back to tie me tightly. "Light it," I heard Surt say. A woman came forward with a torch and ripped the stone from around my neck, her eyes gleaming in triumph. There was whoosh and the wood began to burn. The last thing I saw before the smoke billowed up around me, was Cat hissing, his eyes reflecting the flames that licked at my feet. He seemed to grow in size, his fur rising on his back as he expanded into a jaguar with gleaming green eyes and razor-sharp claws. I heard someone scream.

A second later my pants caught fire, my skin sizzling. I let out a piercing shriek as the flames took me. My skin blistered and peeled off, my screaming seeming to come from somewhere else as the sound filled my ears. Faces were lit up by the flames, laughing, clapping, eyes wide with delight. Surt stood back watching, a smile of triumph lighting up his eyes, Sally laughing next to him.

Darkness, murmurs, searing heat. Raucous laughter. I followed the braid, hand over hand, climbing. *Silver and gold. Gold and silver.*

I DRIFTED, floating. Was I dead? I couldn't feel the fire anymore. My eyes were open but I couldn't see anything. Except...the cord. The cord was there, spun gold and bright silver threads twisted together. "Lucifer?"

"I am here."

"Where are we?"

"In my realm."

"I can't see."

"I'm working on that."

I closed my eyes, resting in the knowledge that he was with me.

34

When I opened my eyes again, I was lying on a four-poster bed in a room painted a very pale blue. A shift in the same color covered my nakedness. Gossamer curtains wafted in the warm breeze that touched my cheek from the open French casement windows. I sat up, examining the colorful blue and brown rug on the wide plank floor, the fireplace flanked by overstuffed chairs. *This* was Lucifer's realm? But when I rose and padded barefoot to the window to look out, all I saw was white that stretched away into nothingness.

I was still standing there puzzling over it when I heard the door open and close, turning to see Lucifer. "Where are we?"

He made a funny grimace. "You are severely injured, Feirin. The healers are attending to you. This is the fantasy world I made in order to keep you calm."

"So...this is a figment of your imagination?" I asked, gesturing.

He nodded. "Burns cover half your body. You nearly died."

"How are you doing this?"

"We have healing powers. You know that."

"But couldn't you just wrap me in your arms like you did with Sam?"

His eyes swirled, meeting mine. "Not with an injury like this. That was a supernatural fire that burned you—Surt's doing."

I moved to the chair and lowered to sit, feeling the soft cushions under me, the velvet of the arms under my fingers. "You are far more powerful than I imagined. But I thought your people wanted me dead."

He shook his head and came to stand next to me. "They believed it was wrong for a light being to be with a human. But you are not human and what you came to do is in our best interest."

I thought of the cord, remembering climbing. "I got here...how?"

His mouth quirked. "You used the cord that connects us to climb into my realm. This is why they changed their minds. They saw you for who you are."

"And who am I besides the dark goddess?"

"You are poised to change the face of the human world."

"By building the forest?"

"No. By opening the portal and bringing the gods back. We have lost our ability to stop evil. We need help."

"I have no idea how."

Lucifer reached for my hand and pulled me up, leading me back to the bed. He pressed me gently down and climbed into the other side, unbuttoning his long coat as he lay next to me. When he slipped it off and reached for me, I began to cry. And when he kissed away my tears and his lips touched mine, I wondered—how can I be here making love with Lucifer when my body is burned and lying somewhere else? But the questions disappeared as he lifted the shift up and over my head and pressed against me, his whispering words of love touching every part of me.

When I woke again a naked Lucifer was lying next to me. Asleep. I'd never seen him sleep. I gazed at the dark lashes that lay against his pale cheek, the arm flung out toward me, his luminescent glowing skin. When he opened his eyes, they were swirling with light. "Am I healed?" I asked.

"Not yet."

"Can you stay with me here?"

He smiled. "Yes. The healers have given me permission to 'distract' you for as long as it takes."

"Does that mean what I think it does?"

"It means we can be together until you are well."

I let out a sigh of relief. This was the first time he'd been given permission to remain with me for any length of time. We were both naked, lying together on a real bed. I could hardly take it in, it was so preposterous. I snuggled close and took his hand, twining my fingers through his. "How's everyone down on earth? What's happening with Surt and the ones who had me burned?"

"You are not allowed to think about that right now," Lucifer answered. "Only healing thoughts, Feirin. And if that means I have to make love to you again, then I will."

I laughed. "Is it such a hardship?"

"Terrible," he murmured before placing his mouth on mine.

"Fee?"

I opened my eyes to see Elena leaning over me, Ted next to her. Behind her I saw the others, the ones who I counted as friends. Had I really been with Lucifer or was it all a dream? I couldn't think, could barely breathe, my body aching with such ferocity that it was all I could do not to cry out. "I...I..."

"Don't try to talk. You have to rest."

"I'm not healed?"

Elena let out a funny sound. "You almost died, Fee. The fire. Don't you remember?"

"I was with Lucifer. The light beings healed me," I muttered.

"Maybe they did. Maybe without them you'd be dead. But you still have burns."

I held up my arm, aghast when I saw the blistering.

When I glanced up, Elena nodded. "What I saw of that fire would have killed anyone else. After the fire burned out, we went to get you down and there was no body, not even bones left behind. I was sick inside and so were the others. We stood there and cried, Fee. All of us. Three days later I found you naked at the edge of the forest on a bed of pine branches, as though someone had placed you there. Your skin had obviously burned away and new skin had grown in, but many burns remained and I could barely feel a pulse. We brought you into the forest and bathed you in the stream. I didn't know if you'd live."

"What happened with Surt and Sally and the others?"

"Once the fire got going, they tried to torch the forest, but it threw the flames right back at them. They left right after your screams stopped. I'm sure they figured you were dead. I certainly did."

I thought of the cord, the silver and gold rope I climbed. I couldn't tell her about that—it was just too hard to believe, even for me. But I did tell her about the room and Lucifer and what he told me.

"Might be that you dreamed it all. Sounds like a fantasy I would like to have if I were dying."

"It was conjured by Lucifer while the beings worked on my burns. I never experienced pain. Until now," I added, grimacing.

"If you feel up to it, I would suggest a trip to the pool. Bathing in the waters will restore you."

But all I could think about was Lucifer and our time together. He'd finally said he loved me, not once but many times. I hoped it wasn't just a dream.

I FLOATED IN THE WATER, my thoughts drifting along with my body. It had been nearly two weeks, the burns pretty much healed. But my mind floundered. Surt was still out there, as well as the followers who'd joined him. Mirabelle, who I'd counted on, was among them. If he returned, he'd bring thousands from the city, all those people I'd basically brainwashed into following him. What had Lucifer meant when he said I embodied both the light and the dark? I had so many questions.

I was pulling on the long skirt and tank top Elena had provided when Ted and Elena appeared. The baskets they'd woven from rushes were filled with red and blue berries. "Some people just arrived," Elena announced. "Not sure where they came from."

"I'll use my intuition to decide if they have evil intent."

Ted chuckled and Elena let out a howl of laughter. "Are you serious? You had no idea the last time, Fee. What makes you think that..."

"Because I've changed."

She stared at me. "Really? In what way?"

"Trial by fire? I'm stronger, but not physically. The strength is inside."

Ted and Elena glanced at one another before turning back to me.

"You're wondering if you should trust me."

Ted did a one shoulder shrug. "You've led us astray several times. This last one almost cost your life. I'm more worried about Surt. He's got a cult following and he's very persuasive."

"What about this portal you're supposedly opening? When is that happening?"

I glanced at Elena to see if she was mocking me, but the expression on her face was serious. "I don't know," I answered honestly, my gaze going to the clear water, the boulders surrounding the pool and the steep rock-strewn path leading up the slope that rose above the timber-line. "I'm waiting to find out."

Elena frowned. "Do you expect Lucifer to suddenly appear and tell you how to do it? I thought this was your calling. I suggest you spend time alone and stop wandering about in a haze, daydreaming about having sex."

Instead of this statement making me angry it made me laugh. "And you think you aren't psychic?"

Elena scoffed. "It's obvious, Fee. You're *obsesionada*."

"Not sure what you mean by that, but..."

"She means you seem drunk on love," Ted said. "Your expression, how you stare off into space, the way you fiddle with your hair."

"Fiddle...do I?" My fingers were there already, twisting a long tendril into a curl that I let fall. My hair was still wet from my bath.

"We need the warrior Fee back."

"That's not who I am."

"What about Surt and those creepy followers who laughed while they watched you burn?"

"I feel almost sorry for them, especially when they discover who Surt really is."

"You need to go after him, Fee. You can't let this stand. Over half our people left. What will happen to them?"

"I know, Elena. I feel terrible, especially about Mirabelle. But if he thinks I'm dead we have the advantage."

Elena picked up her basket, one hand going to her bulging belly. A grimace passed across her features. "You'd best do something soon, dark goddess."

"I'm working on a plan." I turned to pull on my boots. In truth I had no plan.

Once she and Ted disappeared down the trail, I climbed the rocks, perching at the very top to look out over the desert. The air was cooler, the dust settled for once. I saw no cars, no people, nothing but the temple mountains in the hazy distance and the undulating reddish dirt that stretched between here and there. I could even see the ocean from up here. The forest had taken us closer. The expanse of nothingness always calmed me and today was no exception.

I was in a deep meditation when I heard Elena let out a high-pitched scream. I knew exactly what it meant. I ran.

When I reached the shelters Ted was with her, his worried gaze going to me. "She's in labor."

"Where's Maria?" I asked frantically.

"Gathering herbs on the mountain," Elena grunted. "This baby is on the way now, Fee."

"Me? You expect me to..."

Ted grabbed me. "You are all we have," he muttered with wide eyes.

"Walk her around while I boil water and find some clean rags," I told him.

Ted put his arm around her and led her away as I rushed to heat water and tried to quell my fast beating heart. I built up and fire and hooked the kettle onto the bracket Ted had devised. "How dilated are you?" I asked when they came back, not even sure what those words meant.

Elena let out a grimace of pain, bending forward with hands on knees before she was able to answer. "I can't see down there. But from how it feels, this baby is well on the way. My water broke a half hour ago and the pains are very close now."

I stared at Ted, trying to think what to do.

"Get me into the shelter," Elena muttered before letting out another ear-piercing shriek.

Ted grabbed my arm. "Fee, you've been through this—you know what to do."

I had very little memory of the one birth I'd attended. I'd put it out of my mind the second it was over, relegating the disturbing images to the deep recesses of my mind. I took Elena's arm and led her inside. "I need to see what's going on," I muttered, wondering how I would know what to look for. I helped her down on the pallet of hides and had her spread her knees apart. "Is that the baby's head?" I shrieked.

Elena gave a grunt and let out a moan as she pushed. "Should you do that?" I asked, watching the head emerge further. Things were going too fast.

Elena ignored me as she pushed again, completely consumed inside the pain as her ongoing screams began to reverberate. The sounds scared me into action. "Ted, bring in the rags! The baby's coming!" I shouted. Sam wasn't here. I didn't even know the right things to ask.

Ted appeared next to me holding a battered kettle, the rags under his arm. "What should I do?"

But I couldn't answer as I watched the baby sliding toward

me, blood and fluids coming with it. I caught it, trying not to let it slip from my grasp. "We need to cut the umbilical," I told Ted, the only thing I could remember from before. "Do you have a clean knife?"

When I glanced at him his face was white as a sheet. He held out the knife which I took in shaking fingers. I dipped it into the hot water. "Come and hold the baby while I do this," I muttered. "Wrap it in the rags and wipe it clean."

"I can't," Ted whispered.

"Jesus," I muttered, the irony not lost on me. The baby had not yet made a sound.

"Hold the baby level for a minute or two before you cut the cord," Elena whispered. "It's too soon."

I did as she asked, watching his little face contort as the reality of being out of her womb took over. He let out a piercing shriek, his face scrunched.

Elena nodded and let out a sigh.

I took in a deep breath before carefully slicing through the umbilical cord, blood spilling down the slippery body as the baby let out a wail. I held my hand out to Ted. "Rag." He put it in my hand and I pressed it on the wound. But when I checked Elena, I realized that a lot of blood was still coming out.

When Elena tried to sit up, I pushed her back. "Baby's fine but you're bleeding."

"Use the moss," she muttered. "But you need to make sure the placenta is out first. Press on my belly."

"Ted? Moss!" I yelled.

He handed me the substance and took the baby, waiting while I pressed, releasing the rest of the placenta with a whoosh of fluids and blood; it spilled across the hides under her, leaving a dark stain. Elena cried out and fell back, her eyes closing. "What should I do? Elena...what do I do now?"

But Elena was either unconscious or dead. I cleaned her up

and pressed the moss up inside her before I took the baby out of Ted's shaking hands, using the warm water to clean him. He had olive skin and dark hair, dark eyes peering at me solemnly as I wrapped him up in old T-shirt.

Ted was crying, leaning over Elena. "She's dead, Fee. Elena's gone."

I pressed my fingers to her wrist. "She's not dead. I think she fainted."

He turned to stare at me. "The baby—is he...?"

I smiled and handed him over. "He's fine."

It was over an hour before Elena was strong enough to sit up and take the baby into her arms. "I'm too old for this," she muttered, gazing down at the bundle in her arms. She pulled her blouse up and pressed him to her breast, watching him root for the nipple. "At least he knows what he's doing," she murmured, looking down at his dark head nuzzled against her.

Ted smiled and let out a sigh. "Thought I lost you."

Elena smiled at him through her tears before she turned to me. "You did it, Fee. You just delivered my baby."

"I had to, didn't I?"

Two days went by. Elena and the baby were doing fine, but I still hadn't recovered, my nerves jangling every time I recalled the image of the baby emerging and the panic to do what was needed without knowing what that was. My longing to have Lucifer's baby had disappeared that day.

They named him Joseph. "Joe would be happy," I murmured, taking the baby from her so that she could go and relieve herself. When she returned, I was ready for a change of scene. "See you in a while—mountain calls."

Elena nodded. "Go for it. Ted's here to take care of my every need."

Ted smiled down at her. "That I am."

As I walked away, I heard Ted laugh, Elena's murmured response, the mewling of the baby. There was an ease around them, the impression that nothing could touch their happiness.

THE LAST STEEP hill took me up to where the peak waited. I settled into a cross-legged position, my hands on my knees.

But when I closed my eyes, the thoughts I'd been avoiding for the past few days rose to the surface. Surt and his minions were still after me, despite this new protective shield, or whatever it was, that kept him at bay. His power infuriated me, as well as his ability to manipulate. He was dangerous and had to be stopped. It was time to move forward with what I was, to do what I came here for.

The sun was low on the horizon when I rose and stretched to get the kinks out of my knees and back. An owl hooted, another answering before the creature flew silently by. Our eyes met for a brief second as a message was imparted. Owl meant change, and revealing the hidden. I watched until it disappeared into another part of the forest. Something was about to happen, maybe not tonight and maybe not tomorrow, but soon. And it was up to me to stop it. All calm was gone, my body trembling. When I reached for the stone around my neck and found it missing, I remembered its true importance. A woman had ripped it from my neck before they burned me. That stone was my only link to the past. Without it I couldn't open the portal.

35

Peyton appeared from under the trees around midday the following day. He looked different somehow, his eyes haunted and flat.

"Sanctuary is a fucking hell hole," he told me in a hushed whisper. "And Sally is the bitch from hell. She tried to get me to join their cult. The people on the street are like zombies. But I found your friend Jeremy. He and his sister are here." He pointed behind him where a group of hollow-eyed men and women came out from under the trees. Canada and Bruce were there, along with several others I recognized.

When Jeremy saw me, his eyes lit up. "Jesus, Fee, I thought I'd never see you again!"

We hurried toward each other and hugged, my tears landing on the shoulder of the frayed T-shirt he wore. "Isabelle?"

He pointed toward a bedraggled young woman wearing a filthy ripped skirt and a man's shirt that came to her knees. Her hair was tangled with leaves and sticks and the hoop earrings I remembered were gone. She looked older, worn down, her cheeks sunken from weight loss and her formerly sparkling eyes dull. I would never have recognized her. "Isabelle," I said gently, taking hold of her hands.

One look at me and she burst into tears. "Are we safe here? Please tell me we're safe."

"This forest is protected. Yes, you're safe."

"Someone is killing animals out there and just leaving them," Jeremy told me, pointing toward the path leading to the desert. "I saw a bunch of small deer and also what looked like wild boar."

"Who would do that?" Elena asked, stumbling from the shelter into the clearing.

Peyton stared at the baby she carried. "You had a baby," he said stupidly.

Elena laughed. "Yes. Didn't you know I was pregnant?"

He shook his head, swiveling to look at me. "Any other changes I need to know about?" he asked, gazing at my belly.

I put my hands there. "No. NO."

"This place feels good," Jeremy muttered, looking around. "Some serious magic goin' on."

"The forest is enchanted," I whispered, making sure I wasn't heard by anyone else.

Jeremy grinned. "I always knew there was something about you, Fee."

"We've lost a lot of followers because of it," Elena said, glaring at me.

"Fools," Jeremy muttered. "Sanctuary's enchanted too, but not in a good way."

"Did you know that was my doing?"

Jeremy shook his head, frowning. "What are you talking about?"

"Surt made me turn the protestors into automatons to do his bidding. You saw me there, didn't you?"

"I did see you and then you were gone. Those people...they got picked up and taken away."

"To work for Surt."

"We need to get these people settled and then you can question them," Elena said, scanning the tired faces.

I wasn't planning on questioning them; even a normal conversation was out in the state they were in. "They're too exhausted. Food and rest are what they need first."

Elena nodded and headed for the shelter to feed the mewling newborn.

With Ted's help we organized a meal and built up the fire before I announced that I needed some time to contemplate things. No one seemed to pay much attention as I walked down the path away from the firepit.

It was an hour or so later that Elena found me sitting under an enormous cedar tree. "Everyone is settled. Time to screen them."

I stood and brushed the dirt and leaves off the skirt. "If I look into their eyes I'll know who they are."

Elena scoffed. "Really? And how has that worked out for you?"

"I'm not the same as I was before the burning."

She stared at me. "You try my patience, Fee. Fifty followers just turned on you and nearly killed you. What's changed?"

"I cry now."

Elena made a face. "I figured that was hormonal. I'll admit that seeing you in tears is shocking, but I'd hardly call it a real change."

"I managed to deliver your baby."

Elena laughed. "Yes, you did. I'll admit some change has taken place."

"Can you try to trust me?"

She cocked her head to the side. "Maybe, but don't make me regret it."

Once she was gone, I headed to the stream to wash my face and rinse my feet. My stone was missing. If I didn't get it back my mission might never be completed. Delivering a baby wasn't the same as providing a place of safety for a hundred people. Elena was right not to trust me.

I WOKE TO A MEOW, Cat standing next to the tree where I'd fallen asleep. Filtered light crept through the heavy canopy and lit up his swirling eyes. I'd slept here all night. When I sat up my necklace was lying next to me, the facets twinkling. "Did *you* find it?" I whispered, reaching for it. His green eyes met mine as he rubbed against my leg. The leather cord was broken but I tied the ends and slipped it over my head. As soon as it settled into the hollow between my breasts, I felt it. The link to the past. A misty fog was all that separated us now. I buried my face in Cat's fur, thanking him, but instead of being happy about it, he hissed and a second later he melted into the underbrush. "Cat?"

"You saw the cat?" Elena asked, walking toward me with baby Joseph in her arms.

"Cat found my necklace," I said, lifting it to show her.

"That animal is uncanny. Where is he now?"

I glanced around. "He was here a second ago."

She bent to look at the stone. "It's pretty, but I doubt that stone's important in the grand scheme of things. The arrivals are waiting for you."

"How are they today?"

She made a face. "Peyton is spreading rumors."

"What kind of rumors?"

"That you may have lost your mind. Jeremy's been standing up for you, but Peyton seems intent on painting a dark picture of who you've become."

I frowned and hurried to walk beside her. "He seemed fine last night—tired and thinner, but..."

"If he convinces these people that you're the devil, all our goals for community are lost."

"He's saying I'm evil?"

"He's telling them that you call yourself the dark goddess and that you think you've met Lucifer. Those two things together could be construed that way."

"That doesn't sound like him."

"He's still jealous, Fee. He'll never get over you."

I spent the next hour walking amongst the newcomers and looking into their eyes. When I came to Peyton, he refused to look at me. "You know me," he mumbled, turning away.

I grabbed his arm. "Not anymore I don't. What have you been saying? Two people told me that they thought I was in league with the devil."

Peyton let out a laugh. "It's the truth isn't it? You and Lucifer?"

"Lucifer isn't the devil. He's just the opposite."

When Peyton finally met my gaze, I was shocked by the anger in his eyes. "Since I've never seen him it's hard to know what to think. But you are not the woman I knew back in Elysian City. I'm only trying to steer these people clear of sorcery and devil worship."

"If you feel that way, why did you come?"

He shook his head. "Hoped I was wrong. Unfortunately, you're still crazy."

"I'm sorry but you need to leave this forest."

"Leave?"

"Yes, Peyton. I can't have people here who don't trust me."

He smirked. "Most of the ones I brought think you're a fucking witch. Will you kick them out too?"

"If that's true, then yes. They will have to go."

His eyes narrowed and grew dark. "Fuck you," he muttered. I watched him stride down the path and disappear into the bright sunlight. And when I hurried to see where he'd gone, there was no sign of him anywhere. He said *I* wasn't the same? He was not the Peyton I knew.

I was calling everyone together when Elena grabbed my arm. "Can you hold off on the supernatural stuff for a while? They don't need to hear all that right now."

I shook free of her grip. "I'm only doing what I should have done months ago."

Elena was frowning at me when Ted came toward us with Joseph in his arms. "He needs you."

Elena took the crying baby and gave me a dark look before she headed for the shelter. "Hope you know what you're getting into," she warned.

Once Elena was out of sight, I clapped my hands, waiting until I had everyone's attention before moving to stand on a log. "First of all, welcome," I began, scanning across the tired faces. "Peyton was correct when he told you that I'm the dark goddess, but do not assume that I'm evil. I'm just the opposite. I've come from the past into this future time to help mankind rid itself of evil." I lifted my necklace, watching light pour from it like liquid silver. "This stone I wear is a talisman, a link to the gods and goddesses who have been banned from this timeline. But Surt, the god of chaos, is here and wants to destroy everything good. And he will get his wish if you bow to his manipulations. Many of my group left to follow him. Jeremy and many of you here now have seen what he's done in Sanctuary."

I waited for a moment, scanning the wide-open eyes, the expressions that signaled shock. "If you cannot trust me and want to go, that's your choice, but I have to be honest about who I am. I know what I'm saying is upsetting for those who believe in the one God. Maria and Mateo are Catholic and can help you sort through your confusion." I gestured to the smiling couple standing at the back of the group, letting a moment tick before going on.

"I cannot alleviate your fears or perform miracles. All I can hope to do is bring back the gods and goddesses and build a community where we can live together in peace. Everyone will be included, no matter what religion, skin color or sexual preference. So, if you are willing to suspend your disbelief and give me a chance, I will do everything in my power to keep you safe. And if not, then you must leave now. I cannot tolerate those who spread rumors or want to undermine the cause I stand for."

There was stunned silence for several minutes until a whisper began, followed by a roar of approval. Jeremy hurried forward to hug me and I saw a few others approach Maria and Mateo. Not one person left.

36

As the weeks passed, our group expanded to nearly two-hundred. And there were more coming every day. Sam and Sika, their baby and older boy arrived one night, exhausted and underfed.

"The natives are starving," Sam told me, settling Sika by the fire. "Someone is out there killing animals."

"Surt, the god of chaos," I muttered. "He's hoping for recruits to his cause. Nothing better than starvation to make you desperate enough to listen to a madman."

Sika glanced up at me, the six-month-old suckling at her breast. "Natives angry," she said haltingly.

"Surprised they haven't found the forest. Will the tribe come here?" I asked Sam.

"Scattered to the four winds so it's hard to say. We saw vans cruising the desert.

This god you mentioned might be offering food for their services."

I let out a sigh, watching other newcomers join us by the

firepit. "Surt is an ongoing problem. He wants to ruin me, to ruin this place."

Sam frowned, glancing at Sika. "We're lucky only one twin survived. Sika has barely enough milk for one."

"Girl?"

Sam nodded. "Celeste."

"And your boy?"

"Finian, after my father. Sika named him."

"You're safe here and we have plenty to eat. She'll feel better soon. I'm glad you found us."

"This forest is kind of hard to miss. It's got be over 9,000 acres."

"And it's growing."

He stared at me. "Growing? You mean the trees are spreading."

"No, I mean we have a river now and at least two mountains, as well as many streams. And yes, the forest is also spreading outward."

"Is this Lucifer's doing?"

"I'm the one doing it, Sam. It's what I was intended to accomplish all along—to create a safe haven where people can live together in community. I conjured it—my visions are bringing it into existence, but I haven't figured out how to do the most important part—bringing the gods and goddesses here from the past."

Sam stared at the shelters, the trees, the underbrush, the deer racks and hides and the firepit. "You...you say you conjured all this?"

"The forest began with my tears and grew from there. Every time I picture a mountain or a stream or a river, it appears a few days later. The vision has to be elaborate—I mean I can't just think mountain and have it turn up the next day, but if I really see it in my mind, the way it should be, with plants and rocks and caves and boulders and so on, it usually works."

"And the gods part? How did you figure that out?"

"Strangely enough, Surt told me."

I rose to check on the shelters, finding one that would suit Sam and Sika and their children. It was a beehive shape set back under the trees and larger than several of the others we'd built from scratch in the early days. "You are welcome to bunk here until you can build something you like more."

Sam laughed. "What, no conjuring while we sit here watching it build itself?"

I laughed. "It isn't *that* simple."

Sam came close and hugged me, his eyes welling. "You are something else, lady," he whispered.

I remembered him saying those exact words when I first met him. "Thanks, Sam. And so are you." I lifted my stone, holding it out so he could see the light pouring from it. "I thought this was all I needed to bring the gods back, but so far my meditating and visualizing have gone nowhere. I think it's broken."

Sam laughed. "I doubt that stone is broken. Where is Lucifer in all this?" he asked, gesturing.

"I guess I haven't needed him." But I did need him. His continuing absence was more troubling than I cared to admit.

"After your story about being burned and the healing, I'm surprised. Seems you two belong together."

"He can't survive on Earth. I'm not sure how to make it work between us."

"Maybe the answer lies in that stone. Maybe its function isn't what you thought. Or what about that cord you mentioned?"

"It connects us, but it doesn't change the fact that he's a light-being."

"What about going to him? From what you said you can exist in the fantasy world he creates."

"But that world isn't real."

His eyes met mine. "What's obvious sometimes blinds us to what's hidden."

His words echoed, traveling into the deeper recesses of my mind. I was thinking in concrete terms, not in the mysterious ways in which Lucifer and I were bound together. I said goodnight and headed into the forest. It was time to climb the mountain and meditate.

THE WHISPERING WAS LOUDER than usual as I worked through the underbrush, trying to follow the path through the thick canopy. I peered at the trees that leaned toward me, feathery branches brushing against my cheek in the waning light.

When I reached the highest peak, I gazed across the desert as I always did, expecting the waning colors at the horizon, the stars beginning to show themselves. Instead, the entire sky was thick with a haze of red. Fire was my first thought, but when I turned toward the city of Sanctuary in the far distance, a cloud of the same color had been shot through with menacing darkness that churned and spun, alerting me to Surt and the chaos he was wreaking. He couldn't get into the forest but he could certainly destroy everything else. The thought was terrifying.

I had to see Lucifer. He was the only one who could help me now. I visualized the silver cord, imagining it whirling into the air and reaching, reaching. I closed my eyes and climbed.

Fin

AFTERWORD

If you enjoyed this book please leave a review at the site of your choice. It really helps!
If you want to see more of my books or find out about me, please visit my website:
www.nikkibroadwellauthor.com
https://www.nikkibroadwellauthor.com/blog-1

And if you sign up you will be the first to get the news of new offerings or deals!

https://www.facebook.com/NikkiBroadwellBooks/
https://twitter.com/nikkibroadwell
https://www.instagram.com/broadwellnikki/
https://www.pinterest.com/nbroadwell/_

Thank you for reading!

OTHER BOOKS BY NIKKI:

<u>Wolfmoon series:</u>

Moonstone-Book 1

Willow-Book 2

Raven-Book 3

Faery-Book 4

<u>Gypsy series: A Time Traveling Romance</u>

Gypsy's Quest-Book 1

Gypsy's Return-Book 2

Gypsy's Secret-Book 3

<u>Coyote series:</u>

Just Another Desert Sunset

Coyote Sunrise

<u>Summer McCloud paranormal murder series:</u>

Murder in Plain Sight

Saffron and Seaweed

Black and White and *Red* all over

Finlay's Folly

The Night of the Jaguar

The Case of Missing Books

The Bridge

Time Gap

A Witch in Time Saves Nine

The moon in Her Eyes

The Last Keeper of the Light

Rosemary for Remembrance

Burning Night

Raven and Hummingbird series

Siobhan's Secret

Dagda's Daughter

Kat's Conundrum

Raven's Runes

www.ingramcontent.com/pod-product-compliance
Lightning Source LLC
Chambersburg PA
CBHW020935260626
47169CB00006B/1732